INCURSION

GUSTAVO BONDONI

SEVERED PRESS
HOBART TASMANIA

INCURSION

Copyright © 2017 Gustavo Bondoni
Copyright © 2017 Severed Press

WWW.SEVEREDPRESS.COM

ISBN: 978-1-925711-20-2

CHAPTER 1

Tristan woke with a start. He'd slept for centuries and now it was time to die.

His training kicked in. The pod release button was exactly where it was supposed to be, and he pressed it without hesitation.

Nothing happened. The transparent lid of his sleeper pod, deep in the hold of the troop transport ship, should have popped open on hydraulic lifts, but it stayed resolutely where it was. He chuckled. *No matter how many times they tell you that everything has been worked out and that nothing can possibly fail, something always does. Usually multiples of something.* Fortunately, his training covered this contingency.

The lid was a lightweight plastic molding held in place by four latches, two near his head and two near his feet. By unclipping the upper ones, he would be able to bend back the plastic. This method had the effect of rendering the stasis pod useless, but no one was expecting this ship to make a return trip, so the loss was acceptable. In the unlikely event that anyone survived the mission, there would be time to remedy the problems later.

It should have been easy. The plastic was so thin that a child could have pushed it away.

Tristan Polaris Han, a well-trained shock marine, found that he could barely budge it. He rechecked the clasps, and saw that they were both open. There was nothing holding the lid down. *What the fuck?*

There was no such thing as a claustrophobic marine. Those got weeded out early and aggressively, but he was damned if he was going to lie inside a plastic cylinder until Marc or one of the others came along and rescued him. In the corps, there are some incidents that are impossible to live down, and he suspected that getting stuck in a stasis tube was one of them. He pushed against the transparent shielding with all his might. His muscles screamed and, inch by agonizing inch, the plastic gave way.

With a soft crack, it creased about halfway along its length and Tristan let his arms drop with relief. He couldn't see what the lid had snagged on, but it had to have been something pretty solid. He sat up,

1

pulled his legs back towards him and out of the tube, and dropped the eighty centimeters to the floor.

And kept right on going as his legs collapsed under his weight. The floor applied a nasty blow to his head before he could get his arms up to prevent it.

Tristan lay in a daze. He'd been in stasis several times—the nature of interstellar war made it inevitable—but he'd never suffered from stasis sickness. That was something for desk jockeys and transport pilots, not grunts. A marine's body should be able to take up to two thousand years in transit before feeling any ill effects. Afterwards, a week in the gym should get them back in excellent shape.

But here he was, facedown on the metal grating of the floor, unable to stand under his own power.

He realized that the unusual nature of the situation went beyond the fact that he felt as weak as a baby. The revival chamber should have been pandemonium as troops bounced out of their tubes and got into their uniforms. For shock units, the time between revival and battle-readiness within their exoskeletons was five minutes. Ninety seconds to get dressed, one minute to get their ass to the exoskeleton bay, and the other two and a half minutes to get the suit systems up and running.

He'd already been awake for longer than that, and hadn't seen movement from any of the other bays.

That could only mean one of two things: he'd either been woken before the preset time because his tube had malfunctioned, or he was in such bad shape that his crew had decided not to bother with him and gone on to the battle. Neither would explain his inability to move, however.

Tristan turned his head to study the stasis pod beside the one he'd emerged from. To his relief, his neck muscles responded reasonably well, with only minor pain, and he brought the tube into his field of view.

The problem he had now was that the tubes were too close together. Lying beside one made it impossible to see the lid of the one beside it. All that was visible from his vantage point was the bottom of the tube, partially obscured by a mess of refrigeration lines and wiring.

He gritted his teeth. If he'd been woken early, it was extremely likely that he was the only person awake anywhere on the ship. Help was not on the way, which meant that he had to help himself. By extending his arm as far as he could, Tristan managed to take hold of the railing which ran around the tube. These were usually used by maintenance teams to haul the stasis pods around from one place to another, and were sturdy enough to grab onto.

Now that he had a firm grasp of the railing, he knew he had to pull himself up very carefully. His training had extended to the assistance of victims of stasis chamber failure, but he'd always assumed that he'd be the one helping, not the victim in need of aid. At least he knew the problems he was likely to encounter.

If he was correct and his tube had gone bad, then there would be a boatload of problems to deal with, but the most pressing was that he would have lost both muscle mass and muscle tone, to a degree that might cause the muscles to tear with movement that he wouldn't think twice about if he were healthy.

This meant that he needed to move slowly and he needed to ensure that any exertion was spread among as many muscles as possible. For example, instead of pulling himself up by the hand, he should pull with his arm at the same time as he pushed with his legs. If he coordinated it correctly, he would minimize the strain on any one of them. They might all tear simultaneously and leave him to die of starvation on the ground, of course, but at least this gave him a better chance.

It worked like a dream. There was much less pain than he imagined as he brought himself into a kneeling position. He felt a passing dizziness and the sensation of fierce pins and needles in his limbs, but not the searing pain of ripping muscle fibers.

Tristan paused to catch his breath and study his arm and thighs. Visually, at least, his muscles looked pretty much the way they always had, full and strong with just the slightest touch of flabbiness from the forced inactivity, and which the tubes weren't quite calibrated to counteract. He shouldn't be having this much trouble standing.

Emboldened by that discovery and his success in getting off the floor, Tristan attempted to rise. It took the strength of both his arms pushing on the railing, but he was soon upright, albeit wobbling more than he would have liked.

The stasis chamber was closed and locked down.

For a second, Tristan felt relief as his brain registered what that meant. A closed stasis chamber meant that the time to open the tubes hadn't arrived yet, and that his own must have malfunctioned. All he needed to do was to get himself into one of the emergency spare stasis pods and hunker down. Hopefully, he'd wake up in better shape once they reached their destination.

But the feeling was fleeting, lasting only the time it took for his mind to comprehend the other thing his eyes were telling it: under the plastic lid beside him he could clearly make out a human body, desiccated and mummified.

3

There was no sign of decomposition. It was the body of a person who'd been dead in a completely sterile environment for a very long time.

The faded plastic tag on the tube told him that he was looking at the remains of Crista Rigel Wagner. He didn't remember much about her, except that she had dark hair and was hard as nails in training, neither giving quarter nor expecting it.

"Fuck," he said. Speaking was difficult, the words grinding like stuck gears. But he insisted, just to prove to himself that he could, in fact, speak. "What the hell is going on here?" The words echoed around the chamber.

And something came back, a muffled grunt.

He turned in the direction of the sound. He could see a row of ten tubes from where he was standing, and apart from his, two others were open. One was empty, while the other held a marine who'd managed to get halfway out before weakness overcame him.

"Don't move," Tristan said. "I'll be over as soon as I can."

The other man nodded and let himself fall back into the tube.

Tristan took a halting step, then another. It was like trying to walk with rubber legs, but at least his strength seemed to be returning as the muscles warmed up. He proceeded from tube to tube, grabbing onto the rails of each as he went. By the fourth, he was able to walk stiffly and held on only for precaution's sake.

The tubes between his starting point and the struggling man held only dried-out corpses.

"Tristan," the guy whispered. "What's happening?"

"I was hoping you knew." The guy's name was Klaus, and he had just transferred in from another unit. "All I know is that it gets better the more you move." I was standing without holding on which meant that, in my case at least, I was telling the truth.

"Help me out of here."

Between them, they were able to get him unsteadily on his feet. "Hold on a second." Tristan hobbled over to the third open lid and found the unit's young lieutenant, Cora, sprawled on the floor beside her open tube.

He didn't even take a second to admire the view, but immediately knelt beside her to see if she was alive and breathed a sigh of relief when he found a steady pulse. She'd probably tried to walk and hit the ground just like Tristan had.

"Klaus, see if you can get over here. The lieutenant needs help."

4

The man grunted as he approached. It took him a while, and the woman began to regain consciousness. Her eyes flickered open. "Relax, Lieutenant. You took a bit of a bump to the head."

Young as she was, she knew enough not to argue. She just nodded once and awaited further instructions. Tristan found that a bit ironic. Five minutes before, he'd been wondering what the hell he was going to do, and now there were two people waiting for him to guide them.

Well, you had to play the cards you were dealt.

"I'll need to check you for a concussion later, but I can't do that yet. You'll have to try to stand. We can help you up."

Klaus had arrived, already walking without help. He gave what aid he could and Cora was up. She wore her blond hair cropped close, and her body was lean, but there were still enough curves there to distract any male with a pulse.

Tristan kept his eyes firmly on hers and gave her a rundown on what he knew. He finished by saying: "What are our orders, ma'am?"

Her ice-blue eyes didn't blink. "Until I hear otherwise, the orders haven't changed. Every able-bodied marine needs to get to the exoskeleton bay right now."

"Yes, ma'am." Tristan saluted and was about to turn.

"You may want to get dressed first," Cora said with a smirk. "They might look at you funny if you arrive with everything hanging out. Plus, I'm not sure if the equipment is rated for nude use."

Klaus laughed.

***

It took them an agonizingly long time to get dressed. The uniforms, meant to be pulled on easily after a few hundred years in storage, had turned brittle and tore under ridiculously light loads. The boots simply disintegrated when they tried to don them.

Finally, Cora had simply told them to follow her to the exoskeleton bay. They plodded barefoot and in tattered uniforms down the steel tunnels of the ship. First, though, Cora limped from tube to tube, checking that every other member of their platoon was, indeed, long dead. Tristan winced as she read out Marc's name on the label. He'd become a close friend over the course of three campaigns and various training cycles. They'd even volunteered for this mission together.

Then she tried the intra-ship comm system, which didn't even power up.

The corridor was another challenge. It was intermittently lit, and only every second door or so was fully operational. The remainder had to be winched up manually. By the third, they were exhausted.

"At least we're getting our exercise. No need for the two-week retraining period to get back up to speed this time around. I should be good to go once we get to the end of the hall," Tristan quipped as he struggled with the winch.

"I don't think this mission was going to last two weeks anyway," Klaus responded. "From what I heard, we were going to go in, do as much damage as possible, and then fight to the last man. Dead in hours was the general consensus. That's why they asked for volunteers for this mission."

"Guys," the lieutenant said, "this isn't helping. If that were true, don't you think we'd have felt something by now? The *Minstrel* isn't particularly heavily armored. If there were people shooting at us, then we should feel it, shouldn't we?"

"Maybe they're dealing with the spaceborne elements of the fleet first. Shooting down the fighters and the battle station before coming after the grunts."

"We've been awake for an hour at least, and they have no way of knowing which vessels are carrying what. I think someone would have noticed a big ship flying around and taken a potshot or two."

"There," Tristan grunted. "That should be far enough."

They got down on their stomachs and crawled under the half-raised door. To their dismay, just twenty meters ahead, there was another darkened door. They'd come to realize that the ones with power to the lighting also had power to the opening mechanisms. They leaned against it and Tristan said, "I need to get some rest. Do either of you feel up to moving this one?"

"Let's take a few minutes," Cora agreed.

They slumped against the blast door. "Where do you think everyone else is?" Klaus said.

"I don't want to think about that right now. Once we get to the staging area, we can ask anyone else who happens to be there."

They'd walked past the entrance to a few more stasis tube chambers, all sealed. Cora had forbidden them to attempt any detours because they would only slow them down and keep them from carrying out their orders.

"What if there's no one there?"

The lieutenant shrugged it off. "We'll deal with that if it happens. I personally don't think it's all that likely. After all, there are three of us alive out of ten people in our platoon. If that holds for the ship, there should be thousands of troops moving towards their battle armor."

"Or maybe our room had a malfunction and we're the only ones awake."

"I don't think so. Look around: all the lights are on. Well, kinda, anyway. The ship is pressurized. The system wouldn't be spending all this energy and air if we were the only ones using it. It would have powered up our room lights, and our room air and let us deal with things the best we could."

"So what happened? A bad batch of stasis pods?" Tristan asked. That was the biggest nightmare of every person who boarded an interstellar flight. A stasis failure meant that you'd never wake or, worse still, find yourself alone in a ship with five hundred years still to go and no way to get back to sleep. It was the thing everyone tried to avoid thinking of, the part of space travel that required true bravery.

Cora shrugged. "Or maybe we took a hit. Enemy fire somewhere. Or even a space object through our ice shield. The odds of that are about as high as having multiple tube failures, so it's a valid possibility." She looked into Tristan's eyes. "So, marine, ready to get on with it?"

Are you kidding? Not even close, he thought. "Yes, ma'am."

"Good. Let's take turns on this winch. I'll go first."

Five minutes later, there was a big enough gap under the door to allow them to squeeze through.

They entered a fully illuminated corridor which stretched all the way to a door about twice as wide as the ones they'd been using.

"Hope that one works; I don't think I'm up to winching it."

"Come on." Cora strode ahead. When she arrived at the door, she unhesitatingly pressed the big blue button.

Tristan heaved a very un-marinelike sigh of relief when it opened without a hitch.

The staging area, one of four identical hangars within the ship, stretched out before them. It was a colossal rectangular chamber with balconies along each side, each consisting of row upon row of niches, and each niche holding a single armored exoskeleton. The hold held three thousand machines: a hundred per row, by ten stories, replicated on each of the three walls of the room. The fourth side consisted of a gigantic doorway, the only thing between them and hard vacuum.

The room was dimly lit. Lights on the floor gave off some illumination, and there were also lights on the roof that looked like a tiny starscape in the distance. Most of the room was lost in shadows.

"Hello!" Cora shouted.

Tristan was expecting echoes, but the room swallowed the sound. He saw movement up ahead and a voice responded. "Just a second," someone shouted. "We'll be right there."

A few moments later, a small group trudged out of the shadows. Five men and two women approached and saluted. "We're the 74th platoon," a tall, greying man said.

Cora returned his salute. "243rd," she replied. "Or what's left of us."

"Casualties already? Have you been in combat?"

"No. But we had seven tubes fail on us. Did you guys all make it out okay?"

"We lost one man to a fall, but that was after awakening. He hit the back of his head against a corner trying to get out of the tube. Other than that, we're all right, but we seem to have gotten a bad batch of stasis chambers as well. I've never been this weak after a trip, and I've taken some long ones."

"I count only seven. With one dead, that leaves two of you unaccounted for."

"They're inside, checking out the suits." He grimaced. "It's not looking too good on that front. The batteries are all dead and they won't hold a charge for more than a few seconds."

"That's stupid. They told us the equipment was all brand new. No way it can be dead after a four-hundred-year trip."

"Well, we've only tried some exoskeletons on the lower levels, but so far, it's all the same story. One dead suit after another. Maybe when we go higher, we'll have more luck."

"Somehow, I doubt it," Cora told him.

"Yeah. The whole ship looks like it's held together with duct tape. I hope the rest of the armada is in better shape, because if not, we're not going to be much of a diversion."

Tristan smirked to himself. The rumors were true: this was a suicide mission, start to finish. And a diversion at that, meant to draw attention away from more important action elsewhere.

Then he shrugged inwardly. It had never been much of a secret. He'd heard the rumors weeks before launch, while they were training with the new suits. He'd volunteered anyway. The war was going so badly that he just thought it was better to go down on his terms than in some doomed rearguard action.

And besides, how much of a secret could it be if even the platoon lieutenants had been briefed? Those guys were always the last to find out about anything. Even the newest recruits would hear about it days before it reached a single lieutenant.

"Even if the ship was in perfect shape," the greybeard continued, "we don't have any suits. What good is infantry without suits?"

"I'm still not sure what good infantry is in a space war against an enemy that isn't interested in territory, so I'm not the right person to ask. Find a general. Or better yet an admiral; I'm pretty sure they don't care how many grunts get vaped as long as their precious ships don't get damaged. They can probably give you a thousand reasons to send people in suits against relativistic projectiles."

"I hear you, but I'm still hoping the navy people are all right. I have no idea how to fly this thing, much less fix it if it isn't in perfect condition. And I have a feeling it's far from perfect."

The 74th led the three marines deeper into the bay, and demonstrated the suits. As they'd warned, the exoskeletons were receiving power from the ship, but not holding a charge. To make things worse, the lubricant seemed to have petrified in every joint. Every time an exoskeleton moved, a cloud of dried lube flew into the air with a crack.

"Man, I sure hope the maintenance people get here soon," Tristan said.

"Hell, I hope anyone gets here soon. Where are they?" Cora said. Then she turned to her counterpart. "What do you think? Did they wake us up too soon?"

"No. I actually thought we'd been woken too late and we'd missed the fighting. Before we made it here, my theory was that everyone had been killed and we were drifting around in a ghost ship, just waiting for the air to run out. I thought our timer had malfunctioned and the fighting was over."

"But then the exoskeletons would be gone," Tristan blurted.

"Exactly. Either the exoskeletons would be gone or there would be a whole shitload of marines sitting around playing cards, and I don't know about you, but I don't consider the twelve of us to be a shitload by any stretch of the imagination."

A voice from the entrance hailed them and they went over to investigate. Six soldiers who'd lost their CO and three of their friends to some kind of weird stasis tube failure had one question for the group already in the exoskeleton bay.

"Where the hell is everybody?" one of them asked.

"Fucked if I know," was the only reply they got.

9

CHAPTER 2

Melina Tau Osella thought she was out of tears. She believed that they had all been shed when the tiny mining colony gathering heavy elements in the Epsilon Canis Majoris system was suddenly, unexpectedly, overrun by an alien fleet.

Melina had been watching from the pilot's room of a transport with fifteen other children—the only people evacuated from the settlement—as organic-looking landers swarmed over the colony's hull and then, horribly, breached and entered through every weak point.

The terse reports soon turned to screamed descriptions of gelatinous aliens, impervious to beam weapons, consuming everyone in their path. Five minutes after the first aliens had breached the hull, the radio from the colony went silent.

Humanity had, in that distant backwater a little over four hundred light years from Earth, made its first contact with an alien species: a monumental occasion with terrible consequences. At that moment, Melina didn't care that her race would soon be dragged into in a three- and then four-sided interstellar war. Her mind wasn't on the billions who'd perish as a direct consequence of what she was witnessing.

All she knew was that her mother and father had been on that station. As the transport ran for its life, she cried, convinced that she would die of sadness. As gentle hands placed her in stasis, she was still crying. And when she woke, hundreds of years later, she cried for days.

Melina spent her childhood aboard a succession of transport vessels, always one step ahead of the advancing enemy. She grew up in spurts between terms in stasis: a month here, half a year there, and then they'd shut her into a tube. Always running, always crying.

She cried herself to sleep every single night until one day she simply decided that she was sixteen years old, the age at which she could legally sign up as a subcadet in the space corps. The woman who ran the recruiting office thought she looked too young, but her records were so completely muddled after dozens of decades-long space flights that they had no choice but to accept her.

She'd known exactly how old she was: thirteen and eight months. She'd counted every single day since her parents died when she was seven years and four months old. The night they assigned her a uniform and a bunk in a long barracks room was the very last time she cried.

Until now.

Tears fell, one after another, and spattered against the transparent plastic of the stasis pod. The… thing beneath the plastic was long past caring, and she couldn't believe that the desiccated tissue, sunken eye sockets, and rictus grin had once belonged to Nairo.

It couldn't be. Nairo was a smiling, laughing, loving man, the epitome of everything good about humanity. This dried husk couldn't be the same person.

But her tears knew better. They fell onto the lid and rolled down the cylindrical tube and through the grating in the floor.

A hand shook her shoulder. "Come on, Melina, you need to get dressed."

Melina nodded. She was dimly aware that she was still as naked as when she'd left the stasis tube. In the hour since she'd woken, someone had managed to get the ventilation working, and the circulating air was giving her goosebumps.

She hadn't even noticed it. Her brain was in shock, unable to correctly process the loss. They'd volunteered for this mission together, even getting married so that they would be posted to the same ship. They both knew they wouldn't be returning. It was an open secret that this raid was a suicide mission, and that was something they'd both accepted. They had decided to die together—the only thing that had made the fact of Nairo's inevitable demise bearable was that he'd die beside her, probably a victim of the same attack.

In the final moment, as some unspeakable energy weapon reduced the ship to atoms, they would blend together, probably forever, in the resulting ionized cloud.

That was how it was supposed to end.

He wasn't supposed to die before her. What possible eternal connection could she have with the mummified corpse in the stasis tube? She felt that she'd lost him in the most complete way imaginable.

"I don't even know how long he's been dead," she mumbled.

"I'm sorry, what did you say?"

She turned to Laika, the woman trying to help her up. "I said, I don't even know how long he's been dead."

The other woman just nodded, unsure of what to say. She had the haunted look of someone who'd given up trying to understand what was going on and was just along for the ride. "Come on. You need to dress."

Melina allowed herself to be led numbly across the chamber to where her uniform hung. And then be gingerly inserted into the clothing. "You need to be careful with these. They didn't travel well," Laika said.

Melina nodded and let her companion lead her to the pilot room.

11

The buzz of voices raised in argument reached her before they arrived. The room was only half-full, but the twenty people within seemed to all be talking at once. They went quiet when Melina entered. Heads nodded in her direction. One or two people squeezed her hand as she passed.

The concern on everyone's face broke through her daze. "What's going on?" she asked.

Everyone spoke at once, and it was impossible to understand anything. She held up a hand, wincing slightly as pain ran up her arm. "Wait, wait. One at a time." She selected a pilot nearby. "Xsu, you go first."

The man straightened. "No one's really sure, Commander. We lost about a third of our unit in the stasis room. The hangar doors are sealed shut and we haven't been able to get in touch with the ship's bridge crew, or even the maintenance team. All the ships comms seem to be down."

Reflex and years of training as a fighter officer kicked in, and she set her grief aside. "Did you send someone up to talk to them?"

"We did. The compression locks are sealed tight, as if the ship suffered decompression on the far side."

That was standard procedure on carriers, and the *Ismala* was no exception. The fighter bays were often breached in heavy fighting, so ships with fighter wings often had double-hulled structures with airlocks connecting them. They were always sealed in combat and in transit, but they should have opened automatically when the ship was repressurized.

"All right. What else do I need to know?" She scanned the room as no further information was forthcoming. "Where's General Tau Tinini?"

Xsu shrugged, but a junior pilot at the rear of the crowd spoke up. "He's dead. Never made it out of his pod."

The face of her dead lover—no, husband, now—flashed in front of her eyes and Melina pushed it away. *Not now.* "Fair enough. Where are all the rest? We started out with hundreds of pilots. Are they all dead, too?"

"No. We sent the ones who made it to settle in their barracks rooms. Didn't want them messing around in the hallways. Each flight sent a representative."

"Good work. What was the casualty rate?"

Xsu spoke up again. "It's hard to tell, but we've been comparing notes, and we think it was somewhere between twenty and thirty percent."

One out of five pilots dead before a shot was fired... this isn't the way we wanted this to begin, Melina thought. She made an effort to

12

control her expression, however. All she said out loud was: "Xsu, can you get me an exact number? Go to all the birthing chambers and count the bodies. I want to know what we've got to work with. What about other senior officers?"

"A few in the barracks getting the troops together. They told us to report whatever info comes up back to them."

"All right. I need a few volunteers." Everyone tried to step forward or raise their hands at once, and she smiled. "I should have known. The reason you people volunteered for this mission, even though you knew it was a suicide job, was that you volunteer for everything. And here I thought you were all a bunch of heroes."

This got a muted laugh. Melina decided she'd have to be content with that under the circumstances. She chose four random pilots. "Go get a laser drill and some hull discs. I want to find out who's flying this crate."

Hull discs were easy to find. Designed to patch small areas of depressurization, they were assigned to every unit. Anyone who spotted a small breach was to apply the disk to the hole. The patch would be held in place by the pressure differential, and it would also deform into the hole to seal it until more permanent repairs could be made. It was simple, but effective.

Finding a working laser drill, the most basic piece of technology, was another thing altogether. One after another, drills were inspected and discarded. One was dead. So was another. This one was working, but out of focus—you could use its beam to warm coffee, but you weren't going to drill through a bulkhead with it—another one was dead. It took an hour before they found one that would serve the purpose.

"All right. Set it up here, and close that blast door." If they suffered sudden depressurization, the blast door would hold while others sealed its edges and made it airtight.

As one of the pilots drilled a small hole in the airlock, the rest of them held themselves ready, disks in hand, expecting the air to rush out.

"I'm nearly through... there!" the man with the drill said. He quickly turned it off and moved out of the way to allow his disk-wielding companions through.

It proved an unnecessary precaution.

Melina cautiously put her finger near the hole, careful to avoid touching the hot metal. "No breeze. The other side is pressurized. Go ahead and open the airlock." She waited impatiently while her volunteers wrestled with a large circular manual locking handle. The airlock swung open to reveal a well-lit corridor. "Looks like they've got power, at least. Let's get to the bridge."

Three corridors and a couple of staircases later, the five fighter pilots reached the main observation deck and control center, a domed enclosure at the upper front of the ship. There was another, similar space underneath the ship, but that one was farther away. And besides, naval tradition held that the captain was always in the upper bridge.

They found the area full of people in maintenance uniforms, but none in those of ship's officers. "Hello," Melina said. "What's going on?"

A robust man in a ragged maintenance uniform who was giving instructions to a work crew arrayed beneath a bank of instruments glanced her way and then did a double-take as he noticed her uniform and insignia. "Commander," he said. "Am I ever glad to see you. We thought we were the only people alive on the ship. Us and the cleaning staff."

"What about the ship's officers?"

"Taken out by some kind of impact. Whoever designed a ship where the people who can fly it are housed near the hull where any passing asteroid or dangerous radiation is likely to get to them should be taken out and fed to a blob." The man used the popular term for the alien race that had killed her parents and countless billions of others.

"So what are you doing here?"

"Trying to get the instruments back online, especially the comm. Everything's down: microwave, optical, everything. Hell, I'd settle for a radio, if only we could talk to the rest of the fleet and get some semblance of a crew on board."

"The rest of the fleet? Do you know if they're here?"

"I don't know about all of them, but you can see the *Lapland* over there. For some reason, they have their running lights on. I'd estimate that they're fifty klicks off, maybe more."

"That's stupid. We're supposed to be running full dark and in tight formation. Fifty klicks is too much."

He shrugged. "Tell that to them." He handed her a pair of long binoculars.

She looked and, sure enough, the shape of their factory ship could barely be made out, silhouetted by its illumination patterns. A small fraction of the weight on her shoulders lifted. If the factory ship had made it, then basically any piece of the *Ismala* could be repaired, up to and including hull plates. Of course, they had to have enough time to do it. If the enemy located them and hit them first, there would be little to be done.

The thought brought her back to matters at hand. "Any sign of the blobs?"

"No. But they have to be around here somewhere. That's the star we were aiming for."

Kochab hung, bright and blueish, right in the center of the forward viewscreen and Melina growled to herself. *Mission planners are a secretive bunch of assholes*, she thought. *In the briefings, they told us that we'd be approaching from above the ecliptic, but here we are, coming in from the side.*

And then she chuckled. How did she know they were coming in just slightly above the ecliptic plane when there were no planets in sight? The only answer she could give was: *hell if I know. I just know.* And most of the pilots she knew would nod in agreement and leave it at that.

"And what happens if they suddenly appear? Do we have anything online? Weapons? Propulsion? Shields?"

"Not yet. We've been concentrating on getting the radio back online."

"Screw the radio. Get me everything else. Start with the main engines, and work down from there."

"Why? Who's going to fly it?"

"I will if I have to. And right now, it looks like I do. And since I have to fly it, I'd like to have some ability to stop this thing before we smack into that star over there."

"We've got plenty of time. I'd feel better about this if we could call the fleet and ask for a real crew, and not just a bunch of guys who fly things about a million times smaller than a carrier."

"If anyone in the rest of the armada wants to talk to us, they'll send someone over. In the meantime, I want this ship up and running. Unfortunately for you, this is a military mission, and this little badge on my shoulder here says you have to do what I tell you to. So get me engines…"

He gave her a sour look and turned to make it happen.

Melina paused and thought about the situation. "No. Belay that order. Get me scanners first. If I'm going to have maneuverability, I want to know what I'm steering us toward."

She called the surly maintenance chief back to her side. "Tell me. Do you have more people? Eighteen seems like a tiny number of techs for a ship this size."

He shrugged. "These things are completely over-engineered. They're designed to never break. But yeah, I have another two crews resting. Fifteen and sixteen people, because something happened to our stasis pods. Normally, each crew would be twenty strong. We work in eight-hour shifts."

"Good, get them all to work right now."

"What about the shifts?"

"I'll let you know when the first shift is over, but you can bet your ass that it's not going to happen before this ship can participate in a fight. From where I sit, that looks like it'll probably take longer than eight hours, so I suggest you get a move on."

***

An eternity—or perhaps it just seemed that way to her—later, the foreman was back on the bridge.

Dark circles had formed under his eyes. "Nothing works."

"That's not what I want to hear," Melina told him. But the edge was gone from her voice. After his initial resistance, the man had proved to be an incredible asset. He seemed to be in ten places at once, chivvying, cajoling and, when necessary, bullying his people to do what needed to be done.

And she'd also remembered that, like everyone else on the vessel, everyone in the fleet, the man was a volunteer.

He sighed. "But it's what you need to hear. Every sensor antenna is worn to a nubbin. We have only one EVA suit, which we cobbled together from the two dozen we were supposed to have. Even the wiring is worn out. There's something really, really wrong with this ship."

"Do you think we were attacked?"

He hesitated. "No... I don't, actually. Other than the impact damage to the crew quarters, there's no other sign of major violence. If I had to guess, I'd say that the ship was built wrong. There's no way it should be looking like this after this flight. Four hundred years? It should be able to do that trip fifty times before even starting to look this way."

Was it possible? Could someone be selling the substandard military equipment to make a quick profit in the middle of a fight for humanity's survival? Or had the shipyards been infiltrated and sabotaged? Both possibilities made her stomach churn.

"So, is there any good news?"

"We should have forward-looking sensors up and running in about five minutes."

"Thank you." She hesitated for a second. "What's your name, anyway? I know we got off on the wrong foot, but I should have asked."

"I'm Frederic. Just call me Fred."

"Melina." She held out her hand and the man shook it.

"Ready, chief." The voice came from below the console in the center of the bridge. "Try it now."

Fred walked over to the console as one of his techs emerged. He hit the biggest button and it came to life. "That's probably the only piece of delicate electronics working on this ship, Commander. Please take care of it."

Melina sat on the chair in front of the console. It groaned and swayed alarmingly, but held. She began entering commands into the holographic space above the console, calling up views and high-res imagery.

She called back to the other pilots who'd been trickling up from the fighter levels. "Does anyone remember their Fleet Instruments classes? I'm way too old for this."

A couple of the pilots stood behind her and began to point at the commands she needed before Xsu finally lost patience.

"Maybe it might be best if I took over, Commander."

"Good idea, although you'll need to be careful with that chair."

He sat down gingerly and the display began to dance. "What am I looking for?"

"Whatever you can find. Enemy fleet formations, electromagnetic signatures. Any radiation not coming from the star, basically. Also, planets. Tell me where we are."

The foreman stepped forward. "You only have passive capabilities. We don't have any of the active systems running yet."

"That's all right. We can't use the active systems anyway. We want to see them before they see us... and the active systems are extremely easy to detect. They're great for looking through planets, but terrible for hiding. We're definitely trying to hide right now, at least until you give me some guns to play with."

"I'd feel much better about that if the *Lapland* didn't have all its lights blazing."

Xsu held up a hand. "All right. Two planets on this side of the star. One is an ice giant with a boatload of moons, the other is much further in and seems to be a superearth type. Emissions coming from at least three of the giant's moons and also from the inner planet and its moon. There's definitely something here."

Melina turned to Fred. "Can I add another task to your list of priorities?"

The man sighed. "How? You've already got us working on everything at once."

"I need you to get the recorders up and running, and some of the processing and translation mainframes. I want to see if we can run these signals through them and find out if they correspond to standard blob military frequencies, or if we're seeing something else. Our intel is four hundred years old. God only knows if someone else might have hit this system while we were in transit. It might be the Brillans sitting there waiting for us. Hell, it might be a human fleet no one told us about or even the Uploaders. I need to know what we're heading into."

The man looked nervous when Melina mentioned the Uploaders. They were another faction in the four-way war; sometimes a friend and sometimes a foe. They were the only ones that had once been human, until they decided to abandon their bodies and live in a simulated world. It was a strange thing: tens of thousands of people had volunteered for this mission, knowing that they were going to an almost certain death in the frozen wastes of space, but mention the possibility of having your mind forcibly transferred to a giant computer and they turned very quiet.

"Wouldn't you prefer to get navigation up and running next?"

"Who needs navigation? All I need to do is to avoid running into any planets or the star. I can navigate manually. Recorders first. And if a fleet appears anywhere, I'll fly at that and shoot it with the weapons you'll have repaired for me." She turned back to Xsu. "Any sign of a fleet?"

"No. The only radiation is coming from the sources I mentioned. Unless they knew we were coming and hid behind some massive body, there are no other ships in this system."

"That's the first piece of good news I've heard all day. If any of our generals or admirals survived, they'll be delighted to hear it."

CHAPTER 3

The bridge of the flagship wasn't designed to give the general staff a direct look at space through a glass dome. This room was an armored and radiation-hardened bunker buried deep within the bowels of the vessel.

The flagship itself wasn't really a ship, either. Although it sported the name *Heavy Gunship IV*, it was actually a mobile battle station designed to sit at the vanguard of any action and to draw fire away from less well-armored troop transports and fighter carriers.

In consequence, it was only after the electronic viewscreens had been put back online that the bridge began to fill up with people.

Lieutenant Ian Centauri Perez knew he'd only been invited because the two people above him on the Recon staff had failed to survive the trip. Though he would have preferred to have every able-bodied person available to fight the enemy, he didn't really mourn his superiors too much. His wing commander and her own superior had both been humorless harridans. He suspected that his unit, which had been signed up wholesale, was one of the few consisting of troops who hadn't volunteered to be there.

And now, he'd been field promoted to CO, and the issues that were inevitably going to come up were his to deal with. Great. Those two shrews hadn't even had the decency to die at a convenient time.

At least the admiral seemed to be discussing high-level stuff with the upper command of the fighter wings and ground troops, and they probably wouldn't need him to participate much.

"So the fleet is completely out of formation, but mostly accounted for?" the admiral asked. He was an old man, balding and liver-spotted, who looked like he'd volunteered because being killed in a suicide mission would likely only shorten his life by a few minutes.

"Yes, sir. Only the *Troubadour* is missing."

"That's twelve thousand troops less than we set out with. And I suppose we still haven't got an accurate count of how many troops didn't make it out of stasis on the *Minstrel* and *Bard*."

"Not yet, sir. They're still counting. The good news is that they overestimated the dead in the first reports. Seems like a lot of troops were alive, but caught behind sealed doors. They're finding more and more able-bodied soldiers as they get their systems back online."

The admiral nodded. "All right. How about the fighter wings?"

"*Dart* and *Centauri's Courage* report that their fighters need extensive repairs. They estimate that in the best of cases, they can build a single fighter with the parts from four others. They want the factory to build them more." The aide giving the report paused, checked with a small man seated beside him with headphones on, and continued. "We still haven't been able to reach the *Ismala*, but they're probably all right. They've got their engines up and running and have closed formation with the *Lapland*."

"Well, somebody is looking alive at least. They're the only ship in the fleet that has engines right now."

"*Banshee* says that they should have power to the drive pretty soon, maybe in a couple more hours, and the captain wants to know if he has permission to range ahead once the engines are up."

"No. Not yet. I know she's our scout ship, but I don't want him to move out until he has his cloaking working. Without that, it's better to do the scouting with a ship that can defend itself."

The aide relayed the order as the admiral turned his attention to the other side of the room where a knot of senior officers was conversing. "So, what's the plan?"

The general in command of the fleet's complement of ground troops responded. "We think the best idea is to go after the two moons on the ice giant which have been emitting radiation. There's a couple of reasons for this: the first is that I don't want to leave anyone behind me, not even automated systems. The second reason has to do with securing resources for the *Lapland*. From what I hear, they're going to need a lot of raw materials for the nanofactories to repair our ships and suits, and the giant and its moons are a good place to get them: they're on our way and probably less heavily defended than the inner system."

"I like it, plus they'll probably be less well-defended than places further in. Do we have enough working suits to take both of those moon-based installations?"

"No. We're planning to disable one from the air and only send ground troops to take the other."

The admiral nodded. "Good. When do we start?"

"Whenever the fleet can move and we have enough suits and fighters."

"Okay. I'll keep you posted on the repairs." He turned to another aide. "Any sign of the enemy fleet?"

"No, sir."

"Good. We got here before them. The spies weren't sure, but they did say that they thought we might have a few days' window before the blobs arrived, based on their departure date and the speed we'd seen from their ships. We were lucky there." He stood straight and surveyed his audience.

Ian knew the admiral was now speaking for the benefit of everyone in the room. He leaned forward to listen. "I know that each and every one of you signed up for this mission in the expectation that it would be a suicide job."

Not me, thought Ian. *I was press-ganged.*

The admiral continued. "But for once, luck seems to be with us. Maybe, if we can remove their ground support and hit them by surprise, we just might be able to destroy the enemy fleet."

"It's ten times bigger than ours, sir," someone pointed out from the shadows in the back.

"True," the admiral responded, unfazed. "But they think they're arriving at a staging position that's secure. As far as we know, they're unaware that we can send spy probes through space folds and get information about their movements faster than light—or at least when they left, they weren't aware of that. The enemy definitely won't be expecting us to be here before them—all the warning they'll get will be whatever time they have from the moment any message sent from here reaches them and the time they arrive. With luck, they'll all be in stasis, and no one will read the info until it's much too late."

"Still a pretty tall order."

"That's what you signed up for. To give your life to buy the people of Tau Ceti a little more time."

"They've had four hundred years. How much more time do they need?"

"Well, as much as we can give them, plus any damage we can do to the blob's fleet. Reinforcements scrambled from all over, and retreating fleets have been diverted to Tau... but some of them will take another ten years to get there, some of them a hundred."

"Sounds like Tau is pretty much screwed."

Silence met this pronouncement. Even the guy who spoke seemed uncomfortable with what he'd said.

The admiral sighed. "I hope not. Tau Ceti is the last stand before the enemy reaches Earth. Even a slow fleet can cross that gap in forty years. If we lose Tau, we'll have to bring everything back in to defend the Motherworld." He slapped a hand against a console. "We have to hold Tau, no matter what the cost."

The talk made Ian dizzy. How anyone could plan a war in which the battles happened hundreds of years after they'd been planned, and it was nearly impossible to communicate with the commanders once they set off, was beyond him. What if peace was declared, but the commanders didn't know? Entire systems might be destroyed, millions killed before word reached them that the war was over.

Of course, from what he'd gleaned listening to the admiral, it seemed that mankind now had access to some kind of fold technology which allowed electronics to move through space more efficiently... but how many of them were there? And how reliable? They'd all heard of the research being done, and dreamed of putting fleets wherever they wanted to instantly. That would change the course of the war, obviously. You could attack unprotected systems while the enemy fleets were in transit.

He was glad he didn't have to coordinate any of it. If it was up to him, he'd probably just order the entire fleet to find a nice empty system with a nice empty planet to colonize, turn off all its electronics, and hide from the galaxy until it all blew over.

The admiral was still speaking. "If we manage to inflict significant damage here, even if we all die doing it, it might mean the difference between Tau's defenses holding against this fleet or not holding. It might be the difference between Tau being reinforced before the enemy can send another fleet in its direction and Tau falling. That's why we're here."

He pointed at the screen, empty of markers denoting enemy ships. "And we've been lucky so far. The installations here are undefended from space. We know the blobs are always tough to kill on the ground, but if worse comes to worst, we'll hit them from orbit. At minimum, that should make it tough for them to refit and refuel." He let them think about it a few minutes. "We have had a very lucky break, and now it's time for us to take utmost advantage of it."

Heads nodded around the table.

"Who's in charge of Recon?"

Ian started, but tried to cover his surprise. "I am, sir."

"Maintenance tells me they have one of your flyers ready for action. It's the only space-worthy smallcraft in the fleet, which means that you just got volunteered for some flying."

"Yes, sir." But his mood darkened. He felt that he was getting volunteered for stuff more often than he would have preferred.

"We need someone to fly out to the *Ismala* and see what their status is. Can you get there?"

"In a Recon Flyer? Of course."

"Good. Tina here will... where's Tina?"

"Over here, sir."

"Don't hide from me like that." He shook his head in anger. "As I was saying, Tina will get you down to the hangar. She can get you anything you need from the maintenance crew. If she doesn't, let me know about it and I'll have her tossed out of an airlock or something."

He followed the woman off the bridge and into a corridor. She was an attractive woman, perhaps thirty years of age with shoulder-length red hair, which was a welcome change: it seemed that every other woman on board had cut her hair in some variation of utilitarian shortness. Her uniform held no rank, and wasn't from one of the service branches, just regular ship's crew.

"The old man sure was hard on you."

"Well, someone needs to run messages. I guess he just wants me to understand how important this job is."

"I'm sure there are other ways of doing so."

"Possibly. Come this way. The lifts are still out of order, and we don't have time for the main stairs."

She led him into a small service corridor which alternated short drops via pole from level to level with metal rungs set into the walls.

"Going down seems easy enough, but I'd hate to have to come up this way."

"It can be a pain," she replied. And then maintained a stubborn silence all the way to the hangar.

"Here you go. The maintenance people don't like me, but the admiral's probably told them to give you anything you need. Still, I'd better come with you just in case."

"Seems like the admiral's message got through to you. You're treating this as an important task."

"Hell, I think everyone here knows how important everything we do is, even the small stuff. Why volunteer if you didn't?"

"What makes you think I volunteered?"

"Because the only people who were forced to come along were the crew of the factory ship. And they were only obligated because they have expertise which the fleet couldn't get elsewhere. Nanotechnicians don't exactly grow on trees."

"That's not quite right. My entire unit was volunteered by our CO. No one asked us whether we wanted to come."

"What? That's impossible."

"Not particularly. I'm here, and I most definitely didn't volunteer for this. I had a wife and child, who are both probably dead hundreds of years ago now. We were told that not coming meant court martial, and that the whole concept of everyone volunteering was just something the military was saying to keep the civilian population from panicking. I only found out that the volunteers were real when I woke up here."

She stopped in her tracks. "Oh, my God. Did you tell the admiral about this?"

"No. And what he doesn't know won't hurt him. I'm sure I can trust you to keep my secret."

"What makes you say that?"

"The way he treats you. I bet you'd be happy to keep him in the dark"

"Probably not. He can be pretty cranky, but that would still be a really lousy way to treat one's father."

He swallowed, but before he could answer, a maintenance tech in mechanic's coveralls, tattered and broken like every other uniform on the ship, approached. "We've managed to get this one flying, but I wouldn't try anything too fancy."

Ian looked over the flyer. It looked fine, solid and gleaming, but if there was one thing that he knew from experience, it was that the techs knew these birds inside and out, and a pilot ignored their misgivings at his own risk. "Why, what's wrong with it?"

The mechanic scratched his head and looked it over. "Nothing, in theory. It's just that all the parts we use seem to be worn out. Brittle. We took the ones that worked best and also tested the ship as much as possible, but when you don't trust the parts, you never feel quite right about the ship. All I can say is that it works for now, and it passes all the tests."

"All right, let me try it on for size."

It was a standard Recon flyer. This two-person unit was the backbone of the corps. It could drift through space completely undetected in standard patrol and observation trajectories. It was designed to leak absolutely no radiation. Even its surface was painted with a special treatment that reflected most wavelengths in precisely the same way that a random supercool space rock would.

Communications were by tightly focused line-of-sight laser modulations, which were about as difficult to intercept as anything could be.

Ian knew from long experience that flying a real Recon mission in one of these things was uncomfortable as hell, and when you were two-up, privacy was inexistent.

But they did their job very well. Ian knew he owed his life to the thoughtful, thorough design's performance under real surveillance conditions at least twice over, both during the same battle.

He had a soft spot for these little flyers, even if the fighter jockeys insisted on calling them 'beetles,' on account of their insectoid appearance. And he trusted them with his life—they'd delivered the goods before.

He climbed in and powered it up. Although he knew he technically hadn't flown one of these for four hundred years, his muscles remembered where every toggle and lever was, and he soon had it hovering gently in the hangar. "How's it look?" he asked the tech over the radio.

"All right so far."

"OK, then let's try it in space. A few klicks to the *Ismala* should be a good test. Open the hangar door."

"Can't. The ion air shields aren't working yet. If I open the main door, we'll vent all the atmosphere. Can you fly it out of the airlock?"

Ian sighed. "If I have to."

"You have to."

It was a tight fit for a flyer, but the cargo lock was big enough that an experienced pilot could navigate it without knocking off his antennae. Five minutes later, he was in space, gingerly testing the thrusters: if one of the stream nozzles failed, there was enough energy in the fuel cells to atomize him.

Everything seemed to work correctly, but the tech still felt the need to tell him: "I'll feel a lot more comfortable if you keep everything under sixty percent load."

"All right. Steering for the *Ismala*."

The flight was uneventful, even boring. Ian feathered the throttle and approached the carrier from above, waggling his extremely stubby craft at the startled crew in the bridge. This was strictly forbidden by every single regulation in the book, but with the *Ismala*'s comms out of commission, it was the only way he could think of to let them know he was there.

He made his way to the upper landing pad, touched down, and let his pressure tube find its own way to the airlock. Once it was safe to do so, he opened the inner hatch and descended into the carrier, delighted to find that light, air, and gravity were all present.

Also present was a woman. In her late thirties, with short dark hair, she had rings under her eyes. That seemed to be the norm. Everyone on *Heavy Gunship IV* sported a set just as dark.

But there was something about this woman that made Ian suspect that more than exhaustion was at work. Her look was tinged with barely controlled grief. She fought to keep it under, but Ian could see it lurking just beneath the surface.

"I'm Commander Coloni, of the fighter wing," she said. "What's going on out there?"

He shrugged. "All I can really tell you is that they're pulling the fleet back together as fast as they can. Most of the ships seem to have been pretty badly damaged in transit. If the enemy fleet had already been here, they would have cut us to ribbons before we could even move... or know they were out there."

"Yeah, I gathered that. Good to know everyone's alive, though."

"Not everyone. We lost the *Troubadour*." She nodded, taking this information, the loss of a full third of the ground troops, without blinking. He went on, "The admiral sent me over here to find out how you were doing. Your comms are down."

"We're working on that. We had other priorities."

"More important than getting your orders from the admiral?"

"If he's offended, I'll apologize later. I just thought that in a battle zone, it might be better to actually be able to move and fight back before worrying about the other stuff. I know exactly which ships are on my side, and I was planning to shoot at everything else."

"You? Why you? Where's the captain?"

"He turned out to be allergic to asteroid strikes. So did the rest of the regular crew. Turns out, I'm the ranking officer now. First thing I do once I get the comms up is to ask the admiral for some regular navy types. This tub is a bear to fly. We nearly crashed into the *Lapland* as we were moving back into formation."

"I'll make sure to mention that to the admiral."

"No need. You're not going back."

"What? Admiral gave me orders to tell him what I'm doing here."

"I know. And I'll apologize for that as well. But my maintenance people have forbidden me to let your flyer off the hull. They told me that fixing the comms would normally take hours, but patching into your ship's system would take minutes. So the good thing is that you won't need to wait to watch the admiral tear me a new one."

But the admiral didn't comply. Far from berating her for stealing his only working flyer, kidnapping its pilot and motoring around incommunicado, he commended her for taking swift action and getting her ship closer to fighting form than anything else in the fleet. He also said a few choice words about the men who designed the ships.

Finally, he asked her to honestly tell him when she'd have a complete fighter wing for him to use.

"Not until the factory starts sending us parts. The maintenance team thinks they can salvage maybe one in five, but it's going to take them weeks to build them. We don't have too many mechanics on this crate."

"Yeah, *Dart* and *Centauri's Courage* are singing the same tune."

"This makes no sense, Admiral. For so many ships to fail at the same time, in the same way... I've never seen a single ship fail on such a short jaunt, much less several. Hell, I've never even *heard* of something like that. And I've been in this war quite a while."

He chuckled. And then self-consciously realized what he'd done. "I'm sorry. It's just that when you get to be my age, young lady, claims of being in the war for a long time become matters for humor. It's been a good chunk of my life."

"With all due respect, Admiral, it's been *all* of mine. I was at Epsilon Canis. I'm pretty sure I've been fighting the blobs, or running from them, since before your great grandfather was born."

His eyed widened and she saw him repeat her name under his breath one time, and then another and another in succession, as if trying to place it. Out loud he said: "So that's where I heard your name. Tau Coloni. I would say it's an honor to serve with you, but I imagine you've heard it a bit too often."

"Plus, I no longer find honor in being next to people when they're vaporized. I've lost too much for this war to be anything except for something I want to forget about... even if that means dying during a suicide mission."

"Fair enough. You might get your wish pretty soon. I've ordered an assault on the moons of the ice giant."

"When?"

"As soon as I have enough suits and dropships. Two days, tops."

"We can't get you fighter support in two days."

"I know. Concentrate on the big guns for now, in case the blobs have ships hidden behind the planet or something."

"And if they've got fighters?"

"All the way out here? Without carrier support?"

"Yes."

"Then the shock marines are going to have a very bad day."

CHAPTER 4

He'd gotten a viewport this time. It almost never happened that way, because the squad lieutenant and sergeant traditionally got the two window seats, with the lieutenant getting planetside, and the sergeant getting shipside. The thinking was that by having the decision makers have a view of the battlefield beforehand, they might see something that they could use to the platoon's advantage.

But that only applied when the platoons were at full strength. Each dropship held ten suits, the exact size of one unit. The math worked perfectly.

Of course, on this drop, units had been haphazardly melded together, and the assignation of seats was pretty much random. That meant that Tristan got a view of the pale view ice giant floating serenely in the distance. It was nearly a million klicks away, but he could still feel the power of its presence. It was an impressive chunk of frozen gas.

Awe pushed aside the fear of the forthcoming battle for a few moments. He wondered how there could be a war in a galaxy where resources were nearly infinite and space was not at a premium. Fear? Lack of an ability to communicate with enemies? Or were humanity's enemies truly so implacable that coexistence was not an option?

The questions were well above Tristan's pay grade, but the sight of a massive blue-white planet hanging in the darkness made him wonder. He spent some weightless minutes following the contours of the ring system with his eyes, attempting to count the number of distinct rings. He gave up at ten.

Then, the dropship shook and brought him back to the present. The moon they were approaching was more like a small planet. Perhaps half an Earthmass, it was big enough to have a methane atmosphere with weather patterns. The gas buffeted the unstreamlined dropship as they approached the surface at high speed.

As the shock marines converged on the selected landing zone, other dropships appeared in the viewport. Tristan could see four of them, black spots against the rusty red sky. They closed formation. The spots became recognizable shapes just as a sudden gust of wind or pressure change buffeted them.

When the shaking stopped, Tristan saw that one of the dropships was in trouble. Small chunks of hull stripped away before it finally disintegrated into a cloud of debris and fell back, out of view.

Tristan knew that the exoskeletons could withstand the fall, and most of the troops should survive, unless whatever had taken the ship apart caught them, too.

He spoke over the Taclink. "We're under fire. Dropship four... no, three, destroyed."

"The suits?" It was the voice of their dropship driver. Tristan felt respect for the man. One of his colleagues had just bought it—the drivers were the only people on board without exoskeletons—and he was still asking questions relevant to the success of the mission.

"Impossible to tell. They fell back behind us. It didn't look like an explosion. More like the dropship took some damage and the atmosphere peeled it like an onion."

"All right. Thirty seconds to touchdown."

Tristan braced himself. The transport was shuddering violently now, and the suits were rattling like ball bearings in a tin can. Things would only get worse. Dropship braking was legendary: the pilots would wait until the last second to apply a combination of backwards thrust and air braking, thus giving any ground troops shooting at them the smallest window possible. The G forces were extremely high, and the guys in the exoskeletons often passed out, something which the pilots in their G suits enjoyed immensely.

When that happened, the exoskeletons would simply inject you with a compound that brought you around immediately. Tristan had once asked what the side effects of that mule kick were, and the sardonic medic had quickly replied: "I have no idea, but I imagine they're probably less than the side effects of standing around on a battlefield without being able to move." He was probably right, even though a single dose of the stuff was enough to keep you awake for three days afterwards.

"Brace yourselves, fellas. Braking in five... four..."

It felt like he'd been kicked in the back. His eyeballs made a bid for freedom, doing their best to jump out of their sockets and splatter against the suit's visor.

It only lasted for three seconds. "All right, folks. Get the hell out of here before they start shooting at me. Remember, I'm not wearing armor."

"Probably serve you right for giving us a fake countdown," one of the troops replied sourly.

"Didn't want you tensing up. Now get out."

They didn't need to be told twice. Or even once for that matter. No one wanted to be stuck in an immobile dropship while the enemy demonstrated how good they were at blowing up static targets. Almost before the floor had finished retracting, the troops had released the magnets holding them to their clamps and were dropping to the frozen surface.

"It's some kind of rock. Good footing and doesn't melt," the team's first-footer reported.

"Perfect. What's the friction?" Cora asked him. She'd been given command over the remnants of her own unit and two others that had lost officers.

"Zero-point-eight of Standard."

That was pretty good for a world this far out from the star. At least they wouldn't slip all over the place as they went.

"Roger. Proceed towards the target."

Their objective was a small building which scanners had shown to be the entrance to a large underground complex. It was just on the other side of a small ridge which they'd landed behind because it was the only cover available for miles.

Two marines scaled the ridge and reported back. "No enemy fire, and I don't see anything that looks like it could be a weapon. All I see is a dark spot on another dark spot, even in thermal imaging. The facility is nearly as cold as the terrain around it."

"Something shot down one of our dropships, soldier."

"With all due respect," Tristan chimed in. "How do we know it just didn't stop working due to faulty parts, just like everything else?"

"We don't. But we can't discard the possibility that someone out there is taking pot shots. Now shut up and get moving."

The scouts moved ahead and Cora and Tristan replaced them at the top of the ridge.

"They're right," Tristan said. "The building looks just as cold as everything around it."

"I can see that for myself. Maintain radio silence."

One of the scouts' voices came in through the net. "The entrance looks to be clear."

"All right. Get inside. And be careful."

Cora motioned for Tristan to follow, and he moved out. The icy ball in his stomach had been replaced by excitement. He'd been on the ground against the blobs before and knew that a well-guided exoskeleton could deal with most of what the aliens had in their ground arsenal.

It was a pleasure to be loping along in a powered suit after some time in stasis. The exoskeleton made easy work of the cold rock and topsoil—its combination of heated rubber pads and crampons allowing excellent grip—as Tristan loped along.

When he reached the entrance, he studied it in detail with his helmet's thermal imaging function. The door was hangar-sized, and the area inside the building was big enough to hold one of their dropships, or some other kind of small transport vessel.

"Are we sure the radiation signals came from here? I'm not getting anything at all."

"The techs on the *Minstrel* were pretty certain, yeah. But the way those ships are working, who knows? This place might have been abandoned ages ago."

"I'm going to look at the far end." Tristan knew he would run the biggest risk. The scouts would be advancing carefully along the two lateral walls, trying to spot defensive measures, but it was always necessary for someone to go down the middle, in the time-honored tradition of every marine corps from the days of ancient Earth onwards.

Some guys liked to take it slowly down the middle, but Tristan took it at a run. Anything nasty would see him regardless of what strategy he took and moving quickly meant that they might miss, and it also gave him some velocity he could use in his favor while taking evasive action.

Three-quarters of the way across, the lights went on inside the chamber, a dull reddish glow. Tristan instinctively jumped to one side, rolled as the suit landed, and pulled into a crouch. He held his hand on the trigger and moved his eyes to control the suit's scanner system. There was no movement, and nothing seemed to be shooting at him.

"You think the motion sensor only activated the lights?"

"That might make sense. All the way out here, you might not get visitors too often, so you can't keep the lights running all the time. And the few who did come probably wouldn't know where to look for the switch. But I'll admit that it would make more sense for a civilian installation."

"Look, as long they aren't shooting me to pieces, I'm fine with this being a civilian place. That will make it easier to blow up." Tristan covered the final few steps to the far wall. "There's some kind of sliding panel here, probably a door."

"All right," Cora said. "Hold there. I'm trying to coordinate with the platoons from the other two dropships. One of them crash landed. No casualties, but they're gonna be awhile. The other crew is on its way to help."

"Any news regarding the crew whose lander broke up?"

"They're not in Tacnet range, and we're not allowed to use anything the enemy might pick up from orbit."

31

Tristan swallowed. On the ground, he would take whatever the blobs threw at him. Hell, when his blood was up, he welcomed the challenge. But getting taken out while helpless in the dropship was every marine's worst nightmare.

"All right, Tristan, everyone who's gonna be here is here. Scouts say the walls look clean. Do you see any way to open the door?"

"No. Blank wall all around it. I'm giving it a push. Nothing."

"Try sliding it."

"Okay." He pushed to the left, but the panel didn't budge. On pushing to the right, his suit sensors picked up a tiny movement. "Looks like that might work, but I'm gonna have to force it. If they don't already know we're here, they will when I'm done with the door."

"Do it."

The material gave way with a loud groan, the first sound Tristan had heard in the methane atmosphere. He pressed against the wall, hoping that any murderous barrage of projectiles or energy would fly right by him.

Nothing happened, so he stuck his head into the hole, pulling it back out quickly. "Dark as hell in there. Gonna take another look with the suit light."

Actinic white beams cut through the room, nearly blinding after the dull red glow of the facility's native illumination. Tristan pointed them into the darkness beyond the gap he'd made and found another wall about six feet away. Then he pointed the beams downward.

"Looks like we found an elevator shaft," he informed his team. "Goes straight down farther than I can see with this light. I count three levels that can be accessed, but there are probably more further below."

"All right, give me a second. We've got this place secured, so we'll leave a couple of sentries to welcome the stragglers from the other shuttles when they get here. The rest of us will go in."

Tristan knew he was going to get into trouble, but toggled his radio. "What? Why? If we drop a charge or two down this shaft, we'll destroy the installation completely without risking any of our lives."

"Orders are orders, soldier. If you like, you can stay up top doing sentry duty. If we get massacred down there, you can drop a charge."

"Absolutely not, ma'am. I want to go down there."

"Thought so. Now use your head. The general needs to know what we're up against. No way to tell him if we just blow everything up. And besides, I don't know about you, but this just doesn't feel like a blob installation to me. They must have stolen it from someone."

She was right. Tristan had fought rearguard actions in the evacuations of two systems. He'd been tasked to hold positions in the face of nearly overwhelming blob attacks. Though he'd never been inside a blob installation—the settlements they were abandoning were invariably human—this certainly didn't feel like their tech. And the light seemed a bit weak for their preference.

"You're right. I apologize."

"Save your apology. No use to me now. But how would you feel about going down that hole first?"

He looked down into the shaft and chuckled. "I don't feel at all good about it to be honest, but I guess someone has to. Do we go to the bottom and work our way up? Or downward from the top?"

"Just go as far as the first stop. We should probably try to figure out how to use this elevator at some point."

"Not while I'm inside, please."

He hooked a line to the suit of one of the scouts who'd made it as far as his position and jumped into the shaft. His exoskeleton had braking rockets, so he considered it best—as he had when crossing the hall—to move as quickly as possible. He overshot the landing by ten feet, hovering below the level of the door as he checked for defenses. Nothing there.

He'd assumed that the door mechanism would be visible from inside the shaft, but the sliding panel looked exactly the same as the one above. He decided against trying to get a grip on it while hovering on suit jets.

"I'm going to have to blow the door."

"All right."

He fired an expanding shrapnel round into the thin metal. In the enclosed shaft, the noise reverberated loudly enough that his suit's audio receptors damped it automatically. The shot punched a round hole about the size of his hand into the material, and then it was just a case of using the suit's servo-assisted claws to pull the door away.

Tristan stepped into a hallway built for some creature shorter than humans: if he'd stood there without his suit, it would have been a close fit. The suit had to bend nearly double to advance. He stopped at the first bend in the hallway and looked around the corner to see another stretch of hall that ended in a door. A cross-corridor bisected it about halfway through.

"All clear. Send in the cavalry."

Suit after suit entered the corridor from the shaft, Cora and the sergeant from the other dropship leading the way. "Cover us," the lieutenant said. She advanced with one of the scouts, moving cautiously. Their beams created long shadows in the darkened hall.

They reached the spot where the other corridor crossed the first and looked carefully around to each side. "Short halls that end at open doors. We'll have to split up to check all three rooms. I'll start with the one in front."

Cora strode across the intersection and the place suddenly came alive. Gunfire from the cross-corridor, accompanied by a bright light, slammed into her suit and threw her down the hall and out of Tristan's sight. Projectiles also glanced off of the scout's suit before he dove out of the line of fire.

"Lieutenant!" Tristan said.

There was no answer. He ran into the hall, selecting his weapons as he went, and ignoring the sergeant's shouted order that he stop. Tristan dove across the intersection, fast enough that the shots that came in his direction missed by wide margins and fired randomly in the direction of the attack.

Once across, he played back what his cameras had recorded and cursed. "It's just a ceiling-mounted swivel gun. And I'd guess it's probably automated and activated by a motion detector. It shot at me, but it's not shooting at the lieutenant."

He selected a frag grenade, set the timer for a second after release, and lobbed it into the cross-corridor, up near the ceiling. He knew that he wouldn't have to hit anything; the fragments should be enough to take a weapon out.

Tristan dove across the hall again. There was no fire this time. He crawled back, staying low, and inspected the weapon. It was a wrecked mess. "OK, the intersection is clear now."

The sergeant approached, held a hand into the intersection, and then walked up to the gun. He motioned for Tristan to join him.

"Hold your light steady on this for a minute," the man said.

He poked and prodded at the gun before pulling it out of its mooring, bringing a mass of wiring with it. "I think your lieutenant is right. This isn't blob tech."

"Not ours, either."

"No. Definitely not. But whose, then?"

"Brillan?"

"We'd better hope not. We can hold our own against the blobs, but the Brillans have kicked our ass every single time we came anywhere near them. If they took this system from the blobs while we were in transit, then we're in deep shit. And so is the blob fleet when it gets here."

"Might be Uploader."

Tristan saw the sergeant shudder beneath the exoskeleton.

"We'll figure it out later. Might be some poor suckers the blobs conquered and ate. Whoever owns this, we need to disable this installation now and worry about it later. You should check on the lieutenant. She got hit hard."

Tristan hadn't worried about it, mainly because the Tac computer wasn't reporting her as dead. Those suits could take quite a beating. But if she was all right, she should have been up and about already. He went to where she lay.

His pulse quickened. Cora's suit was bent into an unnatural shape and he could see light areas where the automated repair systems had patched the skin to keep it pressurized. It didn't look survivable.

He hooked into her diagnostics and saw that the suit had injected her with coma-inducing drugs in an effort to keep her alive long enough for help to arrive. She was in bad shape.

"We need a Medevac here," Tristan said.

"Hate to remind you, we haven't got a Medevac shuttle up and running. Maybe one of the dropships can pull her out, but you're going to need to get her back upstairs. We need to move forward."

Tristan was torn. On one hand, he desperately wanted to feel that he was actually doing something to fight the enemy. On the other... there were only three surviving members of his original ten-man unit. He was damned if he was going to let that number fall by one.

And Cora didn't have a hell of a lot of time.

"All right. I'll try to get her out of here."

"Good luck."

"You, too. Watch those intersections."

Tristan forgot about them. Shock marines could take care of themselves.

He turned his attention to Cora. The diagnostics said that she was stable, but all kinds of red lights which he wasn't trained to evaluate were blinking at him. "Hang on, Lieutenant."

It was nearly impossible to be gentle while wearing an exoskeleton, but he did his best to avoid bumping her unnecessarily as he dragged the inert suit down the hall towards the elevator. Now came the tough part.

Tristan hooked a diamond monofilament line to her suit and let it play out behind him as he powered his way up the shaft. Once he reached ground level, he began to pull the line back in. He winced as Cora's suit overbalanced slightly and banged into the far wall.

He managed to get her up without further mishap, and put her suit on his shoulder, aided by the taller roof of the hangar area. He approached one of the sentries and spoke to him. "Any news on how we're getting out?"

"Pickup in thirty minutes."

"Are any of the dropships still in the area?"

"The one that crash-landed is just getting off the ground."

Tristan called the ship. "Are you in good enough shape to do a Medevac?"

"How many?"

"Just one."

"Hang on."

Less than a minute later, the wounded dropship, wobbling noticeably, flew into view. "Hook her up, but I really wouldn't want to carry anyone else. Not sure how well this thing is going to hold together."

"That's fine, just get her back upstairs as quickly as you can."

The ship left, leaving Tristan to look out over the dark landscape and the stars, hard and bright through the thin atmosphere. The stark emptiness gave him the answer he'd been searching for earlier: warm, hospitable places were few and far between. When you had one secured, logic dictated that you had to defend it against anyone who might covet it. Even if they weren't showing any signs of aggression.

Without warning, a dark shadow flew out of the open door of the building and disappeared into the sky. Thermal imaging showed it as a slightly warmer spot against the cosmos, moving at spectacular speed.

Thirty seconds later, exoskeletons began to pour out of the door. "Move it, guys. You don't want to be within four hundred meters of this place when those charges go off."

Tristan followed the sergeant as they ducked behind the ridge they'd originally used as cover for the landing and then ran a few hundred meters further for good measure. The suits could cover ground extremely well.

"What was that thing?" Tristan asked.

"I have no idea. It was sealed inside some kind of containment field on the lowest floor. We broke some equipment to see what the hell would happen when the field went down and this thing flew out and began shooting at everything in sight. Only got one of the troops, but there wasn't much left of him after it was done. Took out a bunch of computers and crap and even a column. Looked to me like it was firing at random."

"Well, what did it look like?"

"Black and wingy and very, very pissed. I was happy as hell when it took off. That's when I ordered the men to place charges. There were a bunch of those containment fields in that bunker. And by a bunch, I mean a few dozen. I definitely didn't want to have to fight my way out of there against an army of those things. I thought it would be a better idea to blow them to bits."

As if to punctuate this statement, the charges went, shaking the ground.

"How many charges did you use, Sergeant?"

"Every one I had, soldier. Every fucking one."

CHAPTER 5

Irene's heart beat loudly in her chest as she came up behind Houssein. He was perusing the results of the radio carbon dating analysis and scratching his head. Even if she hadn't known exactly what was troubling him, it was comically obvious that he was very puzzled by what he was reading.

She took a final look around the lab. Tall tables cut it into four square work areas and computerized monitoring equipment was stored neatly along the walls on wheeled trolleys. Only one piece of equipment was in use, the dating machine, and that one had been pushed off to one side as Houssein read its report. The most important thing was that there was no one there except for the two of them.

Good.

The knife in her hand was nothing special. She'd asked the factory for a batch of cutting blades suitable for the infirmary robots on every ship in the fleet. They'd shipped out earlier that day. The technology was thousands of years old—even the material itself was just medical-grade stainless steel—but sometimes a simple tool was still the best thing for the job.

She did it exactly the way they'd taught her. Approaching from behind, Irene put her hand over his mouth and pulled his head back. Houssein's hands went straight up to try to pull her away, and she reached around him and drove the blade between his ribs into his heart. He collapsed without a sound.

Again, Irene looked around the lab. Still no one around. Of course, considering how many of the *Lapland*'s crew had failed to survive the trip, there was little reason for anyone to walk into the space that Dr. Houssein's had selected for his use, but her nerves were screaming that she was being watched, despite all the evidence to the contrary.

Reassured on that point, she quickly hid the man's body in a storage locker and mopped up the surprisingly small amount of blood. She'd need to dispose of the corpse soon enough, but there was no rush. No one would open a cupboard in here until his absence was noted, and that could take several days. Houssein had not been the most gregarious of men in the best of circumstances, and his reaction to the fleet's situation had been to lock himself in the nearest lab and work without speaking to anyone other than the people he absolutely needed to interact with.

Fortunately for Irene, she'd been one of those people. As one of the few surviving computer and nanotech specialists, she had access to what all the workstations were doing, and was on call to give the researchers support when needed. She thought it would be a nuisance that they'd be asking her, a top researcher, for what amounted to menial tech support. But with the passage of time and admin access to everything that went on in the ship, she realized it was a godsend. She'd known exactly what Houssein was up to and when the man needed to be eliminated. Taking action was just the natural continuation of what she was there to do.

She hadn't imagined that her hands would shake as much as they were now that the deed was done. Granted, she'd never killed anyone—in fact, the very reason she was there was to stop violence in all its forms—but she hadn't thought that it would affect her so much.

Irene took a few deep breaths to steady herself. Logically, she knew that what she'd done was necessary. The life of one man paled into insignificance when compared to the judgment of history upon mankind. And that was what she was there to attempt to salvage—although, in all honesty, it was probably too late for that.

Her attempts to get herself together were undermined by the memory of Houssein's hand which gripped hers, and then losing strength as the blood poured out of his heart. He'd been warm when she took his neck but, by the time she hid his body, he'd felt cool to her touch. Or perhaps it had just been her imagination.

Irene picked up the printouts, still lying where the researcher had dropped them. The data was exactly what she'd seen when she was using her admin access to eavesdrop on what Houssein was doing: radio carbon analysis of several supposedly new parts which had inexplicably failed from all over the fleet. The synthetic lubricating oil was a perfect organic compound on which to run radio-carbon testing.

A weight left her shoulders. No matter how badly she felt about having killed the man, it was justified. She hadn't made a mistake, hadn't misread his research and murdered him for no reason. The scientist definitely suspected something was amiss with the mission—something that Irene herself had been warned was a remote possibility—and these results would have led him down a path that eventually would have indicated action from the fleet's leadership.

She'd managed to get to him before he could share his suspicions. The bigger question now, and the thing that Irene knew she would have to watch out for, was whether Houssein had discussed his thinking with anyone else. She thought it was unlikely. The guy simply hadn't liked to have any human contact. But it wasn't impossible.

In a ship as laden with scientists as the *Lapland* was, any passing comment could be extrapolated into a working theory within days.

Of course, that wasn't her biggest problem. Worse still was that, eventually, another scientist would find himself thinking along the same lines, and then a third. She might be able to keep the genie in the bottle for a few more days, considering that everyone seemed to be more focused on getting the factories to produce again than investigating more general issues, even if these last made no sense. Perhaps she'd even have a couple of weeks, but after that, the truth would emerge, and she would have to take drastic action if she was to keep the people in charge of the fleet from realizing what was going on and taking remedial action.

She'd initially feared that the previous day's successful attack on the alien installation on the ice giant's moon would seem too easy and arouse suspicion, but the presence of an unidentified enemy unit which had attacked the marines and then escaped and made its way towards inner planetary system had confirmed that there was an effective alien military presence within the sector.

It would all be moot when the blob's fleet failed to show up over the next few days. The admiral was well aware that he had a window of less than ten days when he launched. It was only a matter of time before he understood that there was something very unusual going on.

Irene glanced back at the printouts. There were a lot of zeros in that analysis, more than she was expecting. One number jumped out at her: two hundred and fifteen thousand. Clearly, her comrades had somehow succeeded against all odds.

What, exactly, they'd succeeded in doing, she still wasn't certain.

She walked out of the lab, confident that her handiwork wouldn't be discovered before she had a chance to return and take care of the body. The nice thing about being on a nanofactory ship like the *Lapland* was that disposing of organics was child's play. All you had to do was to feed anything you wanted to make disappear into the raw materials chute for one of the machines. If you happened to be the system admin with access that allowed you to turn off the alarms meant to keep people from disposing of murder victims in the machines, that was even better.

But she couldn't afford to rest on her laurels. There were dozens of extremely smart people on that ship. Granted, most were working to get the factories back at full production—they hadn't been immune to the general failure suffered by the fleet—but that wouldn't keep them from trying to understand things at a more fundamental level.

Irene returned to her assigned workspace to find that two of the more insistent had sent her personal messages through the project management system.

One scientist showed his utter lack of people skills. His message was curt and to the point:

Have you got the navigation charts up and running yet? It's been three days. Shouldn't take that long, don't you think?

Another was more diplomatic, but said essentially the same thing:

Hi, Irene! Just following up on the Nav charts. I'd love to know if you have any idea when they'll be running again. I think we might need them for some important research pretty soon.

She responded to both messages with a response explaining how the code had, inexplicably, become corrupted at a very basic level. It was utter nonsense, but with the way things had been going with every piece of technology in the fleet, it would buy her more than enough time.

In reality, the Navigation charts, the standard software system in which every star position was listed and simulated in three dimensions was working perfectly. Or it would have been, had Irene not gone into its interface ports and swapped around some permissions that made it impossible to run.

Of course, she was only able to affect the ones on the *Lapland*. Eventually, someone on one of the other ships was going to get around to doing some more strategic thinking about fleet elements scattered in other places, and they were going to realize that something, somewhere was very, very wrong.

When that happened, things would get extremely interesting.

***

Like the rest of the *Minstrel*, the infirmary was cobbled together with parts dragged in from all over the ship. A motley assortment of machines painted in different colors—even various colors on the same piece of equipment where working bits had been combined to form a functioning whole—whirred and pinged to themselves.

They were arrayed around a small bed which held an even smaller figure lost in the sheets and tubes. She turned to study him as he approached.

"You look like shit, Lieutenant," Tristan said.

Cora gave him a weak smile. "I probably look a hell of a lot better than I feel, soldier. I should have died, the first battle casualty in this glorious defense of humanity, but instead here I am, broken in pieces and suffering. And they tell me I have you to thank for that."

He hesitated, not sure what to say. She laughed and went on. "I'm just teasing. I'm really grateful to you for pulling me out. The doc here

41

says it was a close thing, that any more damage would have needed nanobots to heal, and we don't have nanobots. I wish we did, though. Normal medicine hurts like hell."

"I'm just happy you're going to be all right, Lieutenant."

"Will you please stop calling me that? We're two of the only three survivors from our unit, and you just saved my ass down there. I think we've gotten to the point where you can refer to me as Cora when we're not on duty, don't you think?"

"I suppose so, ma'am." Then as he realized what he'd done and that he was about to catch hell for calling her 'ma'am,' he quickly amended. "Oops, sorry. Old habits. What I meant to say was I suppose so, Cora."

"There, doesn't that feel much better?"

It didn't. It made him feel vaguely uncomfortable. Like every other shock marine, he'd had the importance and sanctity of the chain of command beaten into him. It had been explained, time and again, that he would sometimes have to take orders from green junior officers, and the reason that was so was that, just as they'd had soldiering driven into them by the best system humanity had been able to devise, their officers had been taught what they needed to know in order to make the right battlefield decisions. Even under fire for the first time, an officer was expected to fall back on his training, to react by instinct, and to do what was best for the unit and the war effort. It was the uniform that mattered, not the individual.

Even worse was the fact that he had a vivid memory of seeing Cora naked and unconscious in the stasis chamber room. Even after waking under the worst conditions, the woman had looked fantastic. She was lithe and muscular, as all marines were, but still managing to keep the hint of an hourglass form worthy of any soldier's dream. The fact that her face was prettier than the ones in most of his dreams just made it worse.

He could forget about all of that and respect her as a CO, but if she wanted to be friends… that wasn't going to be easy.

But this wasn't the time or place for that kind of thinking. He was at the bedside of a fellow marine, one that had taken a serious beating in a role that might otherwise have been his.

"I guess," he said. "Other than badly, how are you feeling?"

"Frustrated. They won't tell me anything. What happened out there?"

Tristan glanced at the doctor, which was a mistake.

"No, no. He's one of the ones who won't talk. If you know what's good for you, you'd better start telling me what I'm asking."

42

He hesitated again and the doctor broke in. "Go ahead. She's going to live, so anything she does now to get agitated or whatnot will only make her convalescence longer. It should be pretty painful, too. She's got a couple of muscle tears that we can't quite immobilize."

Cora glared at him, but the twinkle in her eye told Tristan that she wasn't really angry.

"All right. It was pretty much a cakewalk."

"You call that a cakewalk? I very nearly bought it out there!"

"I know. And a guy from one of the other units actually did get snuffed. But it still wasn't what we were expecting. There didn't seem to be any organized resistance other than automated stuff like what you found and the strange flying thing."

"What strange flying thing?"

"Nobody's sure, or if they are, they haven't shared it with the grunts. Something. About man-sized but shaped like a flying wing. The advance team released it from a containment field and it went berserk."

"It attacked them?"

"It attacked everything. Some good weapons on it, too. Blew one of the guys to bits, suit and all. But it did most of its damage to the existing infrastructure."

"Some kind of robot drone?"

"I barely saw it. They ran into it when I was busy pulling you out. It shot past and out into space like it had never heard of the concept of gravity. But the guys say it didn't act like a drone."

"What the hell does that mean?"

"They say it seemed like the thing was angry as hell. There was something alive in there somewhere."

"Any idea where it went?"

"The sensor people here on the ship say they managed to track it as far as the orbit of the inner gas giant before losing it. They told me that maybe the sensor array on the *Heavy Gunship* might be able to pick it up, but good luck trying to get them to tell us anything we don't need to know."

Cora nodded. "And I suppose there's no sign of the enemy fleet?"

"Not yet. We've been lucky. I hear the admiral's trying to guess where they'll enter the system so he can lay an ambush. The word is also that command is confused about where the support infrastructure is. The fleet we're expecting has about seventy-five ships, and a lot of them are big bastards. We haven't seen anything that resembles even a small orbital shipyard, much less something that could deal with the kind of volume coming this way. It's hard to cloak a facility that size. The blobs certainly couldn't do it."

"They've had four hundred years to improve their technology," Cora reminded him.

That was something they always drilled into every soldier fighting for humanity: be prepared to exit the stasis chamber into a galaxy that bore no resemblance to the one you'd left. While you were in transit, there were people sitting still who had time to tinker with stuff. And that stuff could get you killed.

"I think it's more likely they had time for the Brillans or someone to beat us to the system and blow them out of the sky," Tristan said. "But that doesn't make any sense either. We'd be able to pick up the residue of the energy weapons; there would be evidence on the planet. And the little installation we blew up didn't seem like something that had been built over the ruins of another facility. It was a perfectly neat little setup."

Cora shrugged. He could tell that she was getting tired. He stood and patted her hand. "Whatever the reason, they're not paying us to think about it."

"Hate to be the one to break it to you, but they're not paying us at all."

"Get some rest. You'll be up and about in no time."

"It doesn't feel like it. Will you come visit me?" Again, Tristan felt uncomfortable, this time at the vulnerable, needy tone of her voice. Cora had been a tough customer, an officer he was happy to follow. But getting wounded seemed to have changed something inside her, broken the steel of her personality, made her a human being, not an officer.

He knew what would happen if she let it, and he'd been hurt before. Shock marines didn't have long shelf lives—and officers weren't necessarily assigned to the same unit after they finished a mission.

Of course, none of that really mattered. It would be the ultimate folly to fall for a girl during a suicide mission—especially one who'd shown a tendency to charge into danger without taking elementary precautions. One of them would be killed, and in his experience with other couples in similar situations, the other wouldn't last much longer.

"I'll definitely come if I can. They're talking about hitting the surface of the superearth further in the system."

"When?"

"Within the next two days or so. They've got the *Lapland* pumping out parts for dropships and fighters as fast as they can. They don't want to give the enemy any working facilities."

"Damn. Looks like I'm going to have to sit that one out."

As if there had ever been any doubt about that, Tristan thought. *You're going to sit the whole campaign out, and probably die right here in the infirmary when the blob fleet finally gets here and overruns us.*

***

"Let me guess, you volunteered me, too." Melina couldn't tell if Ian was livid or simply resigned to his fate. The man kept a poker face as she told him about the *Ismala*'s role in the following battle.

"Actually, no," she replied. "You're free to go to the rearguard. In fact, since you didn't volunteer for any of this, I can issue a recommendation to put you on the *Lapland* when she evacuates."

"The *Lapland* is leaving?"

"If they can, yes. The rest of us volunteered for this mission. We knew what we were getting into. But the factory ship had to come. So while our orders are to fight until either we are crushed or the enemy is defeated, the *Lapland* has orders to run as soon as they think that they won't be able to get us any more material."

"Plus, factory ships are too valuable to sacrifice?"

"I see you're a cynic."

"I had some great teachers," Ian replied sourly. He looked her in the eye. "All right. I'll take you at your word and run when you go in, but I still don't understand why you volunteered the *Ismala*. You should have asked to stay in orbit and let the *Dart* do the close support for the moon assault. You don't even have a real crew. All you have is a bunch of fighter pilots."

"For this mission, I actually prefer a fighter crew. They'll understand how the battle is evolving better than a naval crew would. And considering the fact that I'm going to be down there, I want my support team to know exactly what they're doing."

"You think it's going to be a battle?"

"Yes. Have a look."

She waved her hand over the console and a holographic schematic appeared showing the superearth in green, about a meter across and one small red dot which approached the orb at a shallow angle which became first an orbital trajectory and then a dive. "That dot is the thing that the marines saw."

The planet came alive all of a sudden. Lines came up off the surface and blue dots materialized. Everything converged on the red interloper, which held for a few moments, even causing some of the blue dots to wink out, before finally being destroyed.

"We picked up the presence of both missile defenses and ground-based fighter units. No energy weapons as far as we can tell, but even without them, that reaction from the planet means that we're heading for a serious furball down there. We need to clear out some of the defenses or the marines are toast."

"Better you than me," Ian said. "Were you serious about getting me reassigned?"

"Yeah, although we could use your Recon experience and your flyer."

"I'm pretty sure you can find someone to fly it, can't you? Someone with more experience in combat situations. He'd know where to point the sensors."

Melina didn't know whether Ian was being ironic or not. He was extremely hard to read. "I could, but the thing about Recon flyers, so I understand, is that the hard part isn't guiding the ship, but actually using the instruments. For that, you'd be invaluable. Don't forget that you seem to have become the most senior of the Recon people on this particular mission."

"I'll think about it," Ian said. "And thanks for understanding about me not being a volunteer."

Melina watched him go. He seemed a little less bitter, but she was damned if she could read the man. But she thought about what he'd said.

When she volunteered the *Ismala* for close combat support, her team had cheered and she'd believed that the decision had been a popular one. The problem was that she'd seen a lot less enthusiasm among the maintenance teams and support staff. It was then that she remembered that, though they were all volunteers, her own crew would mostly either be flying the *Ismala* or flying their fighters while the rest of the people on board would be at the mercy of a less experienced flight team. Being in control of your destiny was very different from being in someone else's hands.

This made her wonder why she'd done it. As Ian had said, the logical thing would have been for the *Ismala* to hold in orbit and to let a navy crew who knew all about flying carriers in combat situations take the *Dart* into battle. It would have made no difference to her: she was going to be leading a fighter wing.

Maybe she was doing it for the memory of Nairo. By throwing everything under her command into the face of the enemy, she felt she was matching his sacrifice, even though she knew full well that, had he survived the trip, he would have told her to do exactly the opposite of what she was doing.

46

It was too late to change anything, though. What was done was done.

CHAPTER 6

Pol was an analyst, the lowest-ranking member of the enormous bridge crew of the *Heavy Gunship IV*. He was so low on the totem pole that while his peers buzzed with the excitement of the raid that was about to begin, his own task hadn't changed: get the star chart and Nav system up and running.

While lieutenants relayed orders and aides reported troop status, he tried to concentrate in the din. The numbers made no sense; there had to be a mistake. He must have somehow installed the modules incorrectly and crossed references somewhere. The problem was that he didn't know where, and in theory, it shouldn't have been possible anyway.

He tapped his neighbor's shoulder. Li was barely senior to him, but had a better understanding of the ship's systems.

"What's up?" the man asked in his soft voice.

"I really don't know. Look, we're in the HR8799 system, right?"

"Of course."

"All right, so when I bring up that system on the simulation, it tells me that yes, there's a superearth in the system, but there are also six giants and another couple of smaller rocky planets closer to the star. We don't have any of that in this system. It's also telling me that the brightest stars that should be visible are here, here and here, but none of those is on our readouts."

"So there must be some mistake. Some of the files probably got crossed."

"I know. But I can't find where the errors are. I checked the backup database, and it shows the same thing. That means that either there was a mistake when they compiled the original, or the program is wonky and it's looking up the wrong system."

Li thought about it in silence for a moment. Pol knew that his friend was weighing the possibilities against each other. Both were equally likely. The database held billions of stars and planets, and there were countless errors. On the other hand, every single system on the ship was working badly, so that couldn't really be discounted either.

Finally, he spoke. "I think it's probably a configuration issue. The one system they would have checked before the mission launched was HR8799. That one has to be correct. So we run the deep diagnostics again."

"That could take another day." They'd already done it twice, and found thousands of errors each time.

"Even so... wait! I have an idea. This system actually had a human base here once, before the blobs came. It was a small installation and they had had to run like hell to get out alive, but there should still be an entry in the reference library, and it might have a chart. We can use that one while the system sorts out the bugs."

"You see, that's why I like working with you," Pol said. "I wouldn't have thought of that in a million years."

"Next time it happens, you will."

As Pol searched the reference base, which was even slower than the star chart system had been because no one had bothered trying to clean it up yet, the noise in the bridge died down. The assault on the superearth was about to begin. The two carriers and one of the troop transports— they didn't have enough functional dropships to send both—were approaching the planet. The bridge crew were idle: they no longer had anything to coordinate but were not yet receiving battle reports to analyze. Everyone watched the displays raptly.

Pol remembered the recording they'd been shown of the battle between the unidentified alien craft that had attacked the marines during the strike on the ice giant's moon and the planet's defenses. The ships were still about thirty minutes out from where the moon's defense had begun to fight back. He put his head back down and tried to search for the file he needed manually.

After an interminable interval, he snorted in disgust. The scroll would take forever—there were just too many files. He typed in another query request and, to his surprise, the file he needed came up. Pol quickly transferred it to his own personal memory and, just to be safe, messaged it to Li as well.

Once it was securely in a space where he was confident that he could access it whenever he wanted to without going into the deep files, he opened it up. Li had been right; there were four folders listed, and one was labeled 'HR8799 chart.'

Pol opened that one and stared at it, slack-jawed.

Five seconds later, he'd gone to the command chair.

"Not now, analyst," the admiral growled. "I'm busy."

Pol held his ground. "I'm sorry, sir, but this is important."

"More important than a large space battle about to start?"

"It might be. We're in the wrong place."

"I don't think it's a good idea to try to teach me about fleet tactics, analyst."

"No, not in the wrong place on the battlefield, sir. We're in the wrong place altogether. This isn't the right star system. We're not in HR8799."

"What? That's impossible."

"I checked and double checked. There's no mistake. We need to pull the attack force out and figure out where we are."

"I'm afraid it's a bit too late for that. They just engaged." The admiral gave Pol a glare. "I hope to hell you're wrong about this. Of course, I'll toss you out of an airlock myself if you are, but I'll be extremely relieved and happy when I do it. We'll talk about it after the battle. Now get out of here. I have troops to command."

***

Tristan knew that the moon's defenses were serious. Even with the fighter corps softening them up, they'd been told to expect a certain amount of fire coming their way. They'd been told that the vicious black wing that had terrorized them had only lasted about a minute under the defensive fire. It wasn't the most comforting feeling. At least his unit hadn't drawn the really short stick: attacking the planet; it was safe to assume that if the moon was a fortress, the planet would be a nightmare.

All he could really do while the dropships were in orbit was look out the window—he'd been made acting platoon leader by virtue of having managed to stay alive through no merit of his own. His viewport gave him a breathtaking vista of the planet itself, which took up a good chunk of the sky. It was green almost all the way around, with white clouds arrayed in long bands around certain latitudes.

He thought about it for a minute. A green world with clouds probably meant vegetation and abundant water. But then why were there no oceans? Could the water be trapped underground?

Tristan had no idea. He'd never done planetary tactics training, and no one had bothered to tell the acting platoon leaders about the planet's geography and biology. Assuming, that was, that anyone had bothered to tell the real officers. None of the officers had spoken to him about it.

Suddenly, he wished Cora was with them. The responsibility of keeping another nine marines alive was way too big. He was just a kid from Polaris III, raised in the safe, clean corridors of the settlement. What the hell he was doing orbiting an alien world waiting for an enemy fleet to atomize him if he happened to survive long enough? It was madness.

But Cora had always seemed to take it in stride. Even sitting up in a hospital bed with a bunch of tubes sticking out of her, she acted like the platoon under his command was her responsibility. He'd visited her the day before, ostensibly to give her the news that he was now in command of her troops.

"Remember not to send anyone into a place where you wouldn't go yourself," Cora said.

"Of course not. I'll take the riskiest jobs."

"No. That's dumb, and it's also a great way to get your people killed. As the leader, you're the only one who sees the whole picture, with all the Tac channels open. If you get knocked off, the unit loses capabilities."

"Look who's talking."

"Exactly. I should have sent the scouts in. Or I should have sent you. That was a mistake, and I'm paying for it."

"I gotta say I'm kinda glad you didn't send me."

She smiled. "Yeah, I can imagine. Well, at least you didn't get away scot-free. They made you a platoon leader, so now you get to see what a crappy job that is. Being part of leadership is only fun if you get to watch from a situation room somewhere well away from the fighting. If not, you get to share the likelihood of getting your ass shot off with the troops and the additional fun of having to listen to them gripe."

"Is that how officers see us? As things that complain in between bouts of getting killed?"

"Well, that and most of the guys in every single unit I've commanded spent a bunch of time staring at my ass. Quite a few of the girls, too."

Tristan was caught off guard and before he knew what was happening, his instincts took over. "It figures. It's a nice ass." Then, seeing her hard glare, he quickly backpedalled. "I'm sorry, ma'am, that was out of line."

Cora didn't speak for several moments, but then suddenly laughed. "I'm teasing you. Don't be such a baby. Guys always think we don't see them looking. I've seen you looking."

"I'm sorry."

"Don't be. I like it when some men look. Others... not so much."

Tristan was about to ask whether he was one of the men but stopped himself in time. He didn't want to make a fool of himself. An even bigger fool that was. "All right. I'm a bit slow today, you definitely aren't catching me at my best."

"Ah, of course. The perfect thing to say to a girl who's wired into four separate life-support machines."

"I mean that my mind is on the mission, and you kinda caught me off guard."

"Good." She seemed satisfied.

"What do you mean, 'good'?"

"It means that you never had a clue what I was thinking when I was your CO, and it means that, when the blobs down there are trying to shoot your ass off, you'll be thinking about how nice it would be to be in the nice safe troop ship with a good-looking girl. Since I can't really do anything else right now, I think I'll have to be satisfied with that."

Tristan's time was up. He had to get to the next briefing. He was surprised at how reluctant he was to go, and even more at the impulsive peck he gave Cora on the cheek. He would have kissed her lips, but the woman had a tube in her mouth.

"Thanks for coming to see me," Cora said as he walked out.

"My pleasure."

But she didn't let him walk. "By the way, now that you're a leader, you might want to ask questions at the briefing. A good one might be: 'why are the aliens in this system fighting among themselves?' Or: 'who the hell are they, and how do we know which side we want to be on?' Another good one that springs to the top of my mind is: 'where the hell are the blobs?'"

That had been nearly a day before, and no one at the briefing had been able to respond. In fact, the captain giving the briefing seemed pissed at him for asking. Now, he was sitting in a dropship waiting to become target practice for the lunar defenses of an enemy more than a hundred light years from his home.

The planet suddenly lit up with tiny orange blossoms as the fighter attack commenced. He supposed the assault on the moon would be starting now as well. They were supposed to be coordinated.

"Fighter wing deployed," the pilot's voice came in on the Tac channel. "Not too much longer to wait."

***

No one told us there would be this many defenders in the air, Melina thought as yet another swarm of fighters streaked past. *It's a good thing they're not really very dangerous.* She toggled her comm. "Everyone okay back there? Any damage?"

"Nothing major. They seem to be using very small-caliber projectile weapons."

The rest of her team also sounded off. They'd all taken minor damage, but everyone was still in flying shape.

"Commander," an unexpected voice popped in over the radio. "I think I've pinpointed your target. It's a bunker about seven hundred miles north-by-northwest of your current position. Not much radiation leaking outward, but right here above it, there's a whole boatload of emission, all of it aimed straight at the planet. Not a whole lot of activity anywhere else."

"Ian? What the hell are you doing here?"

"Recon. I decided to volunteer myself for something. Everyone else was doing it and I didn't want to miss out. Can't say I think much of it so far. There are things up here shooting at me."

Melina laughed. "Yeah, I noticed that. Thanks for the info. Now get out of there."

"Relax. Recon flyers are the fastest things out here. And we're hard to see, too. I'll be fine, it's not my first furball."

Melina put Ian out of her mind. She had bigger fish to fry. "There's a wing of the enemy flying at the dropships. Get behind them and take them down."

Her flight responded immediately and began to pick off enemy fighters one by one. Soon, there were none left.

"That's strange. The fight with the black flyer made these fighters look a lot tougher than they're turning out to actually be."

"I'm not complaining," one of her pilots chimed in.

"More likely that the black flier wasn't as badass as the marines said it was. You know those ground-pounders: always making up stories to try to look good."

Melina chuckled and let them talk. With full-scale assaults happening on both the moon and the planet, the enemy knew exactly where they were. No need for comm discipline now.

She toggled a channel to dropship command. "Guys, Recon just called in a probable target zone for you. We're going to check it out."

"All right, let us know."

With the four fighters that made up the rest of the wing, Melina peeled out of the engagement. The enemy was surprisingly weak. The rest of the fighter command was using them for target practice, and the tension of the early stages of battle had died down considerably.

They shot across the surface of the airless moon and soon came to the coordinates that Ian had called in.

"Mother lode," Melina said. "The guy was right."

They flew slowly back and forth across the installation Ian had pointed out and studied their sensors. During the approach, the sensors would show just trace amounts of radiation, not too different from the surrounding rock. Then, about a hundred meters out, their sensors would suddenly light up with the force of the energy field around them.

"What is it?"

"Hell if I know," Melina responded. "But it can't be very healthy to fly through this stuff time and again. I'm sending the coordinates to the dropship people. Let the shock marines deal with the radiation."

***

The admiral was studying footage sent through from the moon. The surface was like so many dozens of others he'd seen before: grey, pockmarked with craters, and ground to dust by the millennia. If it hadn't been located in the middle of his battle zone—wherever that might happen to be—he wouldn't have given it a second glance.

"Any news?" the admiral said.

"No, sir," Tina replied. "Same as before. The task force assigned to the moon is still reporting very light resistance, while the troops around the planet are just stuck there."

"No news on what it might be?"

"The teams on *Lapland* are working on it. All they have so far is that it's a force field of some sort. And it was strong enough to stop and destroy the two fighters that ran into it."

Tina shuddered as she said it. The war had been going on for ages, and in all that time, no one had perfected an energy shield effective enough to cover its generator. The rule seemed to be that the size of the clusters of machinery needed to create a force field increased exponentially with the size of the field. All the belligerents were having the same issue. It was actually one technology in which humanity believed itself to be ahead of both the Brillans and the blobs—but the tech was useless in its current form.

A generator for a planetary shield should have been the size of a red giant.

Her father echoed her thinking. "Impossible." He considered for a moment. "It has to be made up of patches. Some areas are covered while others aren't. They're probably mobile and controlled from the surface: when we strike in one spot, the patch of shielding moves to intercept. But they can't cover the whole planet."

"So what do we do?"

"First, we need to test its capabilities. Have the ships move a little further away and hit the planet with multiple strikes, but not concentrate their fire. Make sure that each strike falls on a different part of the shield. That way, unless the planet is fully covered, some of the strikes will make it through."

"And if the coverage is complete?"

"In that case, we ought to start looking for an invisible generator the size of a big star. A gravitational anomaly like that should be pretty easy to find." He grunted. "Actually, if it's a full shield, then what we need to do is to move the *Heavy Gunship IV* into a closer position and pound it. I assume that a force field is like anything else: it can only absorb a certain amount of energy before it breaks up. If the Central Cannon can't break it, then we'll just have to ignore the planet at least until the fleet gets here." He looked around the bridge. "Now where's that analyst?"

"Which one?"

"The one who was talking to me before this all started? The one going on about star charts."

"Ah. I'll get him."

Pol was duly brought into the admiral's presence. "All right. Let's go through this once again, slowly. You believe we're not in the right system."

"Yes, sir. I've checked very carefully."

"Why?"

"Because the planetary system we're in doesn't fit the description of HR8799. I checked two different sources, and both show multiple gas giants here."

"And gas giants can't just disappear. But how about if someone used them for fuel, or reengineered them?"

Pol said nothing, and Tina understood him perfectly: if anyone had advanced enough for engineering on that scale, then the last thing anyone would want—Humans, Brillans, blobs, or even Uploaders—was to run into that civilization.

"It's not just the gas giants, sir. The star is different, too. Much whiter than it should be."

"Then we need to find the error. It has to be an error in our databases, because you can't just miss a star system and land in another one. The odds against it are fantastic. We'd have been in space much longer than our ships could survive."

"Well, maybe the original system explorers made an error when they logged the system. Maybe the colony was somewhere else and simply jotted the wrong number beside the star when they created the record. And since no one has been here since, it just carried over."

"I have no idea what you're talking about, son. But I want you to get in touch with the scientists on *Lapland*—Tina can get you the names and comm IDs of the right people to talk to—and give me a definite answer. Until you do, I'm going to keep operating under the assumption that a very large, very angry blob fleet is about to land on my head."

"Yes, sir."

As Tina led him away, she watched her father out of the corner of her eye and decided to avoid him for a couple of hours. He looked unhappy enough to go through with one of his ever-present threats to throw people out of airlocks.

In order to find something to keep her both busy and far from the admiral, she sat down with Pol to talk to the *Lapland*.

"I think it would be better if I call them," she told the analyst. "A lot of the people on board still resent that they have to be here, and might give you the runaround."

She commed the captain of the factory ship, who, like all the military personnel except for the enigmatic Ian, had volunteered for the mission. "Hello, Maria," she said.

"Hi, Tina, what's up?"

"Need your advice. Who should we get in touch with on the *Lapland* to solve a mystery involving star charts?"

"No one, is what I'd say. The support team hasn't been able to get our Nav system up and running. Bloody annoying way to fly a factory ship, especially when we turn the thing around to try to get back home. Am I supposed to find Sol by blind reckoning? It's stupid."

"All right, we can probably beam you the info we want to analyze. Who would be your best bet?"

"I would say anyone in the astrophysics department. Maybe Hetter or Humahuaca. But I wouldn't call them right away. They seem to have lost a couple of scientists."

"Lost?"

"Yeah, as in can't find them anywhere on the ship. What they did find was human DNA in one of the factory intake chutes. We're treating it as a murder. Or rather, they are. I couldn't care less if they all bumped each other off. Would make for a much quieter trip back."

"All right. We'll call Hetter. Thanks."

CHAPTER 7

Irene sat on her bunk. Her room, like that of everyone else on board, was stark and Spartan. White plastic walls, contoured into the organic forms that had been in vogue when humanity was still building factory ships held no decoration other than the wear that had accumulated over centuries of part-time use.

The other three bunks in the tiny room were vacant. Between the fact that factory ships always went into combat with the bare minimum of crew on board and that a good portion of that crew had died in transit there were plenty of rooms to go around.

That was a good thing. Solitude was exactly what she needed.

Sandrina's death had been unfortunate. Completely necessary but unfortunate. She'd caught the woman in a deserted hallway and had barely had time to clean up the mess and dispose of the body before being discovered.

It was little wonder that her handiwork had been found out almost immediately. In her role as admin, Irene could order the nanofactories not to notice human remains, but the cleaning and maintenance systems were fully automated, and the computers that controlled them were buried behind closed access doors that she didn't have the keys to. Getting them might not be too hard to do, but it would definitely call attention to her.

She wasn't worried about the murder investigation. Everything that pointed to her had been deleted from the records, especially all video from the security systems. The scientists were running the investigation like a bad novel anyway, constantly getting in the way of Hemery, the man the navy crew had assigned to finding out what was happening, and the only competent person on the job. The committee would be extremely unlikely to catch her even if she put up neon signs proclaiming her guilt.

Though it had come as a bit of a shock, the star charts the admiral's people had beamed to the *Lapland*, and which Hetter had taken five minutes to study before proclaiming that they were, indeed, in the wrong place weren't what was troubling her either. She'd never expected the scientists to be kept in the dark eternally, just as long as possible.

No. What she wanted to come to terms with was the mission itself. More specifically, whether the mission was worth pursuing.

Sure, the original goal was a noble one: peace in the galaxy by any means possible. If that meant that humanity had to abandon its current colonies and go into hiding to avoid the war, then that was acceptable. If it meant that humanity was destined to go extinct, then that, though sad, was also acceptable. In fact, it might be the only acceptable solution: the war was a genocidal one in which there could only be one winner. Humanity had shown a historical tendency to go to war with itself, and therefore was a bad candidate to rule over a peaceful galaxy.

For this mission, her assignment had been simple: do anything necessary to keep the fleet from being able to take the fight to the blobs.

Her initial plan had been to feed defective designs into the nanofactories. Her handlers had furnished her with everything from gyroscope plans that caused fighters to crash to marine rifles that jammed.

The star chart data had caused her to change her plans. That discovery meant that the most important task at first was to keep the fleet in the dark regarding where they were. She'd expected them to waste weeks flying around an empty planetary system wondering where the enemy fleet was. A lost task force couldn't get into a fight.

And yet it had. She'd initially dismissed the reports of the marines encountering resistance on the moon of the ice giant as simple and not-very-subtle propaganda, but there was no doubting the fact that the fighter corps and marines were now involved in a major engagement on and around the superearth even as she sat there. The crew had been watching the live feed on a big screen in the mess hall, and she had a feed on her personal screen in the room. The human fighters seemed to be doing remarkably well against the defenses.

The problem was that the defenses shouldn't be there. The only explanation for the fleet not being in the HR8799 system was that her colleagues had been successful in changing the launch parameters.

That had been a major sabotage operation which everyone in the movement had been skeptical of. The depth of infiltration and precise coordination needed made it seem like a pipe dream. If it worked, of course, it would be the pacifist ideal: send a heavily armed fleet off into the cosmos for a long time, long enough that when they returned, the war would be a distant memory.

But her initial optimism that it had worked was waning. If the fleet had been sent on a random course, how come there were enemies here to fight? The system, like almost all others, should have been empty save for some old probes. The probability of finding an armored system by chance was negligible.

Something else was going on. But what?

The first idea that crossed her mind was that the pacifist operation had been discovered and that the false star charts had been put into the database intentionally, trying to confuse and flush out any sleeper cells that the movement might have infiltrated as a backup plan.

If that was the intention, it had worked like a charm in her particular case.

On the other hand, if that was the plan, then why were the powers-that-be acting confused about where they were? Was it part of the same scheme? Did the admiral know exactly what he was doing?

The explanation might be as simple as the fact that some upper-level intelligence operative—the guy who knew what was going on—hadn't survived the crossing. Or it could be as twisted as the fact that they knew there were sleeper agents in the fleet and were going to milk the charade until the very end.

The final option was the most frightening: that they had indeed been diverted, and that, by chance, they'd stumbled into a war that wasn't theirs after a journey of two hundred and fifteen thousand years.

In any case, peace demanded that she get to work. Soon, the factory would be getting orders to replace battle losses. Among them would be requests for gyroscopes and rifles.

Irene stood up. She had her orders.

***

"This is starting to get annoying," Melina growled as another wave of enemy fighters appeared on her screen.

"It's no worse than training simulations."

"Yeah, except we're infinitely more likely to die if we happen to crash into one."

She could almost see the shrug on the other end. "That's what we came here to do," the pilot said. "Might as well take a few of them with us."

"What worries me is that it just doesn't make sense. They've surely figured out by now that the weapons they're using are completely useless against us."

"They've taken down a few of our fighters."

"To balance against the entire wings they've lost? Unless they have millions, they won't be able to do much against us."

"Maybe they do."

"Still doesn't make sense. Why would anyone arm planetary defenses with light-caliber weapons? Are they expecting to be attacked by pigeons? You need to be able to take down a fighter."

The chatter died down as her wing engaged the defenders. Even against weak weaponry, it was better not to get hit, so she circled around to see if she could get behind the enemy.

Once in position, Melina toggled her guns and watched with satisfaction as the defender's fighters began to disintegrate under the barrage.

"Heads up, wing leaders," the Tacnet said. "We've decided that the moon's defenses aren't a threat to the dropships, so the marines are headed your way."

She toggled the acknowledgement button and turned her nose to space. Her flight was one of the ones that were tasked with escorting them down.

"Look alive, people. If the defenders decide the dropships are a real threat, they might throw heavier ordnance at us."

It didn't happen. Her crew escorted the first wave of five troop carriers safely to the ground and turned back to pick up some more.

Suddenly, the fighter directly to her right veered right into her path, clipping her wing and taking a decent chunk of her fighter's nose with it. It then spiraled off in an uncontrolled descent and slammed into the moon below.

The crash shouldn't have been a problem. Fighters were streamlined and equipped with wings for atmospheric work, not vacuum operations, which meant that losing cosmetic pieces was a minor concern. Unfortunately, the impact must have broken something, because the machine began to lose power.

"Guys, I'm out of this one."

"Roger that, need an escort?"

"No. I think I can make it back all right."

"Okay."

She pulled back on the control stick, aimed the nose at the nearest capital ship, and throttled hard. If she made it into orbit, she knew they'd eventually get around to picking her up.

Instead of the acceleration she expected, the fighter shuddered and stalled, falling backwards towards the surface.

Melina reacted immediately. Without an atmosphere, she couldn't maneuver the ship unless some of her attitude jets worked. She tried them one by one and discovered that she basically only had control of the landing attitude adjusters.

All right. She'd take what she could get. In the moon's tiny gravity, those little jets might be the difference between a solid thud and a fatal crash. Timing would be everything, and she still wasn't close enough to the ground to feel comfortable with setting them off. Those rockets had a limited burn time, and she couldn't waste it.

Away to her right, the marines were massing in front of the installation they'd identified. *Great,* she thought. *Whatever that radiation is, I'm about to land right on top of it. I wonder if I'll develop any interesting mutations. At least the marines are close enough to defend me if the ground defenses are more formidable than the ones in the air.*

And then there was no more time to think. Melina hit the control of the attitude jets and felt the fighter slow before impact. She hoped it would be enough.

***

Tristan watched the fighter go down just about three hundred meters away, behind the rim of a crater. He braced for the impact, but didn't feel any tremors, so maybe the pilot had managed to get it under control. He sent the guy his best vibes, but there was nothing more he could do.

He had bigger problems.

Unlike the facility they'd raided on the moon of the ice giant, the enemy installation here didn't have a huge open hangar door. It had one of the small horizontal sliding doors that they'd already seen leading into the elevator shafts back in the outer reaches of the planetary system.

Unfortunately, the entrance was covered by four swiveling guns like the one that had nearly killed Cora. They'd appear out of holes on the upper wall and strafe anyone who got too close. What made them hard to stake down was that you could never tell which one was going to appear; they came out randomly. So you might be aiming at one and get caught off guard by another. A couple of his men had already been caught in the crossfire trying to get in.

At first, they'd blasted the wall around the hole, but that was well armored. Tristan had no idea what material it was constructed from, but the big slugs they used barely dented it.

Then they'd tried lobbing grenades into the holes, but they'd bounced away as if there was an invisible sheet of plastic over the opening.

"All right, men, here's what we'll do." He pointed to four of his troops. "You four are going to start firing at the holes. You'll take the first, you the second, you get the third, and you'll take the one on the far left. What I need for you to do is to start firing at full automatic at your assigned hole. Don't stop until I tell you to, even if it means depleting your magazine badly, do you understand me?"

"Yes, sir!" The answer came through from all four of them and he grimaced. They shouldn't have been calling him 'sir.' He wasn't an officer and didn't want to be.

"Perfect. Wait for my signal." He left the cover of a shallow crater and began to make his way towards the door. He'd marked the spot where the guns activated so, well before he reached it he said: "fire!"

He saw the sparks flying off the armor around the gun holes. As soon as he'd seen enough to know that they were all being fired on, he advanced. A gun came out of the one closest to his position, center right. Before it could fire, however, it was cut apart by the covering fire.

Good, this is working.

In fact, it worked better than he had any right to expect. The remaining three guns attacked him in succession, and each in turn was destroyed. "All right, men, hold your fire."

He stood still for a moment. The automated defenses were just idiotic. Any of the simulations on the ship would have adapted its response to the marines' tactics. Both what he'd seen of the air defenses and the reactions of these guns was puzzling. Why were the automatic responses so basic?

Basic or not, he'd lost two marines to the guns, mostly because of overconfidence. He'd ordered the men to scout the doors, never imagining that the defenses would start right there.

He wouldn't make that mistake again.

"Get a scan suit up here. I want to know if the door is booby trapped."

The scan suit was an unwieldy concoction, but invaluable. Its combination of scanner technologies could look through fifty meters of rock or detect a microwave cooker a thousand kilometers away. It should be able to see through the door without much difficulty.

"Sorry, sir," the operator told him. "All I can really say for sure is that the door itself is pretty thin, but no chance to say what's behind it. The problem is the radiation coming out of the ground. It throws everything off."

"All right," Tristan said. "Back off."

Once the bulky suit was out of the way, he planted a magnetic charge on the door and cursed as it slid off. Non-ferrous metals were a bitch.

He shot the door, set the timer, and wedged the charge into the bullet hole, thankful that the door wasn't made of the same material as the armored gun ports.

Tristan loped back to where his remaining men were positioned and then turned back to the charge.

It blew the door completely off its hinges.

"All right, people. Fire into that hole."

The marines did so with gusto and nothing fired back. Slugs tore chips from the façade, and grenades detonated inside the building.

"Enough. Let's go have a look."

The hangar-like interior was pretty torn up, but looked to be identical to the one they'd already encountered in their earlier assault. There was a wall at the back which Tristan was certain led to an elevator shaft.

"Watch the roof, people. Last time we got caught by one of those cannons mounted in the ceiling."

The roof failed to hold any surprises, but the motion-activated red lighting nearly gave Tristan a heart attack when it activated. It caught him off guard even though he was expecting it.

There were nervous moments in any military operation, but eventually, even under fire, soldiers settled down—or their training took over—and did their jobs. But on this jaunt, Tristan was jumpier than ever. He wondered why; the only explanation he could find was that he wasn't worried for himself, but for the seven other men he still had.

The two he'd lost were probably weighing down his conscience as well, but he couldn't really analyze his feelings about them now.

He also wondered why they'd sent his platoon in first. He was the most junior platoon leader in the first wave. Maybe they thought his troops were the most expendable? In light of how he was already feeling, he decided not to overanalyze it. He toggled the Tacnet. "Top floor secure. We're blowing the door to the shaft and heading down."

"Gotcha. We'll be right behind you."

The shaft was booby-trapped. As soon as they opened a hole into the metal of the door, a barrage of gunfire exploded it outward. A grenade dealt with the offending guns, but the damage had been done. Another of his troops lay on his back, dented suit doing its best to keep his battered body alive. Soon enough, he'd been placed in a medical coma to await evac.

"Going down the shaft. We'll start from the bottom level this time." Tristan informed the other squads. He motioned for two men to enter. "Be careful."

They encountered no further problems on the way down. The door at the bottom was soon open and they emerged into a huge dark area dotted with wide pillars every few meters.

"I wonder what all this is holding up."

"Something heavy. There was nothing like this in the other facility we hit."

They quickly determined that there was little of interest on that level and ascended a ramp at the far end which led to the floor above.

"Holy crap."

"Yes, sir."

The chamber they entered was so large that the beams of their suit lights couldn't find the roof: it was several stories above them.

That wasn't what had made them swear, however. In the dim light a huge... something... hulked in the center of the room and occupied most of the space.

It was vaguely, squatly cylindrical—the exact shape was impossible to guess at in the shadows—and took up almost all the space in the chamber. Tristan took an involuntary step back. The sensation that the thing would collapse on top of him at any moment was overpowering.

"Can you feel that, sir?"

Tristan could. The floor, his suit, even the air around him was humming. It was a tiny vibration, but felt extraordinarily deep. The only thing that could possibly be causing it was the huge structure in the middle of the room. He took another step back.

"Looks like we found what we're looking for."

"What is it?"

"I have no clue. But anyone care to bet against me that this is why we're here?" There were no takers. "Thought so. All right, let's get some backup."

He called the rest of the platoons over the Tacnet, but all he got was static.

"Damn. You and you, go up those ramps and see if you can find anyone. If you do, tell 'em to get their asses down here pronto."

Then he turned to his four remaining soldiers. "Let's get the charges placed. I want them all around the base, and I want them slaved to my command. Got it?"

"Yes, sir."

They moved quickly, placing the charges where the behemoth looked vulnerable. Tristan overcame his revulsion for the huge thing and tapped the metal structure with his suit's gauntlet. It dented easily. "Doesn't seem like it's armored," he told his marines.

No one answered. Even though his troops were less than twenty meters away, they'd already moved out of range. Here, at the source of all the strange energy fields and radiation, their Tacnet was worse than useless. Tristan shrugged. He had a job to do, so he did it. Once he'd placed every charge he'd brought with him, he returned to the base of the ascending ramps. His men had beaten him there.

"Can you hear me?"

"Loud and clear."

"Good. Let's get out of here. Up the ramps you go. I'll do a fast lap around and set the charge timers. An hour should be more than enough. We need to stop at every floor and get the rest of the troops out. There are supposed to be a hundred marines in this assault. We need to warn them off."

They set off up the ramps that led up and Tristan began his lap around the cylinder. His original plan had been to set the timers from the exit point, but he realized at the last second that the radiation would make that impossible. No signal could survive out there. He needed to be right next to each charge to get it to respond.

A subjective eternity passed before he finally finished. Just as he was about to mount the ramp, a sound from above made him glance upward.

Two of his men were halfway up the ramp, engaged in a firefight with some kind of wheeled automated systems. They resembled wide blocks on treads with large gun orifices on the top which they were using to drive the marines back. As Tristan watched, a marine took a direct hit to the faceplate which vaporized his helmet.

"Get out of there!" he called to the remaining man, but it was too late. The defenders ignored the fire that the suit's weaponry flung at them and simply shot him to pieces.

And, pausing only to push damaged machines off the ledge to make room for the ones behind, the column of defenders advanced down the ramp. The foremost took a bead on Tristan, missing him only because he was already on the move.

CHAPTER 8

Tristan ran toward the center of the room, thinking to take cover behind the cylinder that dominated the space. He knew it was hopeless; he wasn't moving fast enough to avoid being hit, and he needed to run halfway around the thing before his assailants would lose their clear bead on him.

He cringed, certain that each step would be his last.

Strangely, the killing blow never came. To his amazement, the treaded defenders had stopped shooting at him. They advanced down the ramp without firing another shot.

It's the cylinder, he realized. *They don't want to hit it.* Then the cynicism that was either bred or learned in every marine kicked in. *Probably because they know that, if it explodes, it will blow this entire moon to kingdom come.*

Wasting an unexpected opportunity was a good way to get killed. The right thing to do was to keep running. The defenders looked robotic to him, which meant that they might be programmed to shoot if they got close enough that the risk of hitting the cylinder became negligible.

The elevator shaft, still sealed on this level, appeared ahead of him. Tristan approached at a dead run, firing all his guns at it as he went. The door was still quite solid when he arrived, but it exploded inward when his suit made contact.

Once inside, he moved up. The remains of his platoon might be in any of the levels above the colossal one that contained the cylinder.

Or they might all be dead. Either way, had to try to look for them.

He used his jets to ascend to the door he needed but refrained from simply blowing it off its hinges. The ease with which the defenders had cut through the marines in the room below gave him pause. Shooting the door would be a good way to advertise his presence and get himself hurt.

So he carefully cut through the thin metal, wondering how long it would take the robots below to figure out that he'd escaped up the shaft and begin shooting at him. He didn't think they'd miss. Hell, in the narrow shaft, it would be extremely difficult to miss.

With breath fogging on his visor, he kept working on the door until it finally gave way.

Seeing that the door emerged into the end of an empty corridor similar to the ones they'd encountered in the installation on the ice giant's moon, he quickly exited the shaft and hoped the robot defenders would have to climb up the ramp. He nearly crossed the first intersection but remembered how Cora had been gunned down and stopped. Toggling the Tacnet on an open frequency, he tried to reach out to any of the other shock marines inside.

"This is Tristan Polaris Han, can anyone hear me?"

He inched forward, careful not to cross the intersection and set off any booby-traps, but there was no answer. The radiation must still be too strong.

Finally, he took a running start and dove across the intersection. To his relief, it seemed that this crossroad wasn't supplied with a concealed cannon. He made it to the ramp and looked down to see a line of defenders coming up after him. One of them took a bead on him and Tristan dove for cover behind a column, wondering what to do next.

The ramp continued to the upper levels. The stretch he could see was littered with pieces of robots and marine exoskeletons. His heart sank when he saw that most of the missing troops from his unit were among the fallen, and there were also several suits that corresponded to other units. His men hadn't died alone, but the numbers hadn't made much difference.

Whatever the defenders were using to shoot people with was pretty serious ordnance. The suits were armored against all small caliber weaponry as well as a number of particle and electromagnetic beams. Even so, they were being torn to pieces, marines and all.

He hesitated. His first instinct was to go up the ramp, pick up any stragglers, and fight their way out, but two things argued against it. The first was that the way the bodies were strewn made it look as if the marines—the ones from his unit and the others—had been executing a fighting retreat down the stairs. Which meant that they'd encountered the enemy on the upper levels and worked their way down, defending themselves from the tanks as best they could as they ran from them.

Which begged the question: were there more defenders above, or were the robots coming up the ramp the main enemy force?

Either way, the second problem with going up the ramp was that the armored tanks would cut him to pieces from behind.

The only real option was to get his ass back to the elevator shaft and try to get out of the facility before the robots wised up and sealed it.

But Tristan still didn't move. Could he really run out and try to save himself while the rest of the shock marines got shredded by the defenders? It was bad enough that he'd lost his entire platoon without really having much to show for it. All he could really hope for was that the defenders would be too busy trying to kill humans in exoskeletons to realize that their precious cylinder was surrounded by explosives that would be going off in about fifty minutes. The loss of life in this building could never be justified, but at least it might be tolerable if the explosion happened, and disabled the facility. Whatever it was. He hoped it wasn't a water treatment plant or something equally non-strategic.

He toyed with the idea of going back down and setting much shorter timers on the charges until the robots cut him down.

Tristan suspected that he was dead either way, so it might be best to make it count. Besides, he had no more time for deliberation; the defenders had nearly reached the top of the ramp.

Sprinting back to the elevator door, he looked down, only to have an enemy positioned at the bottom of the shaft nearly take his head off. Before he could even think to turn back, a bolt caught the elevator door next to him, punching another hole into the metal with a shower of sparks.

What now? he thought, but before his mind could process the question, much less answer it, his training had taken over and he was already in motion.

Tristan jumped into the gaping hole he'd made on the way out of the shaft, careful not to catch on the jagged metal. Then, swerving as wildly as the limited space in the shaft permitted, he shot upwards towards ground level and escape.

Shots bounced off the walls of the shaft, but his erratic motion kept the defenders from scoring anything more than glancing hits. He was very far underground but he should be able to make it out long before the charges went off.

The firing slowed to a trickle and stopped. He seemed to be out of range. The shaft wasn't quite straight: it curved imperceptibly, which meant that after several levels, the shape of the shaft made it impossible to obtain a decent firing angle.

Safe for the moment, Tristan stopped to consider his position. His heart told him to pierce another of the doors and try to find survivors, but his mind told him that the only marine who'd entered the building who was still breathing was Tristan Polaris Han. And if he kept dawdling, even that was an iffy proposition.

He looked up, trying to gauge the distance to the exit. A dim red light moved towards him at high speed and every single threat and impact light on his helmet display flashed on at once.

"Oh, crap," Tristan said. He hadn't wondered about the elevator during the descent, hadn't even considered how odd it was that there was no car inside the shaft. Where it had been when they came in would remain a mystery, but there was no doubt whatsoever that, right now, it was coming towards him at full speed.

Again, he acted without thinking, gunned the boosters on his soles, and used the suit to punch through the thin metal of the nearest elevator door, half-expecting the mad lift to cleave him in two as he struggled to escape.

He rolled out of his dive and shot to his feet, ready to make a last stand against any defenders in the place. But there was no one there, just a space split into what seemed to be work areas. None of them would have been remotely comfortable for a human, but all the elements were there: flat surfaces, buttons, and pads that looked to be computer interfaces. Of defenders, there was no sign.

He caught his breath. The elevator car hadn't hit him. In fact, it didn't even pass by. He looked back into the shaft to discover that it had stopped two landings above him.

"No, no, no," he groaned to himself. The only reason for stopping the elevator car would be to keep him penned in the building. They wanted him to use the ramps—and that probably meant that whatever was waiting for him was confident in its ability to take him down.

Tristan had known when he volunteered that this would be a suicide mission, but he was in no particular hurry to bring about the inevitable.

The momentary lull meant that it was possible to take stock of the situation, though he knew he didn't have much time. Despite the action, he still had nearly four-fifths of his ammo remaining. No more explosive charges, of course, but he could probably hold out for quite a while against the defenders on the floor he was on. The place was a warren of nooks and crannies where, he assumed, workers of some description had once toiled. It was a layout that would favor his suit—large and cumbersome as it was—against the even less nimble tracked defenders.

His principal concern was that holding out wasn't a good option for him. In a few dozen minutes, the entire building would be blown to pieces by the charges his team had planted. If he wasn't out, he would be taken with it. A glorious, fitting exit for a shock marine, certainly, but not one that appealed to him.

The only option was to take the fight to the defenders. He strode purposefully towards the ramp on the other side of the floor, but halted midway; his suit's sensors had identified a group of holes similar to the ones they'd encountered on the building's façade. Gun ports... six of them.

There was no way he'd be able to deal with that. It had taken his entire team to take out the four guns on the door. Six were much too many for a single marine to face, so he made his way back to the elevator door to evaluate the lay of the land. It looked pretty favorable for a last stand. He chose a nook to his left with a straight shot down the corridor and two directions he could escape in when the bad guys got too close.

His breathing echoed inside the helmet as he settled down to wait. They had to come for him eventually, didn't they? They'd been following him around relentlessly—even using the elevator to block his path—so they wouldn't let him get away now.

Tristan quickly double-checked the shaft, just to verify that the elevator was still there and that the robots weren't somehow using it to sneak up behind him.

All clear.

Another look around allowed him to fix the place where he was slated to die firmly in his mind. He'd always thought that shock marines bought it on barren radiation-bathed ice fields around pulsating stars fighting incomprehensible aliens. He, on the other hand, was about to be killed by pedestrian-looking robots that might have been designed by an engineer on Earth, and they would kill him in an office building. The place was carpeted, for God's sake.

That tore it for him. He decided that he wouldn't die there.

Tactics and common sense be damned, Tristan returned to the shaft and began pouring all of his ammo, every single high-caliber slug, into the elevator car. Cursing his lack of explosives, he just let his main guns do their work.

The car began to disintegrate under the barrage. It looked to Tristan as though it was made of the same thin material as the doors to the elevator landings were. It made sense: even in the low-G environment of the moon, a shaft this long would require lightweight cars.

The elevator began to look like lacework in the strong light from his helmet as it lost more and more material to the barrage. Less than a minute after his assault began, large chunks of lift were dropping down the shaft. He would be through soon.

But his time ran out.

A direct hit to the right arm of his suit shut down one of his weapons and served notice that the defenders were there. It took off the huge metal gauntlet that made up the end of the arm and only fortune kept it from removing his hand, in the control sheath that ended just short of the fist.

Tristan dove into the shaft and toggled his jets. Spooling them to full thrust, he shot upward and rammed into the stringy remains of the elevator.

He almost made it. As the suit punched through layer after layer of metallic string barely solid enough to hold its shape, Tristan actually believed that he would be able to break through. His head actually cleared the roof of the car.

The upper levels held firm, however, and only his right shoulder, useless without the hand structure, made it past the roof panel.

He hung there, held in place by the metal and the furiously pushing suit thrusters. His eyes flicked unconsciously to the upper right of his helmet display, where the timer for the charges was steadily counting down the seconds, but in the rush to get out of the office area, he must have toggled something accidentally. That display area was showing him that his oxygen regenerators were working at full capacity—information that was worse than useless to him.

Panic rose. He started thumping the left gauntlet into the elevator car, not aiming for sensitive points or strategic weak areas, just attacking anything in reach. Thump. Thump. Thump. He could feel the vibrations in his suit. If there had been any air to carry sound, it would have been extraordinarily loud.

And how did they manage to keep office workers alive in a vacuum? he thought. And then he focused on the task at hand.

Thump.

This was taking too long.

Thump.

At any moment, the defenders would begin burning holes in his ass from below.

Thump thump thump thump thump.

Something finally gave and his left arm tore free. Tristan pulled himself through the roof of the elevator car and shot up the shaft, fearing that he'd encounter a second mysteriously appearing obstruction as he rose.

But the coast was clear. He made it to ground level and exited through the mangled door, ran across the hangar, and out to the frozen regolith. Only when he was behind a ridge and could cover the door, did he stop and get his bearings.

First things first. How long did he have before the charges turned the facility into a crater and a cloud of debris that would rain onto his head? He cycled through a bunch of status reports and alarms before he finally located the timer. There was still plenty of time, nearly forty minutes.

He regretted having set the timers so conservatively. The hour he'd calculated as sufficient time to evacuate the Marines ended up being time that, if they knew what they were doing, the defenders could use to deactivate the charges.

Speaking of the marines, where were they? "Can anyone hear me? This is Tristan from the 243rd. I'm pretty much all that's left of the unit. Just got out of the enemy installation. Anyone out here?"

"This is Bettina from the 65th. I got posted to sentry duty. I saw you run past just now, I think." The voice sounded very scared and much too young for a shock marine.

"Where are you?"

"Right next to the entrance. Glare was a bitch so I'm in the building's shade."

He looked. In the atmosphere-less environment of the moon, the stark light of the star created deep ebony shadows that looked like they'd been cut with a laser torch. He couldn't find the marine in her suit until he switched to thermal imaging.

There she was. A green blotch over the blues, greens, and blacks of everything else.

"I'd get out of there, if I were you."

"This is my post. Platoon leader's orders."

"Yeah, well that building's about to blow, and your platoon leader's inside it somewhere with a bunch of holes through him. Now get over here."

"Shouldn't we get in there and help out?"

"No one to help. I checked. Nearly got killed for my trouble."

"No one?"

"There were some serious defenses inside. Now will you please get out of there?" He knew they had plenty of time to get clear of the blast zone, but knowing how many explosives they'd rigged was making him nervous. Plus, the further he got from those robots, the better he'd feel.

The marine came reluctantly, but she came. She was about halfway to where Tristan had taken cover when a new voice came in over the Tacnet.

"Hello, can anyone hear me?"

"Loud and clear, who is this?"

"This is Commander Melina Tau Osella. I'm with the fighter corps. Got knocked out of combat, unfortunately. I'm on the surface."

"Yeah, I think I saw you go down. Where are you?"

His display blinked to inform him that he was receiving coordinates through the Tacnet. The fighter seemed to have gone down a little under two kilometers from their position.

"All right. We'll be there in a little while. Hang on." He toggled to the marine-only net. "What do you think, do we rendezvous with her or should we hold here for a while? I'm not really comfortable with leaving the defenders at our rear, but I don't think they'll come out of the bunker after us. My opinion is that we should go."

"How should I know? This is my first rodeo. Hell, they left me outside on guard duty. It doesn't seem that they trusted me either."

"All right. I'm hoping that the enemy facility is going to blow up in a few minutes, so let's move back. If they come out after us, we can have the fighter command pick them off." Tristan set off in the direction of the stricken fighter, with Bettina on his heels.

"Well, that's a lucky break, at least," he said when the fighter finally came into sight.

It had landed right side up and looked pretty intact except for some damage to the nose. He paid particular attention to the cockpit area, relieved to see that it had maintained integrity and that the pilot was moving around inside.

The best thing about the landing site, however, was simply the fact that the pilot had ditched her fighter in the center of a crater twenty meters wide and maybe three or four meters deep. That beauty of it was that the rim would offer a certain amount of cover both against any of the facility's defenders that might have followed them and the hopefully forthcoming explosion.

"Stay here and watch for some tracked cylinders. If any of those appear, shoot them and let me know. You don't want them to see you first, so it might be a good idea to stay out of sight." He loped off to where the pilot was gesturing to him from inside her cockpit.

"Can you do me a favor?" she asked over the Tacnet.

"Sure, what do you need?"

"Display says I'm venting air, but I can't see anything from here, and it's not telling me where. Do you have an oxygen sensor?"

"I do. Let me look around."

It was the work of a few minutes. Waving the appendage— fortunately, the scanner was mounted on the suit's left gauntlet—over the fighter and then following the intensifying levels of trace gas in the air led Tristan to a tiny crack in an air tube. He removed the protective paneling and used part of his own suit's sealant to stop the loss.

"How's that?"

"Worked like a charm. Pressure is building again, and I didn't lose all that much air. Thanks! Good news is that the ship is spaceworthy. I may be able to get off the ground once the mop-up action above us is over. Just running a few more diagnostics."

"All right. See if you can warn the fighters that, if everything goes well, the building over there will be exploding pretty vigorously in…" he checked his display. "A little under five minutes."

"All right, I'll let them know."

Tristan ran back to the crater lip and took cover behind it. "You might want to hit the deck, Bettina," he said. "In a couple of minutes, there may be a bunch of rocks flying around."

She complied.

The final ten seconds of the countdown were agony. Had the defenders found the charges? If so, had they gotten them all? He suspected that, whatever the cylinder was, it was delicate. A single charge should be enough to take it down.

What would they do if it didn't blow? The absence of an enemy fleet meant that they could send through another bunch of marine platoons, better armed and armored against the resistance they were going to meet and a complete overview of the facility's layout. The second time around should be a cakewalk.

But he wanted the sacrifice of the men and women lying dead under the soil of a moon a hundred light-years from their home to mean more than just decent intel. He wanted them to be a part of a human victory.

The ground shook and he smiled to himself. Deep beneath the ground, charges were going off.

The timers weren't exactly perfectly coordinated. Each detonation shook the ground individually, and each represented sweet vindication.

He started to count, not sure how long they would need to stay under the relative cover of the crater lip before it would be safe to emerge. He was just about to crawl up the slope when the ground convulsed and threw him into the air.

A sudden shaft of brightness and debris exploded from the direction of the bunker. In the distance, it created an edifice of light.

"Secondary explosion!" he told Bettina. "Big mother, too. Stay down."

The debris began to fall around them moments later. Small pieces at first, followed by chunks of building material and lunar rock dozens of meters across. Tristan barely dared to move as stones fell all around him, only rotating his head to see if the woman in the fighter had survived the initial barrage. The ship, amazingly, still seemed intact.

The end of falling stones was followed by a dust cloud that enveloped him and didn't allow him to see anything further than ten meters away.

Tristan stood. "Bettina. It's probably safe to get up now. Let's go check on the pilot."

He walked towards her.

"Come on, get up."

But as his remaining gauntlet pulled on the suit, his heart sank. The helmet was dented and deformed, as if it had been impacted by something enormous. Her face was still intact, but the vacuum had already done its job. Lifeless eyes and a rictus of unbearable pain stared back at him.

He turned away, knowing it would be no use to try to close her eyes. They were frozen solid, and his suit wasn't built for delicate operations.

"Marine, can you hear me?"

"Yeah, Commander, loud and clear."

"Oh, that's a relief. Thought you guys were goners."

"Unfortunately, you were half right."

"Oh."

Tristan marched over to the fighter. "Your luck seems to be holding, Commander." There were some new dents on the airframe, but other than that, the ship hadn't taken any damage.

They waited as the dust dropped silently around them. "I'm arranging for pickup for you. I think I'll be able to fly back," the pilot told him.

"Thanks. I appreciate it."

He put the suit into power-saving mode and watched the planet the moon orbited come back into focus as the haze dissipated. Such a green, beautiful thing hanging in the sky.

The position meant that Tristan had a front row seat when the green planet suddenly turned black. Millions of tiny specks appeared on the surface and coalesced into a black cloud that resembled nothing so much as a swarm of angry insects on an agricultural world.

The cloud swirled, grew and then speared off the planet into space.

It headed straight towards the human fleet.

CHAPTER 9

Timini Persei Abdullah double-checked her monitors before calling out to her superior officer. "Captain," she said, and waited for the man's full attention before continuing. "Whatever was stopping us from reaching the planet just disappeared. Our missiles are getting into the atmosphere."

"Good." Captain Silenni was an officer whose long grey hair was tied in a tight braid. Every one of his bridge crew knew his story: he hadn't volunteered for this mission; in fact, he'd been selected for evacuation to regions of space where the fighting was likely to arrive long after his death, but he'd been the commanding officer of the *Centauri's Courage* for so long that, when the ship was pressed into duty, he'd elected to come along anyway. "Tell the fighter commanders to probe the area. If they can duplicate your findings, then order them to hit the planet."

She relayed the orders over the fighter wing command Tacnet and watched her display as the fighters, who'd seemed to be milling about aimlessly, quickly re-formed their ranks and dove for the surface. A couple of exploratory missiles were, apparently, enough for the insane fighter jockeys to decide that the shield was actually down and drive straight into the spot where it had been.

Timini held her breath, half-expecting the blue dots representing the members of the fighter squadrons to disappear, atomized as they slammed into a shield which was somehow still there—or worse, into a shield that suddenly came back online.

But it didn't happen. The fighters raced towards the surface of the planet with no further impediment. Her display wasn't set up to show in-atmosphere action—others were assigned to that role—so she listened in on the command Tac to follow the action. A number of fighter wings approached the enemy and their commanders were discussing the lay of the land. Their voices seemed unconcerned.

"Enemy sighted, northern hemisphere."

"I see 'em. There's a lot of bogeys out there."

"Yeah, but remember what the people who attacked the moon reported. They don't have much firepower."

"They might not need it. I have visual and it looks like a black sandstorm in front of me. How in the world are we going to deal with that many?"

"Very patiently. Just don't crash into them and you'll be fine. I'm taking the twelfth wing in."

"Good luck!"

Silence reigned over the command net for a few moments as the officers switched to their wing-specific frequencies to coordinate the assault with their squadron members. Timini held her breath as she waited to see what the results of the initial run would be.

The tension wasn't unbearable, though. The news from the moon engagement had been encouraging. The defenders were severely limited in their capacity to shoot down fighters, and most of the fighters that had been lost in that action had succumbed to the mysterious failures that everything seemed to be subject to since their arrival. The majority of those had involved computer breakdowns, which was new, but were otherwise the continuation of a pattern. Knowing this beforehand allowed everyone to breathe a little easier.

"Oh, fuck, did you see that?" a voice came through. "The twelfth just got wiped out."

"Wiped out? How?"

"Blown out of the sky on their first run. All of 'em. Whatever these guys are shooting, it's not some watered-down ammo."

"I'm closing in... man, those things are *fast*! They look like that wing the marines saw at the ice giant."

Then there was silence again before a different voice spoke, a nervous voice. "Hello, calling the seventh and the fourteenth? Anyone out there? This is the fifth. We're in retreat, but they're running us down fast. Can you get them off our tail?"

Only silence answered the call.

Timini was brought back to the reality of the bridge by a sudden chime coming from her console. Her screen had lit up. Where there had once been a scattering of blue dots—representing the fighter wings that had gone down to the planet—the display showed a near-solid snake composed of red pinpoints. "Incoming!" she said.

"Direction?"

"From the planet. Millions of them. My system can't give an exact count."

"I see them... Oh, my God," Silenni said. "All forward batteries, fire now, full power. Lateral defenses, full fire forward. See if we can hold them off long enough to turn around and get out of here."

Blinding light streaked past the observatory deck towards the approaching swarm. It blinded Timini, and the ship shook around her with the effort of channeling that much power into energy weapons.

When she could see again, silence had descended on the bridge. Her eyes gradually adjusted to the darkness and she was relieved to see that there was nothing outside. Just blackness.

Then she remembered that there should be much more than blackness in the viewport. There should have been stars, especially the bright illumination of the nearby HR 8799. The planet should have been visible. So should the moon, off to the right.

The black sky seemed not to care what should have been.

Upon closer inspection, Tinini saw that even the blackness wasn't quite right. Where the ebony of deep space was a dark, inky shade, the darkness before her eyes was matte, graphite-colored, more deep grey than black.

And it was moving. Swirls and currents flowed within, as if a pitch-black curtain had been drawn over the viewport and was being shaken by unseen hands. It took her a few moments to understand that what she was seeing was a cloud of attacking spacecraft, too many to count, swarming around the *Centauri's Courage*.

In the silence of the bridge, she felt the carrier shudder. Once, twice, and then more times in such quick succession that she lost count. Alarms bleated everywhere, but except for one or two officers yelling instructions and status reports, the people present were frozen, staring at the viewport.

Glimpses of light, evidence of colossal explosions, made it through the curtain of attacking craft. Smaller sparks from energy weapons and explosions on the ship's hull were nearer at hand.

The crew ignored all that as they watched the viewport. It was made of armored transparent plastic, a meter thick and stronger than titanium. The cloud outside was hitting it with projectile weapons. Every so often, one of the attackers would misjudge a turn and crash into it. Each impact against the huge window was a dull thud that the bridge officers knew meant there was that much less material between them and the colossal energies being unleashed on the other side.

Timini wondered what it would feel like to be torn into wet gibbets by a round designed to penetrate hull armor, the weaponry that had destroyed four flights of fighters in under a minute. Would death be instantaneous, or would she feel the agony as the bullet shattered her fragile frame? She didn't even try to imagine what being torn apart by an energy beam would feel like.

A direct hit to the center of the viewport sent a spider's web of cracks through the central panel.

The next impact landed almost exactly in the same place. Timini saw the plastic panel disintegrate inward with enough force to decapitate an aide sitting directly beneath it, and then the plastic shards, the dead aide, and everything that wasn't tied down began to rush towards the gaping hole in the viewport under the inescapable pressure of the vacuum of space.

Timini never found out how it would feel to be torn apart by a massive round. She did, however, get to experience the agony of being simultaneously frozen, asphyxiated, and having all her blood vessels burst in the vacuum of space. Fortunately, it was quickly over.

***

"Move it, marines. We got a fight on our hands, so look alive!"

As far as Tom was concerned, it was completely unnecessary advice. Swooping black shapes blasted through the corridors, shooting at any structures they could identify in time, crashing into many others. The invaders seemed to be doing as much damage to themselves as they were to the ship. Pieces of black enemy craft littered the staging area.

Unfortunately, the enemy dead lay among the broken bodies of a number of platoons of marines who'd been boarding their dropships when the first wave breached the hull of the *Bard* and had been cut down where they stood. The center of an open square fifty meters to a side was not ideal for taking cover, and the platoons had been cut to pieces, even though they reacted instantly and fired back at the flying attackers. At least they'd taken a few with them.

"What are they?"

"How should I know? They look like the thing in the recording. The one the marines from the *Minstrel* ran into on the moon of the ice giant."

Tom looked at one of the things that had fallen, intact albeit with a hole through the middle, near his position. His companion was right. It was dark and wing-shaped, clearly constructed of metal or carbon composites or something and slightly over two meters long. The body was oval in cross-section, bulging out more in the center than towards the wingtips.

It was obviously something that had been built, not birthed. The lines were industrial, chiseled, sculpted from angles and straight lines. The confusion came when watching them fly around. They didn't look like robots, didn't move like them. They swarmed like something alive and reacted with unpredictability and intelligence. Tom had watched them box five marines into a dead end by attacking them from the side and then, once the marines were established behind cover, suddenly change tactics and hit them from above. All that remained of the troops was the memory of their screams over the Tacnet.

And it was impossible to watch a damaged enemy attempt to get back into the air and escape its tormentors without understanding that the thing had a consciousness that it wanted to preserve.

But whether they were alive or some kind of drone wasn't the issue at hand. What Tom's platoon needed to do was to clear the staging area of attackers as soon as possible. To do that, they needed to seal the blast doors. Maybe if they secured an area, someone would take command and lead a counter attack.

He tried not to think about what such a strike might hope to achieve. The *Bard*'s interior was in vacuum, thanks to multiple holes in the hull. Unless part of the navy crew had managed to lock themselves in a space where they still had air, only shock marines in exoskeletons and those pilots who'd made it to their dropships before depressurization had survived.

Even if some of the naval guys had pockets of air, there was still the question of not being blown to bits by these attackers.

All of which made him suspect that managing to take the ship might only be worthwhile in order to keep the bodies of the dead from serving as food for the enemy.

That was good enough for Tom. He hadn't signed up to watch his shipmates get consumed by the blobs for protein.

He watched a flight of enemy craft race by and, timing it as best he could, he stepped out from behind cover, took a quick shot at the rearmost craft and ran towards the door controls. To his relief, they were undamaged, so he hit the emergency blast door seal button. He had to break through its error-proofing cover to do so, but that was child's play in the powered exoskeleton.

The huge door crashed down, shaking the staging bay. Tom felt the vibrations through his suit.

Almost as soon as the armored panel slid into place, he felt new vibrations coming from it as the enemy began shooting at the door. It wouldn't hold indefinitely, but unless they had something bigger than the guns he'd seen already, the thick armor would take them a bit of time to bore through.

Sealing the door meant that the marines could take the initiative. They carved into the flying enemy with enthusiasm, knowing that the huge metallic kites couldn't run out of the staging hangar, and that they also couldn't be reinforced by the numberless cloud of enemies outside.

Unfortunately, the lack of escape and reinforcement didn't seem to dull the bad guys' fighting ability in the least. They still gave as good as they got, and the highly mobile wings were difficult to hit.

Tom exulted as one he'd shot at veered off course and slammed into a column, disintegrating into small pieces in a shower of sparks.

He glanced back at the door to ensure that the enemy wasn't close to breaking through, and then took a bead on another. By the time the remaining flyers had been dealt with, Tom had two more kills to his credit, and he'd never even been in any real danger; his position far from the main marine lines ensured that he could snipe without drawing undue attention to himself.

"All right, crew, any of those fuckers left?" an authoritative voice over the Tacnet inquired.

"I think we got them all."

"OK. You and you," the voice spoke to people Tom couldn't see, "look around the hangar. If you see anything moving that isn't wearing a suit, blow it apart." There was a pause. The commander, whoever he was, must have been on one of the non-public channels. "All right. It looks like we have four dropships left. That means that forty of us can get out of this crate."

"Where would we go?"

"If we use the all the onboard fuel to power the ships, we might be able to get clear of the battle. Then we'll need to wait for pickup."

"Did anyone survive?"

"Situation is still fluid, but I hear that the *Centauri's Courage* is badly damaged. Well, and the *Bard* of course."

"Lucky us."

"Yeah, did you think you were signing up for a picnic?" Another pause. "I just did a quick head count and there are twenty-five marines in here. We can all get the hell out of Dodge."

"But what about the crew? Shouldn't we at least try to figure out if anyone survived?" Tom, to his horror, realized that the voice was his.

"Look, soldier, if you want to try to fight your way through the swarm behind the door to rescue a bunch of popsicles, I won't stand in your way. In fact, I'll drink to your bravery to the end of my days. But my responsibility is to the war effort, and I won't throw away any more marines than we've already lost. So whoever is coming, get your ass on a dropship. Those doors won't hold much longer."

To his surprise, Tom actually hesitated, thinking of a particularly interesting bridge aide he'd struck up a friendship with since they'd been thawed, but then he turned back and ran towards the rest of the marines.

He'd face the fact that she was dead, and probably some blob's lunch, later. Right then, he needed to concentrate on not joining her.

The dropships were quickly loaded and the outer hangar door blown open using explosive charges. The intention was that the huge, very solid piece of steel could help clear a path for them through the swarm of enemy attackers and increase their chances of getting away.

They needn't have bothered. The side of the ship they emerged on was devoid of enemy presence, and they sped away unmolested.

Tom craned his neck around. The ship he was on had been the last to leave, and he'd instinctively chosen the window seat. Dropship action made him feel helpless enough without also forcing him to blindly accept his fate.

Hanging in space behind them, the hulk of the *Bard* drifted aimlessly. Tom wasn't a starship engineer, but even he could tell that the carrier would never be of further use to anyone. Riddled with holes punched into the hull and still venting gasses which became briefly visible as they froze and then disappeared from sight as they dispersed, it was clearly a dead ship. All human children had downloaded vids of ghost ships drifting through the space lanes with unholy memories on board, and this one fit the bill perfectly.

The enemy flyers—presumably excluding the ones still inside—had abandoned the area. The swarm they'd seen on every situation display before the battle was nowhere to be found. There was no way to tell where they might have gone: finding black fighters against a black star field was a fool's errand.

He briefly thought of the crew of the ship, both marines and naval personnel. There had been thousands. Twenty-five marines and four dropship pilots were all that remained.

Tom reached out to the pilot over the Tacnet. "Any news on a possible pickup?"

"None. Area is way too hot for anyone to fly in. It would be suicide."

"Maybe so, but we need extraction."

"Buddy, just calm down. While we're still alive, there's hope. Plus, you've got much more air in that suit than I do in this cabin. Relax."

"Where are we going?"

"Nowhere in particular. We can't fight those things, so we've decided to put the planet between them and us. As long as they're on one side and we're on the other, we're reasonably safe."

Safe, Tom knew, was a very relative condition. They were supposed to be safe inside the troopship, a well-armed and armored capital vessel. That hadn't worked out so well.

And now their safety depended on a tiny flight of inadequately armed dropships in orbit.

Looking down at the planet, Tom wondered if he'd ever make it off his ship, and wondered how the rest of the fleet was doing. He tried to find the *Centauri's Courage*, but the ship was not in his field of view.

***

"Admiral," an aide on the bridge of the *Heavy Gunship IV* said.

"Yes?"

"It looks like the enemy is pulling away, sir."

"Pulling away?"

"Yes, sir. They seem to be focusing their attack on the moon. Both the *Minstrel* and the *Ismala* report that the enemy has broken off their pursuit. And our forward guns haven't gotten a target in over three minutes."

The *HGIV* had taken a beating, but this was exactly the kind of action the ship was designed for. It was more a mobile battle station, armed and armored to the hilt, and unlike the carriers and troopships, it had done well against the portion of the swarm that had come their way.

"Where are they going?"

"Our sensors have tracked them to the planet's moon, and we're seeing energy release in various sites across the surface. The sites map to the ones where we'd seen installations on our reconnaissance runs."

"So they're blowing up their own installations? Why would they do that?"

The aide shrugged. "Maybe they just want to keep the buildings out of our hands."

Tina spoke up. Her father, as usual, was thinking along strict military lines. The admiral could only see two divisions when he was in action: us and them, blue and red dots. "Maybe they aren't the guys who built those facilities."

"That's ridiculous. Who else would have built facilities around their planet?"

"Someone who wanted to keep them locked up, maybe." She looked around the bridge. "Think about it. The shield thing, whatever it was, went down immediately after our marines blew up the installation that was emitting all the radiation, right?"

"Yes," her father said, but she could see that he'd already grasped the rest of what she was going to say. He was hidebound, but he wasn't dumb. The only reason he let her continue and didn't blurt out her conclusion for her was that he wasn't the kind of man to steal a subordinate's thunder, even if he was kicking himself for not having thought of it first.

"So what if that energy shield wasn't meant to keep us out, but actually meant to keep that black cloud of vampire fighters in?"

Silence reigned as everyone considered the implications of what she'd said. The admiral shook his head. "I'll need to think about that a little later. First, I need to understand what we have left. Fleet status, please."

"Yes, sir," a lieutenant to the right of the admiral replied. "The *Banshee* and the *Lapland* weren't involved in the fighting, and are already at the rendezvous point. The *Minstrel* and the *Ismala* survived, but both are still assessing damage. The good news is that they're moving to the meeting place under their own power. The bad news is that the *Ismala* had to abandon a whole bunch of fighters, and of course, all the marines on the moon got left behind. We don't know if any survived."

The admiral massaged the bridge of his nose with two fingers, a gesture that Tina had seen countless times when she was growing up. It looked like a harmless gesture showing that her father was tired, but to her, it represented the times when he'd punished her for misbehaving; especially on those occasions where he knew the punishment would hurt her.

What he was thinking was clear as day. He wanted to return to the scene of the battle and look for survivors, and to save as many lives as he could. He wanted it more than anything in the universe.

The admiral straightened. "Full retreat. Set a course for the rendezvous point. Tell the captains of the *Ismala* and the *Minstrel* that I want to see them on the bridge as soon as they arrive."

The bitter pill swallowed, her father straightened. "Analyst... Pol, isn't it?"

"Yessir," the analyst replied, obviously expecting the call, but still nervous about being addressed by the admiral.

"Everything I've seen so far, combined with what you told me about this system not being HR8799, makes me conclude that there isn't a blob fleet in this sector and there probably won't ever be. Hell, I'm pretty sure the battle we just fought isn't even part of the same war." He gave the man a long look. "What I really want to know is who just attacked us and whose installations we just blew to pieces. But I'll settle for knowing where the hell we are."

"We're working on that, sir."

"So you don't know?"

"What we're seeing out there doesn't match anything in the star charts, so we're working by elimination. We started at the Tau Ceti base and are working our way outwards. We're looking at the records for all the similar stars that we have on file against this system. We've gone out quite a way and still don't have a match."

"How much is quite a way?"

"I can definitely state that this system isn't within fifteen thousand light years of where we started from."

CHAPTER 10

Melina listened in dismay as the battle around the planet evolved from a surprise attack to a rout and finally to a massacre. She held her breath as the command Tac brought her news of the retreat. Both of the ships around the moon were recalled.

She knew the order was logical, a necessary withdrawal that would save the greatest number of lives and the greatest amount of material, but someone on the bridge must have been against it because the last transmission they sent before flying away was: "If there's anyone in orbit, or anyone down on the moon, hang tight. I'll get this ship back here somehow."

And then the ships moved out of Tacnet range and there was silence on the airwaves.

"We're screwed, aren't we?" the shock marine said.

"Probably. I am, at least. I thought I could fly out of here, but I'm getting all kinds of error messages. There's no way I'm getting off the ground, so unless the ships can get back here in a day or so, I'll be out of air. I vented quite a bit, I'm afraid. And you might want to think about telling your suit to put you into a coma right away. I suppose you can save some of your oxygen like that."

"Crap."

"Tell me about it."

They sat in silence for a few minutes before an unexpected voice reached her over the Tacnet. "There you are! I've been looking all over for you."

"Ian? What are you doing here?"

"Looking for you. I already told you that."

"I meant, why didn't you retreat with the ships? You'll be stuck out here."

"I've got a Recon flyer, so I can survive quite a few weeks out on my own. Plus, I can hide from most stuff and run from anything that manages to see me. That's the beauty of Recon, we don't have to be brave."

"Well, I hope you came to say goodbye, because I've got a few hours of air and no power to the engines."

"So hop on my flyer."

"How? Don't have a suit, either."

She could see the flyer now, coming in to land in their crater, following a spiral descent path. Braking jets stirred up a huge dust cloud and the marine raised his guns in the direction of the ship.

"Down, boy. That's a friend of ours, and he just might be your ticket out of here."

"That's not one of our fighters."

"I know. It's a Recon flyer. Trust me on this, he's one of the good guys."

The man stood down.

"Nice to meet you, soldier," Ian's voice came over the open Tacnet. "Name's Ian. Sorry to sneak up like that, but I didn't know Melina had company. Thought she'd have enough sense to ditch further from the fighting."

"Not my choice. I barely had time to keep the thing upright, much less choose where to fall. I thought I might be able to fly home, but the secondary explosion pelted me with rocks... and I don't think this fighter is going anywhere."

"Not a problem. I'll take you out with me. I've got a spare suit. Might be a bit big on you, but I still think it's better than asphyxiating."

Melina suddenly felt nervous. She'd been so sure she was going to die that fatalism had essentially overcome her, probably made stronger by listening to the destruction of two capital ships and the death of their crews over the Tacnet.

Now, however, the risk of getting an extra suit into a sealed fighter without killing herself made her take interest in the world and feel a sense of dread. She knew there was a procedure for that operation, a way to ensure that she would be exposed to the vacuum the least amount of time possible, sealing the fighter again with minimum air loss, but she'd probably been dozing in class when her instructor had walked them through it all those years before.

If she didn't get the suit, she would die. So if she died trying, at least she wouldn't have to wait around for it.

"All right," she said, punching buttons on her console. Her display was still working and she still had power to the canopy mechanism. That was good. "Once you get to the fighter, I'm going to pump as much of my cabin oxygen back into the tanks as I can without fainting. That way, I'll lose very little if something goes wrong, and we can try again. Then I'm going to close my eyes and pop the canopy. I'll leave it open for two seconds before closing it again, so make sure you're ready to throw the suit in. If all goes well, I should survive."

"Got it," Ian replied. "Start your pumps. I'll be there in a couple of minutes."

Melina did. She brought her cabin pressure down to fifty kilopascals, ignoring the alarms that went off. She should be fine at that pressure, especially since the air inside her fighter was pure oxygen.

She flipped open the acrylic covering that protected the canopy opening switch from accidental activation. She put one hand on top of the button and the other on the one that closed it in and re-pressurized the cabin in emergencies. Both hands were trembling.

Ian walked up to the fighter. The suit he was carrying was bulky enough that Melina decided to leave the canopy open as long as she dared.

"Ready?" Ian asked.

"As ready as I'm going to be. Opening the window in three. Two. One."

Melina closed her eyes and pressed the button and air rushed past her head, to be lost in the vastness of space. She couldn't hear anything else and her ears popped with the pressure change. She had no way to tell whether the recon pilot had managed to maneuver his awkward burden through the opening, but she was starting to feel the cold and the wind was gone. She punched the close button.

Air blasted back in and the pain in her ears was excruciating. After a few seconds, she allowed herself to breathe... and it felt good. Only then did Melina open her eyes.

A ball of ice formed in her stomach when she didn't immediately spot the suit beside her. She turned frantically around to see the yellow bag sitting in the space behind her seat. Ian had intelligently chosen to drop it where it couldn't get caught on anything. "Remind me to kiss you when I get to your ship, Ian. I'd never have bet on it, but you actually turned out to be a decent guy."

"Of course I am. What did you expect?"

"Well, you did come across as a bit of a whiner when I met you."

"I think most of us would have been bitter to have been sent on a suicide mission and leave behind our family without being consulted."

She said nothing. She had lost just as much as he had on this trip, and had mentioned it to no one. Of course, he did have a point about having had a choice. But again, it was hard for her to imagine someone in any of the services, naval, marines, or Recon, not volunteering immediately.

"Soldier boy. I see that suit's damaged," Ian continued. "Can you grip the cargo bar on my flyer?"

"Should be all right. But where are we going?"

"I was thinking of getting us off this moon as quickly as possible."

"Any particular reason for that?"

"Yeah. Long range sensors on my ship tell me that the uglies from the planet are massing nearby. I think they're coming our way and I'd like nothing more than not being here when they arrive. Feel free to stick around and fight them if you want."

"Nah, I'm good. Just show me where to grab on. I'm Tristan, by the way."

"Nice to meet you. I assume you were in the bunker?

"Yeah. All the way to the bottom and back."

"You'll have to tell me about that sometime. Melina, you coming?"

She finished double checking the suit and powered it up. Yellow lights became green as the diagnostics confirmed the seals. "Yes, it looks as though I am."

Melina popped the hatch again, this time without trepidation, and climbed out of the stricken fighter. She paused for a single second to place her hand on its skin, a ritual of thanks that she always observed when a ship brought her back from an engagement in one piece. This time, her thankfulness was tinged with sadness—this fighter would never be carrying anyone else into combat. It had given its life to save hers.

But she didn't permit herself more than a second's reverie. Like Ian, Tristan, and Melina herself, the fighter had come here to be destroyed. She gained nothing by dwelling on it.

Moments later, she climbed into the Recon ship. "I'm driving," she said in a tone that she hoped brooked no argument. She knew that if anyone else took the controls, she wouldn't be able to contain her nerves.

Ian just shrugged. "Suit yourself." He clambered into the seat behind her and fussed with his belts.

"Cabin seal locked, pressure coming in a second. We have atmosphere. Nothing leaking, so you can go ahead and take your helmet off if you like." She pulled off her own. Although it was much safer to fly with a helmet on—you wouldn't die immediately if your hull was breached, for one thing—she hated it. She always felt that it impaired her peripheral vision, and she knew that things she couldn't see in a dogfight could be just as deadly as a depressurization. The reason the fighter corps allowed them the choice was that in centuries of space war, it had been discovered that impacts that opened up the hull of a fighter were usually caused by high-energy weapons that didn't just breach the hull, but actually pulverized the vehicle. There was no real survivability gain in wearing a suit.

"Trooper, hold on for a second. I'm going to pull into a hover. On my signal, grab the cargo bar."

Now where was the button to turn one of these things on? Melina asked herself. After shoving him unceremoniously aside, she couldn't just ask Ian to show her. She hesitated a moment, cursing the armed forces for their continued refusal to standardize cockpit layouts across small craft, and then pushed a recessed lozenge. To her relief, the ship powered up.

Melina powered up, held the ship in place, and waited for Tristan to attach himself to the cargo bar. She lifted the craft a couple of meters and hovered a few more seconds trying to get a feel for what the heavy suit would likely do to the ship's balance before she shrugged and took off into orbit.

"I assume you're an expert on the sensors," she said to Ian.

"Of course. Been living with these things for a couple of years."

"Great. Tell me which way to go, then."

Ian chuckled. "You see that solid black smudge over there?"

"Yeah."

"It's not solid. It only looks that way because there are so many little dots one on top of the other. The enemy ships are swarming."

"Oh."

"So my suggestion is that you fly the other way."

"The other way is towards the planet, which is where they originally came from."

"I understand that, but right now, they're over there."

"What if they left more of them on the planet?"

"We'll have to deal with that if it comes up. I prefer to run from the danger we know is out there."

"I'm with Ian," Tristan chimed in over the Tacnet from somewhere below them. "For some reason, I don't feel happy with the idea of this ship being shot at by anything while we're in space. My vote is to get away from the ones we know are out there, and then see where that gets us."

"All right," Melina said. There was no real option, anyway. Attempting to make a run for the rendezvous point would send them straight through the swarm, and flying in any other direction would likely as not just leave them stranded in space until the eventually got spotted.

She set a course for the planet.

"Holy shit!" Ian said.

"What?" Melina instinctually checked her proximity alarms for any sign of enemy attack. When she saw that space around them was clear, she turned on Ian. "Don't do that. You nearly made me piss myself. What is happening?"

He pointed at the long-range display, where the solid mass of enemies had opened up to become multiple tendrils which shot out from the main mass and shot towards the moon like fingers from a giant hand.

Graphs and charts started spiking to one side of the display. "Someone out there doesn't like that moon very much," Ian said.

"They hitting it hard?" Melina inquired. By the way the graphs were jumping, it certainly seemed that way.

Ian studied the readouts. "Yes... but not so much hard, as often. These jumps look more like something getting hit with hundreds of thousands of small projectiles. When there's a big explosion like our marine friends set off, the charts work on a different scale."

"Can you show me what they're shooting at?"

"Sure." He toggled to a different screen which showed a rotating moon surrounded by clouds of data. "They seem to be blasting every single artificial structure on the planet. The alien ones we'd identified and anything else. By this count, they sent forty thousand rounds into your ship. See? You wouldn't have asphyxiated if you'd stayed."

Melina marveled at the ship's sensors. Her own fighter had excellent short-range scanners but would have been hard-pressed to identify an enemy at this kind of range, much less count shots fired. Of course, Recon flyers were much heavier and less nimble than fighters, despite being unarmed and unarmored. The weight consisted of scanners, shielding, and big, big engines.

"How about we get away from here before they notice us?" Tristan said. "I feel a little exposed out here."

Melina throttled gently, to avoid putting too much strain on the cargo bar and pushed them into an orbit around the planet.

Ian suddenly hit a switch and put a headset to his ear. "You're not going to believe this. We have company in orbit. A bunch of marines. They've got four dropships, too. They say they fought through the swarm and got away."

"Of course they did. They're marines. Those flying things are just fighters. It's not even a fair fight."

"Shut up, Tristan, or I'll jettison the cargo bar with you on it," Melina said. Turning to Ian, she asked, "Can you show me where they are?"

***

The hangar door shut behind him, and Yuri waited for the space to pressurize. He climbed out of the fighter, but didn't open his face shield.

He knew all about hangars that had just been open to space. They were always extremely fucking cold.

A circumnavigation of his fighter made him wince. It was still spaceworthy, which was why he was still alive, but he knew that it was only a temporary thing. When his quartermaster saw the state of that fighter, the man would kill him.

The door opened and two women entered the hangar. They could have been mother and daughter: both had dark hair and olive skin, but one of them was about thirty while the other looked closer to fifty-five. Of course, considering stasis sleep patterns during the war, the younger-looking one could easily have been born centuries before her counterpart. "So, can you explain why, exactly, you decided to come here? The *Ismala* is damaged, but it was good enough for all the other fighters, wasn't it?"

He shrugged. They'd told him that the *Lapland* would be expecting his arrival but, as usual, the fog of war seemed to have intervened. "Admiral's orders. He said he wanted someone to analyze the ammo we were being hit with."

"The ammo from the flying wings? Those were shooting some kind of explosive heavy-metal slugs. Not a whole lot of science to that."

"I didn't fight the wings, fortunately. I was on the moon, fighting the air defenses there. The fighters they had seemed pretty advanced, but their ammo was crap, and the admiral wants to know why. Look at my fighter. They must have hit me fifty times, but I still flew out of there with most of my systems intact. All I really lost was my targeting computer, which is too smart for itself anyway. No one ever uses those things." He turned back to the ship. "The strange thing is that none of the impact holes are anywhere near the computer. It just probably broke the way everything does on this mission."

***

Irene hugged herself against the chill as she studied the fighter. Her heart sank even further. Her own life, and that of others who were likely dead millennia since, had been dedicated to a single cause: keeping humanity from indulging in its vilest passion: the eternal fighting of wars.

War was the single constant keeping humans from evolving beyond what they always had been: tribal savages organized in a society where the strong ruled the weak and in which the population's fear of being unprotected in the face of conflict kept the strong in power. Until war was abolished, there could be no true equality, not true freedom from poverty and slavery.

The politicians said that the blobs had started the war. Of course they would say that. The problem with their arguments was that in the course of human history, all the evidence pointed to humans always throwing the first stone.

In this one instance, for the first time that she knew of, her group had managed to execute a plan perfectly. They'd moved in and somehow managed to divert an entire task force away from a battle, sending them off into the trackless wastes of open space. The success was complete because they hadn't just sent them randomly out to die when the equipment failed; they'd actually managed to land them in a different star system. Granted, it was far away, and granted many had died, but it hadn't been indiscriminate murder. It had all worked out.

But there was still a fighter sitting in the landing bay full of holes. In a supposedly empty star system thousands of light years from the fighting.

To Irene, there could be no more powerful symbol of the hopelessness of striving for peace. In empty space across a good chunk of the galaxy from where they were supposed to be, the task force had managed to get embroiled in a three-way fight with... God only knew whom.

It was too much to digest, so she forced the thought aside. She'd have to analyze what she thought later. In the meantime, there was a mystery to solve. The fighter in the hangar was riddled with holes, but they were extremely shallow and none seemed to have penetrated too far into the fighter.

As they got to work, the pilot excused himself. They gave him directions to the nearest dining area and promptly forgot about him.

Her colleague, a woman named Serena, who had much more experience than Irene did, got straight to the heart of it. She pulled a small fragment of an enemy round out of the hull and held it up in the light. It was long and thin, fragile-looking.

"Doesn't look like something designed to destroy armored enemies, does it?"

"Not in the least," Irene replied.

"So why shoot it at our fighters?"

Irene pulled another one out of the metal. This one had barely broken the skin, but the bullet itself was deformed. She hefted it. "They're not particularly heavy. Light projectiles do a lot less damage. And this one is hollow."

Serena snapped her fingers. "And that's our answer. It's not a weapon in itself. The bullets are only the delivery system for the weapon. Something inside that shell was injected into this fighter and every other one that got hit."

"Something? You mean that it's a biological agent? Why shoot fighters with a biological agent?"

"I don't know."

Irene was thinking. They weren't expecting to be there, and the aliens inhabiting this system certainly wouldn't have been expecting the sudden appearance of a large human fleet. The weapons systems, therefore, weren't designed to stop them but some other kind of attacker. "I think it's because they weren't expecting us. They were expecting an attack from someone else."

"That's stupid. We've been at war with the blobs for centuries. They know how to kill us."

"I'm just trying to read the evidence," Irene said. Letting anyone know that she was aware of the fact that they were in the wrong place would invite unwanted questions. "We need to try to analyze what they injected here. But first, we have a much more pressing problem."

Irene walked to the hangar's communications console and contacted security. "We have a contamination alert. Use full hazmat suits and isolate the pilot who just came in through the hangar bay. Also, anyone who came in contact with him." She hesitated. "You'd better seal off the areas he visited, too, just in case. And lock Serena and me into this hangar. We'll need equipment, but we'll request that as we go. Now go grab that pilot."

CHAPTER 11

"Two hundred and fifteen thousand years?"

"Give or take, yeah."

"That's stupid," Cora said. The pain of walking around with half-healed injuries was much less than the pain of knowing that her entire platoon was now officially dead, and that she had not been able to do a thing about it, not even been present during the last combat mission. Tristan and Klaus had both been on the moon, and once the enemy swarm—everyone was calling them the black vampires now—had put an emphatic end to any speculation about survivors; everything artificial on the surface had been destroyed.

"No," the medical tech that had been performing her daily checkup disagreed. "It's not stupid. In fact, it makes perfect sense once you look at the evidence." He gestured at the equipment around him. "These machines are designed to work perfectly without maintenance after any long trip. That means they should last for five thousand years, easy. So either all the machines were faulty when we left or the trip was much longer than they were designed for."

She'd developed an instant dislike for the guy's knowing smile and his whiny smart-ass tone, but his argument made sense. Stasis pods were another technology that almost never failed in habitual use. They were designed to last forever, piling redundancies upon redundancies. But about forty percent of the pods on the *Minstrel* had failed, killing thousands of troops and crew. If the new estimates of where they were proved correct, it was lucky to have as many survivors as they did.

"Besides," the guy continued, "this comes straight from the admiral. He wouldn't be saying it if it wasn't true."

"The admiral told you? Wow. I didn't know you were friends with him."

"Bosom buddies. All his other friends died in transit." He studied the readout. "You're all right. I'll tell you the same thing the doctor probably did, though. You need to stay in bed. You're pretty banged up and you just had surgery. Yes, the autosurgeons did their job, but you need to let your body stitch itself back together all the way. Give it a couple more days. And you can forget about strenuous action for... well, probably longer than we'll last out here."

"Heard it already. Not interested."

She left the examination room and looked around the hall. The walls were the same luminous off-white they'd always been, but now she could see the tiny cracks in the plastic. Hairline fractures that she'd seen but never consciously noticed before. They took on much more significance now that she knew she was standing in a ship that had crossed just over fifty-three light years of space. Two hundred thousand years' worth of travel.

Cora ran her hands over a crack that extended two meters on the wall. It crisscrossed with dozens of others along its path. This was just one wall, an unstressed segment in a corridor that had been dormant during the entire trip. If that was the kind of damage that two hundred thousand years could impart, then it was no wonder that nothing worked the way it was supposed to.

Her assigned quarters were only a few dozen meters down a nearby corridor, but it was still a relief to get there. She had flatly refused to stay in the infirmary once the primary intervention had been completed, but the truth was that she was in bad shape. So she collapsed on her bunk and let her mind wander, following doctor's orders despite herself.

Her mind kept coming back to Tristan. Ever since she'd been assigned to the 243rd, she'd had her eye on him. He was good looking, but then all marines were—both men and women had bodies to kill for, courtesy of the greatest training programs that humanity had been able to devise over millennia. That wasn't what attracted her to him, however. There was something else about the guy, a quality that told her that he would see the job through, no matter what it was or what it cost him. Shock marines, especially experienced shock marines, were mainly cynics, herself included, but this guy was the earnest type. There was something endearing about that, something that set him apart.

What had started as a simple weighing of the men and women under her command had matured into a healthy respect for his straightforward approach and finally speculation about what he'd be like as a lover. Nothing she'd seen when they were naked beside their birthing pods had lessened her curiosity. Quite the contrary.

And now he was dead, and she was sitting there on the casualty list, unable to go take a piece of the bastards who'd snuffed him.

If it hadn't hurt too much to move, she would have been pacing like a caged animal.

Instead, she fell asleep.

***

Tristan's suit—the hand it still had, at any rate—hung to the cargo bar. He'd been stuck in basically the same position since they'd left the moon, and he flexed his arm to get the kinks out. He was thankful that the gauntlet could be locked into hold position which meant that it held on for dear life without any input from him.

The planet drifted below, green and unnatural, and he felt he should be falling towards it. Every time he looked down, it seemed closer than before, but that was all in his mind. To distract himself from thoughts of falling to his death, he listened to the banter on the Tacnet as the Recon flyer approached the dropships.

"Hey, guys, welcome to the party."

"Looks a little dead to me," Melina responded.

"Don't be that way. Every human in three million kilometers is here," the marine on the other end of the line responded.

"That might be true, but the cover charge was a bitch."

"Can't argue with that. Any news from the fleet?"

The four marine dropships had settled into a polar orbit around the planet, calculated to keep them as far away from the enemy swarm as humanly possible while still staying within sensor range—all without burning fuel. Ian, the only person whose ship was designed for long-range communication, had finally managed to make contact with the admiral's flagship on the way over.

Ian replied. "Nothing good, I'm afraid. They basically congratulated us for being the flower of humanity and wished us luck. They can't come get us."

"Well, we can't go out to them. They're way out in the ice giant orbits. Dropships can't get there."

"I think they know that. Hence the words 'good luck.' I think we're on our own on this one."

"That's easy for you to say. Your flyer can make it back."

"Not with me hanging down here, they can't," Tristan chimed in.

"I don't think it would be particularly healthy to fly through those enemy wings."

Silence reigned for a few moments. Their situation was bad, and they all knew it.

The silence lasted until it was finally broken minutes later by the leader of the marine contingent. "We've taken a decision: we're heading for the surface."

"What?" Melina replied. "Are you nuts? Did you see what just came off of that rock?"

"Yeah, lady, we got a really good look. I don't like it any more than you do, but the truth that everyone except for you two in the fancy Recon ship is going to be running out of air over the next twenty hours or so. We know from the briefing that the planet has a nitrogen and oxygen atmosphere. The fleet isn't coming for us, so we can either take our chances down there or die up here. Not much of a choice, but it's the one we have."

There was silence on the line as the crew of the flyer digested the news. "What do you think, marine? You're the one on the spot," Melina asked him over their private channel.

Tristan didn't need to think about it. His situation was the same one the marines on the dropship had evaluated, and he had no option but to make the same choice. But he was also hanging by one arm from a spaceship. "Can you make reentry gentle enough that I won't get burned to a crisp?"

Melina laughed. "Soldier, I could put a carrier down on that planet and no one on board would even feel the reentry."

"I'll settle for getting down in one piece."

"Trust me."

"Then yeah, I vote to land."

"Ian?"

"Well, I suppose we can't let him die out there, can we?"

She toggled back to the general channel. "We're with you. When do you want to head down?"

"How does right now sound?"

"Terrible, but I guess we can survive."

"Let's hope so. Wanna lead the way? I know those flyers aren't heavily armed, but they're better than dropships. Plus, you can actually avoid stuff and run away if necessary."

"All right. But we may have to keep it slow. I've got this marine hanging off the side of my ship whining that he doesn't want to get fried. Didn't know you guys were so fragile."

Tristan felt the gentle tug of the attitude rockets firing, and then the nose of the Recon flyer pointed towards the green globe below. His stomach suddenly fell behind and he felt the stress of acceleration in his suit. He could hear Ian and Melina discussing the pros and cons of possible landing sites, but he was much more concerned with the atmosphere around him. Air pressure was building up around his suit as they began to encounter the outer edges of the planet's gas envelope.

"Er... Melina, I'd appreciate it if we didn't go too much faster."

"Don't worry. I said I was going to get you down in one piece, and I intend to."

She was as good as her word. Though the wind howled around his suit, Melina feathered the power on reentry to keep the speed just below the velocity that would have torn away his grip and sent him tumbling to his death. How exactly she managed it was not something he would ever ask... mainly because every flyboy and flygirl he'd ever met would respond the same way: a superior smirk and the dreaded question: "You weren't scared, were you?"

Fortunately, his suit was fitted for disposal and processing of bodily waste, so there would be no evidence to the contrary when he told her that he wasn't.

"Not many places to land, are there?" Ian said.

"No. And I'd prefer somewhere with infrastructure to just a big clearing in the jungle. You're better than I am at reading those scanners. See anything you like?"

"I'm still not convinced we want to land anywhere near civilization," Tristan said. "I'm pretty sure I don't need to remind you that we just got our asses kicked by a huge number of things that came from this planet."

"We know that. But if we sink into the mud, we're stuck here until we dig ourselves out. And I don't want to land in the trees, either. A big patch of concrete or some equivalent likely means a safe landing spot."

"Right until the black things blow us off the face of the planet."

"It's a risk we have to take. Besides, I don't see any signs of them here. Ian, any readings?"

"No, there's nothing in the air with us in this hemisphere. Also, I've found a good spot to set down. Marking it on the readout."

"Great to hear."

The ship's course corrections were minute, but Tristan was convinced that each change of direction would be the one to break the suit's grip—or maybe just tear the exoskeleton's limb clean off, quite probably taking Tristan's arm with it. Of course, he wouldn't have much time to miss it: just a couple of minutes before he splattered into the scenery below.

"Wow," Melina said. "You could put a fleet down on that patch."

"I thought you'd like it. There are some buildings on the west, and the scanners read a huge network of tunnels below, so you may want to set down close to the jungle on the east. That way, if we are flying into an ambush, at least we'll see it coming."

Tristan could see the landing field, a large rectangular patch of grey against the green surface, much too regular to be a natural formation.

"Tristan, I'm going to take us down to about three meters up. From then on, I'll need your input to get you down safely."

The marine was having none of it. He'd been hanging by his arm for much too long to want to prolong the torture unnecessarily. As soon as the ship stopped descending, and he saw that the feet of his exoskeleton were suspended about an arm's length in the air, he simply released and dropped the final few centimeters to land with a resounding thud. He moved his arm around in circles and quickly ran out of the way.

"I'm clear, go ahead and land."

The flyer descended onto the enormous expanse, just clear of the trees that, seemingly unchecked for years, were attempting to recolonize the eastern border of the open space.

Tristan studied the floor, expecting to see a concrete surface, but instead, stared down onto what looked like a gigantic slab of dark grey rock. He looked around for evidence that the surface consisted of smaller units joined together, but the surface extended unbroken as far as he could see.

It was also chipped and cracked, and vegetation poked through in places. It resembled an ancient, abandoned parking lot.

The flyer touched down much more gently than he had. "Should we call in the marines?" Melina said.

"Maybe we should see if it's safe, first," Ian replied.

"Wouldn't you rather have them here if it turns out not to be?"

"Good point, but I meant more along the lines of whether the air is safe to breathe, that kind of thing. If it isn't, they should probably save their dropship fuel for some other desperate scheme."

"All right, pop the door and we'll see what happens."

Tristan jumped in. "Don't be stupid. You two have enough air to go anywhere on that thing, so if it isn't safe, you stand to lose the most by opening up. I'll test this."

Without waiting for an answer, he toggled his helmet clamps. Air rushed in through the seal, and he breathed it eagerly. It smelled sweet, ripe with the scent of vegetation, and humid.

After a few deep inhalations, he called to the crew of the flyer. "Well, I'm not sure about microbes, but the air won't kill you immediately at least."

He took a few more steps, and then stopped. He felt an unaccustomed weight on his face, so he doubled back and approached the jungle. A number of dried sticks lay on the landing area near the trees, so he picked one up and dropped it to the ground. He chuckled.

"Gravity is higher than Earth-normal. I'd say a G and a half or so. Have fun walking around without an exoskeleton."

"Yeah, we feel it," Melina replied. "How's the air pressure?"

"Good question. I got some equalization when I popped the helmet, so it's probably pretty high, but haven't been feeling any pain."

"All right. I'm going out there."

The flyer's door opened to reveal two people wearing space suits without helmets. It seemed to Tristan that, compared to when he's seen her in the fighter, Melina's face was sagging under the large gravitational pull from the planet. Ian's seemed to be sagging, too, but it was hard to tell, as he'd only seen the man through a tinted visor. Perhaps the man had always had jowls that made him resemble a bulldog.

They stood together in the soft light and the warm breeze of a world that was completely new to them. The feeling never got old, no matter the circumstances, so they drank it in while they had a few moments of peace.

"It could be much worse," Tristan said.

"Yeah, it usually is," Ian agreed. "I've scouted hundreds of worlds, and can only recall a handful where the temperature and the air permitted us to walk around this way. Pity about the gravity, though. These superearths can be tricky. You can fall and break bones."

"Yeah, that's why shock marines like to take our skeletons with us. Speaking of which, shouldn't we call them down? Don't want to have those guys holding their breath unnecessarily."

Melina uplinked to the dropships in orbit and gave them the all clear. Then she headed towards the jungle.

"What are you doing?"

"I want to see this vegetation."

The forest consisted of unfamiliar species. There were some trees that looked like the Earth-based species that humanity had modified and brought with them to the stars while others were completely different. Particularly unusual was a bamboo-like plant that grew in a latticework pattern, holding dense mats of light-absorbing leaves about head high.

"Good call on the landing site," Tristan admitted grudgingly. "I'd have hated to have to walk through that tangle." He pushed on some stalks until he managed to break one. "Even with a suit, this stuff would make for slow going."

"Yes." Tristan could tell that Melina wasn't really following the conversation. She was looking at the more normal-looking trees and also listening for sounds from within the forest.

"Anything you'd like to share?"

"Not really. I'm trying to see if I can find any clue to understanding the ecosystem here. I don't see any birds, and I haven't seen any insects yet. Or whatever the equivalent might be on this planet. If there are no animals, then trees probably won't be producing fruit. And that means that we may need to get creative when it comes to finding food."

"Maybe all the animals are further in the jungle. Even on Earth they tend to stay away from inhabited areas."

"Look at that landing area, trooper. Does it look like an inhabited place that animals might avoid? It hasn't been maintained in the recent past. Probably not for centuries. Maybe longer if that rock is as durable as it looks."

"Marines are down," Ian said.

The four dropships had landed in close formation around the Recon flyer and the marines, ever slaves to habit, were already posting sentries and organizing a scouting party.

Their leader, a grizzled dark-skinned man wearing sergeant's stripes on his suit, walked over and saluted Melina. "Hello, Commander. I'm Mubarta Sol Mobutu. Wanted to report that we're down and mostly accounted for."

"How many of you are there?"

"Twenty-five shock marines plus four dropship pilots, ma'am."

"Where did you guys come from?"

"We're the last survivors from the *Bard*, ma'am. We had to fight our way out. It wasn't pretty."

Melina absorbed this with aplomb. Perhaps it was the effect of the gravity on her features, but it seemed to Tristan that she carried some great weight with her. He wondered how old she was. It was difficult to tell; she seemed to be in her late thirties.

"Any suggestions on what to do next?"

"I think we might want to check on the building complex on the western end of this parade ground you selected for a landing site. In the meantime, I'd also recommend creating some kind of shelter in the jungle, preferably not too close to the ships. The canopy should keep us out of sight of anything flying overhead. From the looks of it, nothing can fly through that vegetation."

"They can always bomb the hell out of the jungle."

"Yes, ma'am. That's why I prefer not to be right next to the ships. Anyone bombing us will start with that and work their way outward." He hesitated. "But I really don't think we need to worry about being bombed. At least not by the black things."

"Why not?"

"It doesn't strike me as being their style. I think they win battles by having lots and lots of single guns, not by using individual weapons to clear large areas. Granted, those single guns pack a massive punch."

"Which means that, if they can't fly, they can't effectively come after us."

"Exactly. Which might explain why someone decided to shut them up on this planet."

"Huh?"

"Think about it, ma'am. The shield they had wasn't just a defensive shield. After watching what just happened, I'd bet that it was there more for the purpose of keeping those things contained on this planet than to keep anyone out."

"Why would the blobs want to keep anyone locked up in one of their forward bases?"

The marine shrugged, and his suit shrugged with him. "I haven't seen anything that looks remotely like blob hardware here. And I've been in enough fights with them to know what they like to use. I don't know what was on those two moon bases, but I'd bet that it wasn't blob stuff either."

Tristan started. "You're right, Sergeant," he said. "I was there, and it definitely wasn't a blob installation. The defenders looked more like something humans would have designed than blobs. Probably wasn't a human building, though—the doors are the wrong shape for us. But it wasn't blob-made, I'm pretty sure of that."

Melina hesitated, thinking back to the fighters on the moon that had been so ineffective against her own wing. They hadn't matched any of the blob designs she'd seen anywhere either.

"And those wings sure as hell aren't blob craft or we'd have lost this war long ago," the sergeant said.

"So where are the blobs? This system was supposed to be swarming with them?"

"I don't know and I don't care. I've got enough to worry about with the flying wings. And now that I think about it, I don't want to run into whoever was badass enough not only to defeat them but to lock them up intact and alive. What happened to the shield, anyway? Woulda been nice for that to stay up."

"I think I happened to the shield," Tristan said. "And by the looks of the generator they were using to generate it, I have to agree with you: we really, really don't want to tangle with the guys who built it."

CHAPTER 12

"Excuse me, sir. There's a man called Frederic on the comm. He says he's the head of maintenance on the *Ismala*, and that he has something he needs to tell you."

The admiral sighed. It seemed like everyone on every ship needed his input on something. Over the course of his career, he'd come to learn that no one wanted senior officers around. Underlings tended to hide stuff from them and give them only as much information as they thought would keep them out of trouble while, at the same time, limiting interference from above.

Of course, that only lasted until the shit hit the fan. *Then* they all wanted someone else in charge.

For the other man's sake, the admiral hoped the maintenance guy wasn't just calling to give him a status report on the *Ismala*'s toilets.

"Put him through."

The *Ismala*'s comms were still the worst in the fleet, but the voice on the other side could be made out over the static. "Hello, sir, I'm sorry to bother you with this, but with Commander Tau Coloni missing after her sortie on the planet's moon, I didn't have anyone to take this to."

"All right, what is it?" He made a mental note to try to find out who the hell was in charge of the *Ismala*. He had heard that the Tau Coloni was still alive in orbit around the planet with a contingent of marines, but without any plan for the fleet to rescue them, it was unlikely that they'd survive much longer. They were well out of comm range by now, anyway. She'd been a bright one, but he had no time to mourn all the people they were losing, or the ones they'd likely still lose.

"When we first came into the system, Melina, the commander that is, had asked me to record the data our scanners were receiving from the installations on the moons when we entered the system. She told me to run it through the analysis, to see if we could make anything out from the transmissions.

"I'm not an expert on that, so I put some analysts on the task, they confirm that nothing in the system is of blob origin."

"Yeah," the admiral said. "We've figured that out already."

"Yes, sir. I know. I asked them what the transmissions looked like, and they told me that the most similar thing to what we know is binary.

They tell us that these transmissions look like corrupted, or maybe evolved, versions of our own telemetry."

"So you think these installations are human?"

"I have no idea, but if they aren't, they belong to a species that uses computer communications very similar to ours."

"Were they able to tell us what the signals were saying?"

"No, sir. Everything seems to be encrypted."

"Or transmitted in an alien language that we can't even begin to understand."

"That's also possible, sir."

"All right. Anything else?"

"No, that's it."

The man signed off and the admiral studied his bridge crew, lost in thought. He didn't know if the information meant anything or if it was just more meaningless data in a sea of meaningless information. They knew so many things, but they still had no answers to any of the important questions.

No matter. There were much more pressing issues calling for a decision.

The first was what to do next. He was in command of three semi-intact fighting ships, a scout vessel, and a factory ship, deep in enemy territory. The fact that he didn't know who the enemy was and why they were fighting was irrelevant at that point—there was no longer any doubt that they were the enemy.

All the evidence, physical and circumstantial, also told him that there were two enemies in the field, and that those factions were also fighting among themselves: the defenders of the moon installations and the swarm of automated fighters his troops had taken to calling vampires. He saw little likelihood of establishing a truce with either faction; even if they could somehow speak to them, the fact of the matter was that they'd attacked the defenders without warning or provocation, and the vampires had then done the same thing to the fleet.

So what to do?

The *Heavy Gunship IV* had shown that its arms and armor were sufficient to hold the swarm at bay for a while. If they fought long enough, he believed that it might be possible to blast sufficient numbers of vampires that they would no longer be an effective fighting force. Of course, only his most optimistic simulations gave that outcome. But he still believed; it was pretty much all he had left.

Unfortunately, he also believed that there was no reason left to fight. The defenders and the swarm seemed to be involved in their own private war, one which probably had little or nothing to do with humanity.

In fact, after destroying every installation on the planet's moon, half of the swarm had shot off to the other side of the solar system to attack something on a rocky planet on the far side of the star, while the other half was just sitting where they'd been, probably serving to ensure that the admiral's fleet didn't try anything funny.

Logic dictated that they should just withdraw while no one was paying attention to them.

That brought up the next question: where could they go? The nearest human system was forty thousand light-years away, and after nearly a quarter of a million years in transit, there was no guarantee that it would still be inhabited by human beings.

In fact, it was quite possible that the men and women in the fleet, by the sheer luck of the draw, represented the last surviving pocket of mankind anywhere in the universe. The rest might have become slaves to the Brillans, food for the blobs, or simply been forced to upload by the computer-based portions of humanity millennia ago. It was quite possible that his little fleet had nowhere left to go.

Even if he decided to head out and establish a New Earth in some out-of-the-way system, it wasn't practical to do so immediately. The ships were completely worn out after the long voyage, and it would take months to refit. He couldn't ask anyone to step into a stasis pod without knowing how long it would keep them alive.

If he did order them to go into stasis, he wouldn't be at all surprised to have a mutiny on his hands.

And besides, what if one of the people who didn't make it all the way to the destination was Tina? He hadn't been able to stop his daughter from signing up for this suicide mission, but now that it seemed that survival was an option, he wasn't going to throw her life away for no reason.

While he'd had a mission and orders relevant to that mission, those had been paramount. But now that the original scenario had gone out the window, he would do everything in his power to keep his people alive.

And if anyone wanted to argue the point, or thought that everyone would be better off if someone else was in command... then he would step aside and smirk at them as they got their wish.

"Admiral, the captain of the *Minstrel* needs to talk to you."

The admiral sighed.

***

Irene studied her audience. Several of the people in the room were attired in full hazmat suits. Most weren't. As equipment had been brought into the hangar—which now resembled an enormous lab more than it did a place to store vehicles, some of the scientists bringing the machines had volunteered to help and had remained. If there was danger of contamination, they were willing to risk it.

Most of the people watching, of course, weren't in the room with her, and not even in the ship. They were the officers of the other ships in the fleet, none of whom had wanted to come to the *Lapland* until the team managed to establish what, exactly, the compound delivered by the defender's bullets was.

After all, if they were so confident of it that they didn't bother using high-caliber rounds, it had to be something pretty devastating.

She could feel the cold scrutiny of the camera as she began. She had to pause, clear her throat, and start again. "We've run an analysis of the dust inside the casings, and, as far as we've been able to determine, it's biologically inert. Unless there's something really exotic going on, we shouldn't have any problems with disease."

A ripple, possibly a sigh of relief went over her audience, even though most of them knew what she was going to say. Many had been part of her analysis team, and that was the first thing they'd tested for.

Irene continued. "From that conclusion, we moved on to an attempt to understand exactly what the powder that was delivered consisted of, but all we really found was that it's mostly carbon with a bit of aluminum and other metals thrown in. Not really much to work from, and not poisonous or otherwise dangerous in its current molecular configuration.

"We were pretty much stumped, until we decided to examine the fighter itself. As you already knew, the bullets caused little more than superficial damage to its armor." She pointed to a small fragment of computer board lying on a workbench to her right. "But what you see on the screen is a magnification of circuitry we removed from the fighter. This area here is deeply pitted, and it should be smooth. We found residue of dust with the same composition as that delivered by the bullets beside this circuit."

Irene let the audience digest that information. Blank faces told her that her next words would make them sit up and listen.

"But this part was in a part of the fighter that didn't receive any damage. It was fully one-point-five meters away from the nearest bullet hole. Somehow, the dust moved through the ship and attacked this circuit—the most intelligent part of any fighter's system: the targeting computer." She held her audience's gaze, moving from one anxious set

107

of eyes to the next. "I believe that what we have here are nanobots designed to find and destroy complex computers while ignoring those that function beneath a certain threshold."

That caused a stir. "That's impossible," one man in front said. "Even with all the nanofactories on this ship and the best nanotechs that humanity has, we couldn't build something like that."

"Well, someone did. And they've been shooting us with it. The only reason it wasn't devastating is that most of the computers on the fighter aren't good enough to be worth attacking. The only one that got damaged was the targeting computer which, because it needs to be able to predict what multiple targets flown by unpredictable sentient beings will do, is just one step below being self-aware."

She paused again, this time for dramatic effect.

"What we have here is a weapon designed to attack artificial intelligences."

There was another shuffling in the room, but no one spoke. They all seemed to be waiting for her to say something more. She shrugged. "That's it. We can all relax, because the nanobots were inert before they got onto this ship. And none of them attack people anyway."

There was a smattering of applause. Some people came and thanked her, but that was all she got. It was strangely anticlimactic. People began to file out, and none of the ones who'd brought hazmat suits into the room with them took them off.

Only the analysts who'd worked with her and one other man stayed behind. The man was large, with short-cropped iron-grey hair and a scar over one cheek, obviously something he hadn't had time to get removed between postings.

"Miss Sol Vianini, my name is Hémery," he said, holding out a hand. "I'm with the security team. Would you mind coming with me?"

"What for?"

"I'd like to ask you some questions regarding the disappearance of two of your colleagues."

Irene's heart jumped into her throat. "Oh, yes. I heard about that. Are you sure I can come with you? I thought we were under quarantine."

"Didn't you just explain to us why that's no longer necessary?"

She laughed, hoping the man couldn't see just how nervous she was. "Yes, I suppose I just did. Of course I'll come."

***

Hémery studied the woman sitting across the table from him in the otherwise empty cafeteria room. Every scientist he'd interviewed had reacted the same way to his questions. Nervous at first, and then growing defensive, as if each of them felt the need to prove that they weren't guilty.

As he worked his way down the list of people who'd come into contact with the two missing—probably murdered—researchers, he'd come to the conclusion that they were all jealous of each other and did, in fact, want all of their peers to die horribly, preferably as soon as possible.

He was also convinced that every single person who'd been questioned during the process could have given him valuable information if only they'd felt like cooperating, but their guilty consciences meant that they kept everything to themselves. Or maybe it was just the cynic in him that had him seeing ghosts.

Irene Sol Vianini had been left for last because she was locked away from all contact with the rest of the ship while investigating the possible contamination brought aboard by a fighter.

He'd wanted to speak to her sooner. She was about halfway up his list of suspects because she'd known both the missing scientists and her area of expertise had, to a certain degree, overlapped with theirs. Of course, what they were actually working on—and why they'd even been assigned to a combat sortie—was anybody's guess. It had been explained to him more than once, but he still couldn't understand what each of them did. He'd never understood nanotech.

But he understood people, and immediately saw that Irene was preparing to go into exactly the same pattern. Her pale, freckled face was suddenly flushed, whether from nerves or anger, he couldn't tell.

So Hémery changed tactics. He leaned back in his chair and asked her an unrelated question. "How does a pretty girl like you end up on a suicide mission aimed at the center of the blob advance?"

It worked. She gave him a sharp glance, mixed with an expression of surprise. "It's been a long time since anyone called me a girl," she said.

He smiled. "Maybe, but I'm a lot older than you are, so I stand by the question."

"All right. I got dragged into the war right out of college. A friend of mine was doing his doctoral work in nanomachinery and he told me that there would be good corporate money in some new stuff that was coming down the pipeline, so I changed my specialty from particle fields to nanotech. Three weeks after that, we got the news about the blob attack on Epsilon Canis Majoris. A year later, I was working in a factory ship. And, four major campaigns after that, here I am."

Hémery felt his smile fading. Maybe his new tactic hadn't worked after all. He was getting the same feeling from this woman that he'd gotten from everyone else. They were pretending to answer his questions, but they were all hiding things. He couldn't imagine what Irene might be hiding in her answer to this most innocent of questions, and couldn't even imagine how there could be anything to hide. But she was definitely lying.

OK, next idea, then.

"Yes. Here you are. So, as I said, I'm investigating the disappearance of Houssein Tau Hunter and Sandrina Polaris Zvereva. I know you had contact with both of them."

Her eyes, if possible, grew shiftier. "I knew them both, yes. I was actually closer to Houssein than to Sandrina—she usually kept to herself, and was much more into astrophysics than the rest of us. So she would usually be in the high-energy room. No. I didn't have much in common with her."

"Then tell me about Houssein. "Who might have wanted to get rid of him?"

"Houssein?" She thought about the question for a few moments. "He was always more concerned with his work than with what anyone else was doing. He was mainly working with materials. I think he was trying to understand why so much stuff failed when we arrived here. Of course, now we all know exactly why, but we didn't then. I think that's what he was working on, at least. You should probably check his log."

"We did. There wasn't much there. Most of the memory was faulty, and we don't even know whether that's because it was intentionally obscured or because everything seems to be faulty." He decided to try another tactic... again. Perhaps this time he would have better luck. "How are you organized on board? I mean, who decides what each of you studies? Do you get orders from the admiral?"

She looked at him like he was crazy. "Why would we do that? We only respond to military authority when it comes to keeping the fleet supplied with the raw materials we need. The machines are pretty complicated to run—despite the years we've been using nanofactories, they're still much more similar to experimental installations than to a factory in the conventional engineering sense. Everything changes as we discover new ways to make them better."

"Better in what way?"

"Faster, or able to create more complex pieces with less materials. Anything that gives us an edge, really."

"And the efforts aren't being coordinated?"

"There's no need. We're all specialists in our field. The ship is—or was before the pods went bad on us—crewed by a well-balanced group of scientists who should be able to manage any optimizations needed on the fly. If each of us works in our chosen field on the problems that appear within that field, then we should be capable of dealing with any requests that the admiralty might send over."

"Requests?"

She smiled, and he felt that the conversation was finally approaching some semblance of honesty. "We don't take orders from the military. Of course, we also don't want to die, and the people who fly the *Lapland* do take orders from the military, which means that they tend to take us into some pretty ugly situations. At the end of the day, it's usually in our best interest to solve the admiral's problems and to solve them quickly."

"Would you take an order if it came to that?"

"Of course I would. I didn't enter this service in the belief that my work would be put to civilian uses."

Hémery could tell how much it had hurt her to admit that. She seemed fanatical in her conviction that the scientists were organized in the only possible way, and that everything was perfectly rational. Just like all the rest. No wonder they were killing each other off. Maybe they were just trying to save the blobs the trouble of doing it for themselves.

"And Sandrina? Do you know of anyone who wanted her gone?" He already knew the answer to this one, but needed to hear Irene's take.

The scientist laughed. "Sandrina? I think we all wanted her dead. The way she pranced around shaking her ass at anything male was just disgusting. And from what I heard, she wouldn't stop at just shaking. She wanted to test drive every member of the crew." Irene smirked as if she'd said something clever. It was probably an in-joke among the scientists, one that every one of them had already repeated to Hémery when he'd asked them about the dead scientist.

He shook his head. The rumors were probably true, and after having studied pictures of the missing scientist, he found himself wishing that her proclivities had extended to crewmembers outside of the science ranks. "Anyone in particular who hated her?"

"Not that I know of, but you should probably ask any of the married women. Or even the ones with a new shipboard relationship. None of the men said no to Sandrina, and she, for her part, knew how to keep her mouth shut, so maybe a wife of a married man found something out that the rest of us didn't know about."

"All, right, I'll look into it." He already had, and it had been frustratingly inconclusive. "Is there anything else you can think of that might help me?"

"No."

"Could you tell me where you were when they disappeared?"

"When did they disappear?"

"We're not sure," he admitted. He'd been trying to trap her, and by the way she looked at him, she was aware of it.

"Well, if you manage to figure it out, let me know and I'll try to tell you where I was. Probably in my cabin. Either there or in my lab. That's where I usually am."

"Thank you. If I think of anything else, I'll let you know."

He sat there wondering. The tracking records on Irene were incomplete, but they were also incomplete on at least three others, not counting the two missing researchers who seemed to have been erased from the data stream.

Hémery sighed. This interview had left him feeling exactly the same as all the others. He was certain that Irene, like most of her colleagues, could cheerfully have killed the missing people under the correct circumstances—especially Sandrina—but probably hadn't.

He wished he could ask for a transfer to one of the marine ships. When they killed themselves—over cards, sex, or drugs—it usually took all of thirty seconds to identify the culprit. The difficulty was usually to convince them to come quietly and that the dead trooper hadn't had it coming.

He scratched his scar and wondered what to do next.

CHAPTER 13

Tristan felt an awful sense of déjà vu as the team approached the hangar on the east side of the clearing. In design, if not scale, the place could have been the twin of the ones on either moon. The only real difference was that the sky was bright with a greenish tinge as opposed to the darkness they'd experienced on the previous missions.

"Why do I have the feeling that this place isn't going to make me any happier than the other two I walked into?" he asked himself over the Tacnet.

"Stop whining, trooper. You're still alive and in one piece, aren't you? I'm not even sure we're allowed to pay you for the hours unless you can show us some injuries," Sergeant Mobutu replied.

"I guess you're right. Besides, I actually think that you guys are probably in more danger than I am. After all, the last time I landed, everyone else bought it and I only lost a piece of my suit."

"This time you've got better marines with you, kid."

"Time before that, my CO got herself so dented that they had to take her suit off with a can opener and toss her in the infirmary."

"Yeah, saw a recording of that. We won't make the same mistakes she did."

Tristan wanted to defend Cora, but held his tongue. He knew the rules, and breaking them meant that he would probably get tagged with an accusation of being in love with her. He couldn't say whether he was or wasn't, but there was no way he'd give the marines an opening.

He found it strange that these men and women on the surface of an alien planet, with no ability to leave and with no food or water supplies, would be more concerned about razzing the newcomer to their ranks than worrying about their continued survival, but he wasn't surprised by it. Every single shock marine unit he'd ever been a part of was exactly the same way. It was expected that the men and women who made up the platoons would die before admitting that they were afraid. And a good way to take your mind off the fear was to rib the new guy.

As they approached the hangar, they began to notice signs that everything was not exactly as it should be.

In the first place, the wide opening of the facility entrance had once held a colossal door. This had been blown apart and pieces were strewn hundreds of meters in front of the aperture. The marines had to pick their way over twisted metal spars.

"Wait," the sergeant ordered, putting up a hand as a sign for them to stop. "Is anyone else worried about the fact that this debris was blown away from the facility?"

"No," one of the marines pitched in. "That just means we don't have to do it ourselves. Sounds good to me."

Mobutu didn't toggle the Tacnet, so Tristan couldn't tell if he actually sighed, but the way he slumped inside his suit was clear enough. "I think what the sergeant meant to say was that he's concerned that whatever blasted the door blasted it from the inside."

"Yes. Thank you. Glad one of you was paying attention."

"Coming this close to getting my ass shot off twice made me sensitive to that kind of thing, Sarge."

The truth was that, until Mobutu had mentioned it, Tristan hadn't recognized the implications of the debris pattern. But once it was pointed out, it became extremely obvious. There was no wreckage right in front of the facility, but, beginning about ten meters away, the debris field spread outward in a semicircular pattern.

Grass had begun to grow around some of the bigger pieces, where the weight of falling metal had cracked the surface of the parade ground. The debris, likewise, was corroded and the edges worn away. The explosion had clearly happened some time before. Probably years. It hadn't been caused by the events of the day before.

"Something hit this door very hard."

"Hope it's not still in there."

The company halted and the sergeant assigned two troops to scout ahead. They entered from either edge of the gargantuan opening, and hugged the walls as they penetrated the facility.

Holding back a couple of hundred meters, Tristan watched them and marveled at the size of the structure. From a distance, it was difficult to gauge scale, but with the tiny men dwarfed by the building, it left no doubts about what they were looking at. While the hangar structure around either of the moons he'd seen action on would have been just about large enough for Ian's flyer, this one could easily have swallowed the *Minstrel*.

The scouts disappeared into the darkness, but soon enough they were back on the horn. "Guys, I think you can come in. If there was anything defending this facility, it's dead now."

"What do you mean?"

"Hard to describe, but you might as well come have a look."

The scouts were right. The hangar looked as if it had been torn to shreds by something big and angry. Chunks of building material were strewn everywhere, and even the ceiling seemed to have come under concentrated attack. It was so badly damaged that it took Tristan a few moments to realize that the destruction was a result of attacks on gun emplacements similar to the ones he'd encountered so often in the other facilities.

The back wall, the one where the elevator shaft was inevitably located, had a ragged hole in it. They sent a scout to have a look.

"Big elevator shaft here. Don't see the lift in it, but it might be at the bottom. This thing is very deep. It's also pretty chewed up. Not sure what it was that hit this facility, but it was not happy. They shot at everything."

"Thanks. Let's get back outside."

"What?" a marine asked. "Aren't we going inside?"

This time, the sergeant did sigh over the Tacnet. "Why in the world would we want to do that? From what our friend Tristan tells us, going in these places is a good way to get hurt, and there's no real value in doing so."

"So why even come out here?"

"To make sure it wasn't a threat."

"I understand that, but shouldn't we find out if the threat is still inside?"

Tristan spoke. "I can tell you what's inside. It's a containment facility for those flying wing things. Like the one on the moon of the ice giant, but on a much bigger scale. I wouldn't be surprised that this is where the swarm—or at least a part of it—was locked up. We don't want to run into them down there. Trust me on this."

They discussed his idea as their suits loped back to where the ships and pilots had been left behind. The trek to the facility under the huge gravity and without the benefit of suits would have been too much for them.

"Not much of a prison, if you ask me."

"Maybe it wasn't meant to be, or maybe it was part of a system. The guys who locked the wings in here had to know that, sooner or later, one of them would get loose. And then…"

"That one probably broke out a couple more, until the defenders were swamped."

"What I don't understand is why bother to lock them up in the first place. If you had them under control, wouldn't it just be easier to destroy them? I mean, why go to all the trouble to lock up drone fighters?"

"Who said they're drones?"

"You saw them back on the *Bard*. There was nothing alive in there, just a bunch of circuits and stuff. Besides, they're not big enough to be crewed."

Assent met this statement from the shock marines who'd fought the swarm in the crew ship's hangar. Tristan wondered about it, though. His impression of the one he'd seen on the ice giant's moon had been that of a living thing running for its life. The way the swarm moved reminded him of flocks of birds he'd seen on videos of Earth. Granted, he hadn't inspected one up close, but he found it extremely difficult to reconcile what he had seen to the idea of them not being alive and intelligent.

"I guess the real prison was the planet itself."

"Or maybe the whole system."

"It still makes no sense," Tristan said. "We broke through the defenses really easily. A fighter wing and a couple of marine platoons. That doesn't sound like the kind of security you want around the shield meant to contain a planet full of those... things. Hell, how long do you think a rescue crew would have taken to break them out? You saw what they did to the *Dart* and the *Bard*, even with fighter screens."

"You're right. But what other explanation is there?"

Melina spoke up. "Maybe all the wings were on the inside of the shield and there was no one left to spring them. Hell, that's what I would have wanted if I'd been the one to capture them."

This set off another round of argument. "But how does one even capture a fighter drone?"

"And why?"

It went on, like all marine bull sessions when no one was shooting at them, for quite a while. No one was any wiser at the end of it.

***

"Sun's going down," Ian said. He and Melina had tried to make themselves comfortable in the flyer. The seats weren't fully reclinable, but even reclining in the tight space and sub-optimal angle was better than trying to stand around and do things in the high gravity.

"I can see that," Melina replied. "The question is, what is night like on this place? All I really know is that it lasts about sixteen hours."

"To be honest, unless that swarm comes back, I think the marines should be able to deal with whatever the planet throws at us. We still haven't seen any signs of animal life, much less anything that might pose a threat to modern weaponry."

"I'm not particularly concerned about animals. Hell, I wish there were animals here. It might give us some hope of finding food." She ignored the rumbling of her stomach. They had some energy bars in the flyer's stores, but not enough to keep them going for long, and certainly not enough to share with the other people stranded on the surface.

Ian looked into her eyes. "You think we're gonna make it?"

"I've known I wasn't going to make it since before I boarded the *Ismala*," she replied.

"Then why come? Why throw your life away?"

She sighed. "I know you didn't volunteer, so I guess you probably won't understand, but the truth is that I never thought of it as throwing my life away. I believe that what we came here to do is meaningful, and that we're the only chance that a lot of people had."

"But how can you think that way? In a war where hundreds of years might pass between the time your orders are given and the time you actually carry them out, everything might have changed. The action might be meaningless."

"You might be right, but those are the rules. We didn't start this war. We don't want to fight it, and I'm pretty sure we don't actually understand it. What motivates a blob, or a Brillan? Even the Uploaders? What makes them want to force every other human in the galaxy to join their way of life? All you can do in that situation is take the course that seems best."

"I'm just saying that you might not choose a suicide mission in those circumstances. Especially if that mission is just a delaying action that might be moot by the time you actually get to wherever it is that you're supposed to be fighting it. It seems like such a waste."

She sighed and a single tear rolled down her cheek, catching Ian completely by surprise. He continued hastily. "Um, of course you're probably right. Ever since I woke up here, everyone around us has let me know what an asshole I am for not having volunteered. Maybe they're right."

Melina wiped her eyes and gave him a wan smile. "You're sweet, but I'm not crying because of what you said. It's because nothing makes sense. Where are the blobs? Where is the fleet we're supposed to be fighting. We know blob weapons, we know their tactics. Nothing we found here looks like their stuff."

"Maybe they lost this system in the time it took us to get here. When their fleet arrives, we'll have the war we were expecting. Plus all this other stuff."

"Somehow, I don't think so. I think we're missing something."

"What can we be missing? Do you think the blobs turned their fleet around mid-transit? Maybe they got word of what was happening here and decided to abandon the system?"

"Well, that might explain it."

He could see that Melina wasn't convinced. "But you don't think so."

"No. Not really. It's just too much. This planet, this whole system, is a prison system. Why would anyone take it from the blobs just to turn it into a jail? And the timeline? Four hundred years? It seems to me that this place has been here longer than that. A few centuries, at least. Look at this floor. Nearly indestructible, but the grass is getting through. I think there's something else going on."

"But what?"

She shrugged, and suddenly broke down completely as sobs racked her frame. "I didn't think I'd live this long. If I'd known we might make it through, I probably would have thrown myself out the nearest airlock when I woke up."

He had no idea what she was talking about. He hesitantly put a hand on her arm. "Look, I know it looks bad, but we'll make it."

"I don't particularly want to make it. I wish the air defenses around that planet had put up more of a fight, or that I hadn't been grounded. I'm pretty sure I could have taken a few of those wing things with me before they got me. They fly pretty well, but still think I could have shot some down."

"Don't talk that way. Why would you want to die?"

"Because I'm sick of it all. I've been at war since I was a kid. I watched my parents die, and I thought my world would end. But then I became a pilot. A good pilot, and I kept many, many people alive so they could keep running from the blobs. I don't think I missed a single major posting during the Long Retreat.

"I've fought them all. The blobs. The Brillans. Hell, I even caught an Uploader spy flyer once and blew it to hell."

Ian grunted. Being discovered by a fighter was every Recon officer's worst nightmare. Normally, spy ships were fast and well-endowed with sensor tech, but sadly lacking in the weapons department. Trying to outrun missiles and projectile weapons was a sucker's bet.

"But even though I always went nose-first into the battle, even though I led my squadrons from the front every single time, I've never suffered so much as a bruise in battle. I've watched my wing mates get burned to atoms, torn to shreds, and thrown out of their ships to die in vacuum, but I've never gotten hurt."

"Did you want to?"

"I never wanted to get hurt but, deep down inside, I think I've always wanted to die. It was the only way I could think of to make the war end. I couldn't run from it. I certainly couldn't end it. Even if I took a slow ship away or landed on one of the new colony worlds and lived out my entire life in peace, I would always know that there was fighting going on somewhere. Fighting for the lives of people being evacuated somewhere, or to try to keep a besieged colony alive just a few more weeks, praying for reinforcements to arrive. And I'd know that the units doing the fighting could always use one more good pilot. I wouldn't have been able to live with myself."

"But dying? Life has so many possibilities."

"I've never known about them. I was too young to learn anything but battle." She paused. "And by the time I found out about everything else, and about love, it was too late for me. I was committed to the course." She laughed bitterly. "I thought I was so lucky when I finally met someone who felt the way I did. We would live fast and die young... well, we wouldn't die old. I should have known it would end like everything else: him dead and me perfectly unscathed."

Ian didn't know what to say, so he kept silent.

"And yeah, I did kind of look down on you for not volunteering to be here. I will never understand the thinking behind that. I wasn't afraid to die—what's one person compared to so many millions? But at least I guess you did the right thing in the end. In answer to your question, dying doesn't concern me in the least. The problem is that I wasn't expecting to have to face my death alone."

"Well, there's a bunch of marines and a recon guy who'll probably die with you if it comes to that, I guess."

Melina didn't reply, and turned away from him to gaze out of the forward viewport.

Ian decided to leave her to her thoughts and, ignoring the discomfort of high gravity, walked into the warm night. One of the marines was standing guard beside the forest and he walked to where the man was peering into the woods. As the hulking exoskeleton came into view in the dim greenish light from the moon, he realized that it was missing one hand: Tristan.

"Can you see anything?"

"No. But even weirder is the fact that I can't hear anything."

Ian listened. The marine was right, the night was completely still. He grunted his agreement.

"I've been on jungle worlds before," the trooper continued. "They're always hell on wheels. Hot, humid and sticky. But that's not the worst part. The bugs are the worst part. There are always insects, flying around everywhere, buzzing in the night. You get used to them gradually, and then, after a while, you learn to rely on them. No one can sneak up on you at night in a jungle. You can always tell that they're coming a mile away just because half of the jungle's insects go quiet all of a sudden."

Ian listened harder. The silence was eerie. Only by listening hard did he manage to discern any sound at all: the soft whisper of leaves in the wind. "Melina thinks that the trees must have evolved so that they don't need any pollinizers. They are either asexual or self-contained."

"I didn't know she was a botanist."

"I don't think she is. She says she never knew what to do with her downtime when she was in ships, so she would read whatever she could find in ship databases. One of them had a bunch of biological textbooks and nothing else, so she read those."

"You getting close to her?"

"Hell, no. I think if she could, she'd toss me out an airlock for failing to volunteer for this insanity. She's really intense. Besides, I'm married. Or at least I was when we left."

"That was a long time ago."

"It seems like a couple of weeks ago to me, trooper."

"Yeah, I guess it does. I'm sorry."

"I had a kid, too. A little girl. You should have seen her. Blonde and adorable and completely perfect in every way. I can't understand why anyone would volunteer and leave their kids behind."

"Not sure too many people did. I certainly didn't. I came because it was just another mission, and I swore to defend humanity to my last breath when I signed up. I didn't have anyone to leave behind—my folks died of old age while I was asleep in transit before my first mission. Everything I own is on the *Minstrel*, in one bag inside a locker."

"No special someone?"

"Lots of 'em. Most of them were marines from one platoon or another. Some were navy, although they always get weepy when you ship off on another carrier."

Ian laughed. "I don't know why I bother talking to you combat types. You're all nuts. Ground troops or fighter pilots, makes no difference."

"I guess the probability of getting yourself killed every time you suit up does that to you."

Ian sobered immediately. "Yeah. I can see that. Don't mind me. I always get bitter when I remember that my baby girl has probably been dead of old age for three hundred years."

They stared into the silent jungle, barely visible as a dark smudge in the moonlight. Tristan finally broke the silence. "I know you don't want to be here. Hell, I wouldn't in your place. But I'm sure glad you were still on the battlefield after the fight on the moon. I'd be dead now if it wasn't for you. So would the commander over there."

"That might have made her day."

"Could be. But it wouldn't have made mine. I don't care if you volunteered or not. You're all right in my book. Thank you."

Ian didn't reply. He stood behind the marine as the man looked out into the night. They listened for crickets, but there weren't any in those woods.

CHAPTER 14

A mass of melted black casing, wires and circuits thudded to the floor beside her.

"Be careful with that!" Irene said.

"Sorry," the forklift operator replied. "I was trying to lay it down as gently as possible, but something failed in the controls." He looked critically at the wreckage he'd delivered. "At least I probably didn't damage it any more than it already was."

Irene had to concede the point. The mangled remains of the vampire were unlikely to yield much in the way of useful data, but it was the only one they had to work with. It had collided with the *Heavy Gunship IV* during the last battle and become lodged in a protuberance. The admiral's men had retrieved it and sent it to the *Lapland* for analysis, where it had literally landed at Irene's feet.

She sighed. No one seemed to realize that anyone with a slight grounding in nanotech and computers could have successfully solved the riddle of the defender's bullets, which meant that she'd effectively been promoted to the position of go-to person for anything the admiral wanted answered by the *Lapland*. Irene had handed most of what was requested off to others, but this time it seemed the problem actually did involve her own area of expertise.

Then again, she thought, studying the wreckage critically, *this one might be beyond anyone's know-how.*

There was no use in complaining. She'd been trained to take large problems a single step at a time, and the first step on this one was to try to get an idea of how the small pieces on her floor had once fit together. There was no chance of rebuilding it completely, but there should be enough parts to get a feel for it and fill in the gaps with educated guesses.

She picked up the nearest piece, some kind of circuit board, and placed it on a random place on the bench. She would build the rest of the machine up around that part.

Irene worked in silence, picking up pieces and making her best guess at where they might belong. As she moved through the pile, her mind wandered.

She remembered the impassioned meetings with her fellow pacifists. They were a secret organization in name only, since they congregated openly and most of their members made no effort to disguise where their sympathies lay. There was no real reason to hide. Most people in human space would have preferred a sudden outbreak of peace, but most thought they had no choice in the matter.

The difference was that Irene and her friends believed that everyone had a choice, even if that choice meant making sacrifices.

Her biggest frustration was with how people reacted to the war. The attitudes were split just about evenly into two camps: those who were angry at the blobs and wanted to push them back into whatever interstellar hole they'd crawled out of and those who bemoaned their fate and seemed to be waiting for the hammer to fall.

Irene knew that the best way to fight the war was not to fight it at all. Run, hide, leave behind the people who couldn't be placed onto ships. War, she reasoned, could only breed more war. Why couldn't people see that? All of human history was sending the message loud and clear.

But no one she knew would accept it. Every single person in the colony except for the few who attended the weekly meetings thought that it was some kind of imperative that they fight back. Running from the fight wasn't just something they saw as impractical; they actually believed it was impossible. Literally impossible. As in that even if they attempted it, the war would find them anyway. And humanity would be exterminated.

That was ridiculous. It was a huge galaxy, and the blobs only controlled a tiny fraction of it.

So Irene had dedicated her life to doing things that could make fighting the war more and more difficult for the government. At first, they were ridiculously little things like sleeping with a marine on the night before he was supposed to ship out and drugging his drink so that he missed his transport, but gradually the group allowed her into slightly more interesting missions.

They stole paperwork and re-filed it so that ships were sent to stars far from the fighting. They infected an entire batch of shipboard food with slow-acting bacteria, causing a carrier to return to base two weeks after launch.

Finally, they decided to try to interfere with the task force.

Irene had been asked to volunteer for the mission. Her qualifications in nanotechnology and electronics would make her a valuable addition to the factory ship team.

And then they trained her. They taught her how to hack into protected systems and how to kill people with weapons and her bare hands. When she commented that she'd joined the movement to prevent violence, not instigate it, the answer was that they were just giving her tools, and that the situation might come up where one death could prevent hundreds, thousands, or millions. Even, if she was unlucky and her comrades failed, an instance of combat.

She'd promised herself that she wouldn't let it come to that but, as soon as she was awake on the *Lapland*, it took her a short time to realize that her promise was in vain. She'd had to kill two people who had realized that something had gone very, very wrong with the navigation, and that would have caused the fleet to turn around and go back.

Irene hoped that the delay she'd caused could justify taking two lives. It was hard to tell how many lives might have been saved.

She didn't regret a thing. The cause of peace was important enough that no sacrifice was too big, not even the sacrifice of having to use violence.

Then, she asked herself, why was she doing her very best to further the war effort—whichever war they were currently involved in—by analyzing the fragments of the black fighter?

She had no answer to that. All she knew is that the same sixth sense that told her that two of her fellow scientists had to die in order to keep her mission alive was telling her that there was something extremely evident that she was missing with regards to the vampire flyer. The feeling of being on the verge of a huge discovery drove her on.

The pile of rubble on the workbench had grown, and the parts were arranged in such a way that the outline of the fighting machine could be made out. She shuddered as she studied it. Even in its dilapidated state, the shape of the flyer exuded menace. It wasn't a machine that could possibly be confused for anything other than what it was: a predatory form pulled from the nameless fears of primeval man.

And that was it. That was what had seemed wrong to her: the shape was too perfect. The vampires actually looked like things that would haunt your nightmares.

Like everyone who had ever been part of a military expedition, Irene had been trained in everything about both the alien species that humanity had encountered. The blobs and the Brillans were undoubtedly horrific, but had you not known what they were, had you encountered one on a far-flung planet, it wouldn't have set off any alarm bells. These flying machines, on the other hand, almost seemed intentionally designed to frighten human beings.

In a galaxy the size of the Milky Way, of course, it was possible that something like that would happen coincidentally. Delta-winged shapes were very maneuverable, and many species would use them. Black was a good color to paint things if your enemy happened to see using the visible portion of the electromagnetic spectrum. There were countless logical reasons for the machines to look the way they did.

But that didn't account for her feeling. She just couldn't shake the sensation that the design was specifically aimed at humans. All logic pointed against that conclusion... but it was still there, in the back of her mind.

She called in two tech specialists. "Hi, guys," she said when they arrived. "Thanks for coming."

"You're welcome. What's up?"

"I'm trying to do an analysis of the computer that was flying this fighter. There's quite a bit of exotic circuitry in there. Enough that I'm concerned that they might have a certain limited amount of artificial intelligence."

"How can you tell? If it was our tech, I could see it, but with alien stuff..." the man shrugged.

"Let's assume it's equivalent to ours, but a bit more advanced. If we find anything to the contrary we'll modify the assumption, but let's work off that base for now."

"Works as well as any other, I guess. What's the plan?"

"I just want to see if we can identify from this mess what might be memory and what might be processors. Once we have that, we can regroup. There's too much for me to evaluate alone. Just be sure to scan at low power. If we can find anything that might be working, I want to see if we can make it sing for us."

One of the techs gave her an incredulous look. "You want to make this stuff run?"

"Sure, why not? It's damaged, but some of it must be in working order. We just need to identify which parts."

"But we don't even know what it's designed to run on."

"I have a hunch that these are binary circuits."

"That might make sense, they're the easiest to design after all. But that still wouldn't allow us to talk to it or read the memory. We have no clue what the base software might be."

Irene smiled. "I have some ideas about that, too. Let's start by sorting the bits, and we'll go from there."

And another little voice asked: *and how, exactly will this advance the cause of peace?* She ignored it.

***

Cora fumed at the man, but she did so in silence. Major Tau Rodchenko had a reputation for being timid: a brilliant desk jockey and not such a good field commander, which probably explained why he was still alive when everyone else with any rank at all had gotten themselves first killed and then blown up in the attack on the moon installation. The fact that he was now in command of all the ground troops on the *Minstrel* was a major disaster... pun intended.

"One of our guys is down there," she said. "Not to mention every single marine who survived the attack on the *Bard*. We can't just leave them down there to die."

"We don't know that they're dying. The planet is supposed to be an ideal place for life to take hold. Besides, even if I wanted to do this, I'd still have to clear it with the general and we'd both need to get the admiral to sign up for a rescue mission. We only run the soldiers; the ships belong to the navy."

"That's all I'm asking. I know how the chain of command works for something this big."

"I don't think we can elevate this one, Lieutenant. It's too risky."

It was the third time he'd said the same thing. "All right, sir," she said, standing. "Thanks for your time."

She walked away and immediately strode towards her room. She'd only found out that the man who'd survived the moon installation assault was Tristan the day before, and since then had been completely unable to think about anything else. A sleepless night of ideating and discarding one plan after another had left her exhausted, but armed with what she believed was a workable scheme.

There was no way that she would take the major's overcautious stance on this issue lying down.

In a breach of pretty much everything that had been drilled into her at officer school, she put in a direct call to the senior officer of a different service—a man who had more to think about than anyone else in the fleet.

Cora chuckled to herself as she waited for the connection to go live. People who volunteered for suicide missions weren't particularly concerned with court martials. It was a wonder that discipline had held out for as long as it had.

"Yes," a strong voice assaulted her as the image resolved into the familiar features of the admiral. "What is it?" He looked down at the information on the bottom of his screen, "Lieutenant Sirius Almir."

"Hello, sir. I'm sorry to disturb you, but I've created a plan to rescue the marines stranded on the planet."

He gave her a look that had all the warmth of the cold vacuum of space. "And why isn't this coming to me from the general?"

"Because Major Tau Rodchenko has flatly refused to consider the idea, sir."

"I assume he has technical reasons for turning you down. Why come to me?"

"With all due respect, sir," she said, hoping her tone and face showed exactly how much respect she had for the major. "I suspect his reasons are political rather than technical."

"Did he tell you that?"

"No. But it's difficult to have technical objections when he didn't listen to the plan."

The admiral sighed. "I should really cut you off right now and have someone escort you to the brig. But I won't, because everyone from the fighter jockey flying the *Ismala* to my own daughter has been pestering me to send a mission out to get them. But no one has any idea how to pull it off, so if you have a semi-workable plan, I might not bust you back to private for insubordination and spectacular disregard for the chain of command."

"Yes, sir. I propose we take the *Banshee* in. She's designed to avoid detection and fast enough that we can take a long route in a short amount of time."

The admiral gave her a look that made his earlier expression seem warm and fuzzy. "I hope this is a joke, Lieutenant. The *Banshee* isn't rated for atmosphere operations."

"Yes, sir, I'm aware of that. But she is designed to carry a dropship via external link with only minor compromises to her stealth and sensor properties, and only a two percent reduction in acceleration."

The leaned back in his chair. "Are you sure about that?"

"Certain, sir. They covered it in officer school. Everything above a Mark Five LSS uses the new design, and all the Mark Fours that have been in dry dock since the modification came online have been retrofitted. I believe the *Banshee* is a Mark Seven."

"You remembered that from officer school?"

Cora chuckled. "No, sir, I looked it up last night. One of the stranded marines is the last survivor from my platoon."

The ice was gone from the admiral's face. "I see. And how are we going to get them all up on one dropship?"

"We may not need to. They have four of their own dropships down there, so that adds up to two more than we need to get everyone off. They may have enough fuel to make orbit with the dropships. If they don't, the one we take can make multiple trips down to the surface. Banshee is big enough to hold everyone. It'll be tight, but not impossible."

"But that would leave everyone exposed while you make the trips up and down to the surface."

"Yes, sir. That's the main risk to this plan, but it's the best I've been able to come up with."

"Is it a risk you'd be willing to live with if it was your own ass on the line?"

"Yes, sir."

"Good, because if my team tells me it passes the feasibility analysis, you're leading this crazy stunt."

"Me? I think I might be out of action for a few more days."

"Yes, Lieutenant, you. The choice of marine officers is currently between you and the major. Even though you were injured in the first attack, you're still a better choice than that guy. I'll have the *Lapland* send you nanite treatment packs for whatever is still bugging you."

"We've got the medical nanite facilities back up?"

"Yes. We were expecting people needing medical care following the attack on the moon and the planet." He paused, eyes cast down. "Which means that we've got a lot of unused medicine to share."

"Then I'd be happy to do it, sir."

"Good. How many men will you need?"

"The fewer the better, maybe a couple of shock marines for ground support, suits and all. Any more and I won't be able to bring everyone up in three runs."

"You have them."

"Thank you, sir." She gave the admiral a crisp salute.

"Don't thank me yet. I meant what I said about the feasibility study. Even though this is the first plan I've heard to try to get them back that has even a remote possibility of succeeding, if the eggheads crunch the numbers and decide that the probability of failure is too high, you don't get to leave."

"I understand that, sir. That's not why I thanked you. I thanked you for acting the way an officer should."

"Ah. All right, then."

***

The admiral signed off and turned away from the screen. The lieutenant's call had reached him during one of his off hours, in which he was actually in the captain's quarters—commandeered by the admiral for the trip.

He wrote a quick summary of the plan and sent it off to the analysis team. Despite the fact that he admired the girl's spunk, he was serious about not risking ships unnecessarily. If the probability of success for the mission proved too low, he'd discard it as quickly as he'd discarded the two plans he'd thought of himself. He had to weigh the effectiveness of his fleet against the lives of the soldiers abandoned on the planet.

Of course, he also needed to consider the morale boost that would come with a successful rescue. Right now, his troops were tired, confused, and scared. Most of them knew that they were well beyond the outer bounds of anything humanity had explored before, and that there was no realistic possibility of going back—assuming there was even anything left to go back to. Even the tiniest of successes would be a godsend.

He sank down onto a chair. He was too old for this. He'd expected to wake from stasis to find himself staring into the jaws of a huge enemy battle fleet. His fleet would then do some damage and hopefully wreak a lot of havoc, mainly because no one was expecting them to pop up suddenly.

And then they were supposed to be wiped out to the last man and woman, leaving nothing but carbon and hydrogen fumes for the blobs to feast on. A clean, glorious end which might or might not achieve something, but which was all that humanity's forces could do against the advancing aliens on such short notice.

To think that he was in officer school when the first news of the massacre on Epsilon Canis Majoris reached them. It was difficult to comprehend after all his years that officers on Tau Ceti II were trained to fight against other humans. He'd taken courses in psychology, hours and hours of it, to understand what an enemy commander might be thinking. All the colonies were at peace with each other, but human history had taught them that it couldn't last.

The fleet that had rushed from several colonies at once to attempt to stop the blobs had taken that baggage with them, and it hadn't taken long for the invaders to make them learn the error of their ways.

He'd been a gunnery lieutenant in the very first battle of humanity's fleets against the aliens. He'd been assigned command of a partially automated battery facing away from the main battle lines, and was only expected to see anti-fighter action if the enemy employed small craft to swarm around the bigger ships.

All he could see from his position was the support fleet: three huge hospital vessels and myriad transports and mail ships which wouldn't participate in the fighting. They'd been placed out of the way, behind and to one side of the well-armed main fleet which had already begun to pour its long-range ordnance into the enemy in front of them.

The admiral's first indication that the blobs were defending themselves was when an enormous enemy battle cruiser, venting gas from a dozen direct hits, flew past his position and headed straight for a hospital ship.

He was so surprised that his battery only managed one shot before the blobs moved out of range.

He also got a ringside view as the blob cruiser, soon joined by six more, calmly incapacitated the three hospital ships and sent boarding crews aboard to harvest the doctors, nurses, crew, and patients for their protein.

The battle ended with a stalemate and the outnumbered human fleet moved back to the next system, but what affected the admiral most from that day was that the enemy had assaulted the hospital ships. Deep inside, he'd been certain that hospital ships were sacrosanct, that no one would ever stoop so low as to attack one.

That was the moment he finally understood that he was no longer fighting anything he could comprehend, and that if he wanted to succeed, or even to survive, he needed to adjust to that.

And he'd been doing it well, probably better than any other human, for the rest of his life.

He'd earned the chance to have it end quickly and without complications.

The universe, as usual, had other ideas.

CHAPTER 15

Tristan trudged thankfully back onto the flat stone of the parade ground or landing field or whatever it was that they'd been camping on. He'd spent the past four hours hacking his way through the dense forest surrounding them. In order to conserve the ammo he still had, he'd used his suit's good hand—conveniently reconfigured as a cutting edge—to slash through obstacles.

The suit made the movement effortless, but it was mind-numbing work which had yielded no reward. His path had described a long loop out into the trees and back and simply confirmed what they already knew: there was no recognizable animal life and no fruit on the trees in the vicinity.

He was just one person, however, and he hadn't wanted to get too far from the Recon flyer and the pilots in case anything threatened them. Another, larger group, led by the sergeant had struck out in the opposite direction, exploring a small river valley beyond the ruined installation.

His stomach rumbled. "Any luck?" he called over the Tacnet.

"Nothing at all. The trees keep getting thicker, especially the short spiky ones, but we haven't seen anything that looks like a fruit or an animal."

"Maybe we can eat the trees."

"You're welcome to try, marine. Be sure to let me know how that works out for you."

"Yeah, right." He ambled over to where Melina and Ian, along with the dropship, pilots were sitting. They'd chosen a clear area of the stone-like flooring material under the shade of one of the tall trees. "How's it going?"

"The gravity's a bitch," Ian replied, "but at least there aren't any mosquitoes. That's something at least."

"I wouldn't mind a bug or two. I'd eat as many as I could catch."

The night had passed without incident, but it had been more than three Earth days since anyone had last eaten. Water, of course, wasn't a problem—both the marines' suits and the Recon flyer were designed to recycle all excreted liquids, which could really stretch out their water supply.

Food, on the other hand, was turning into a serious issue.

"We've got an idea," Ian told him.

"What?"

"When we were coming in, we saw another major facility a few hundred klicks north. We chose this one because the landing pad was bigger, but maybe the other one isn't as badly torn up. And if it isn't, there might be something to eat inside."

"There's two things wrong with the plan. The first is that if it isn't demolished, the facility will likely be full of defensive weaponry. The second is that any food inside will probably be thousands of years old."

"You're right," Ian conceded. "But unless you have a better idea, we need to try this. We've already discussed with the sergeant and he said to take a couple of volunteers on the flyer and go have a look. It's just a ten-minute flight."

"All right, count me in. Might as well finish getting the rest of my suit blown apart if there's a chance for some food at the end of it."

Another of the marines who hadn't gone out into the jungle, a kid named Tom, also volunteered, and the two of them grabbed the cargo bar. Ian jumped into the copilot's seat. Melina, as usual, was driving.

The trip was much less harrowing than the descent from orbit. Tristan was confident that, falling from their current low height, his suit thrusters could probably scrub off enough speed for a soft landing. Falling from orbit had been a very different proposition.

They touched down on a small square of the same stone-like material and studied their surroundings. The smaller patch was just large enough to accommodate their flyer, while trees encroached on every side. The facility they'd come to see was a small stone cube with a tall narrow slit for an entrance, just wide enough for a single person to enter without brushing against the sides, but tall enough to accommodate two people—one standing on the other's shoulders. The suits would have to enter the facility sideways.

"Doesn't look like much," Tristan said.

"Don't let the entrance fool you. There's a huge complex underground," Ian replied

"What is it with these guys and building things underground?"

"Maybe they wanted to avoid being shot at by things in the air," Melina replied. She walked over to the cube and ran her hands along the walls. Shallow, flaked holes dimpled the surface. "If this was done by the flying black things, then this stone is a lot harder than it looks. They barely scratched the surface... and they use some seriously heavy slugs."

Tristan wondered how the things could maneuver so quickly while carrying such destructive ordnance. And then he wondered what would happen when they ran out of bullets... he was pretty sure they would come back here to reload.

Maybe getting underground was a good idea.

The design of the entrance worried him as he led the way into the corridor which spiraled down into the dark. It was clearly a defensive measure, something that was driven home when the tall thin passageway suddenly became a wider—albeit much shorter—square. The suit could crawl through, but he'd never be able to stand.

"What's this all about?" Ian asked.

"I think it's meant to keep something out," Tristan replied.

"But what?"

"I'd bet on the flyers," Melina chimed in from behind. "Their wings won't fit into this square tunnel, so even if they got this far by flying sideways through the part before, they'd be trapped inside. I doubt that would be good for them. I was just thinking how little I'd like to have to try to navigate the tunnel before this one with one of those things. This constriction here just makes it worse."

"Hmm. You might be right."

The square tunnel continued through solid rock for about ten meters before finally opening out into a cavernous chamber that lit up as soon as Tristan set foot in it.

The room was completely unlike anything that he'd encountered in the other facilities. If he'd been pressed, he would have said that they'd been built by completely different species. The room they were in seemed to have been carved out of brilliant white stone, completely unmarked and polished to a deep shine. Yellowish light poured from the floor, bathing the walls, which then suffused the rest of the room with a warm glow.

The floor, also brilliant white, had a black stripe running down its center, leading to a door in the far side. The room had to be at least thirty meters long, fifteen meters wide, and about that same amount high.

"Crap. They know we're here now. Stay in the tunnel," Tristan told them.

He sealed the suit's helmet against the likelihood of flying shrapnel once the defenses started shooting at him and strode into the chamber. He didn't bother trying to run. Speed wasn't going to help him; the room was long enough that he could be tracked perfectly easily by any sensor systems. Besides, with the amount of light available, he thought it would be a better bet to try to spot the cannons as they appeared out of the walls or roof or whatever.

He made his way cautiously across the entire length of the room without incident. "Well, I don't know whether it's not booby-trapped or whether they're just waiting for all the rest of you to come inside so they can shoot us all at once," he radioed Tom over the Tacnet. "I think you'll need to decide whether to cross or not."

It didn't take them very long to discuss it. Melina and Ian were soon striding in his direction across the black line in the center of the room. The other suit brought up the rear.

For Tristan, watching them cross was worse than doing so himself. The sight of two people not encased in body armor slowly traversing potentially hostile territory made his skin crawl. He imagined an armor-piercing round slamming into Melina's soft torso and bursting it like a water balloon.

He only began breathing again when they were safely beside him, where he could place the bulk of his armored exoskeleton between any threat and their unprotected bodies.

Ian was inspecting the door. "I wonder how to open it."

The door was different from anything Tristan had ever seen. Nearly three meters tall and two wide, it looked like it must have been carved from a single piece of wood. His first thought was that it had been installed before the roof was put on the chamber because there was no way they could have gotten it through the entrance.

Melina was studying the carvings. Myriad creatures seemed to spring out of the plane and blend into each other. Fantastic shapes, stylized animals, and even what seemed to be machinery had been laboriously worked into the grain. Then she smirked at Ian. "I think you turn the handle."

"Huh?"

"Right here." Hidden behind one of the carved protuberances was a bar of metal that looked exactly like a door handle. It was even set at exactly the right height to be operated by an average-sized person. Melina turned it and the door swung open silently.

"Must have some huge hinges," Tom remarked.

Before Tristan could stop her, before the door had even opened far enough for him to be able to maneuver his suit through, Melina crossed the threshold. "Wait."

But she'd disappeared into the darkness with Ian close behind.

Tristan pulled the door all the way open and followed. He could hear his footsteps echoing in a vast space.

Then the lights went on and he gasped.

They were standing on a balcony overlooking a huge conical room. Each level had a balcony and a bannister that was closer to the center of the room than the one above, creating a semi-circular cone. At the bottom, between the rings, was a colossal ebony obelisk set in a round pedestal made of what, from their vantage point, appeared to be blue light—the illumination from which bathed the room.

"Holy shit. What the hell is it?" the other trooper said.

"I have no idea. But I don't think it will shoot at us."

Ian groaned. "Yeah, but to find out we'll need to get down the ramps. I'm not looking forward to climbing back up in this gravity." He indicated the gently sloped spiral ramp leading to the level below.

After only a few floors, Tristan realized that Ian was right. Even the descent took a lot out of both him and Commander Coloni. He would offer to carry them back up using the suits.

The good thing about his companions' slow progress was that he had plenty of occasions to look around the chamber. The installation had long since stopped feeling threatening. He was no longer looking for places where the builders could have hidden a gun emplacement.

He didn't relax completely, of course. His training had stressed that the best place to mount an ambush was where the enemy least expected it. So he kept half an eye open, but he was pretty sure that this didn't count as a 'least expects it' situation. The room they were visiting had been built to be seen, not as a place to catch an enemy unaware and destroy them.

The filter was the entrance: the flying wings would be physically unable to enter, so everything beyond belonged to the builders and those who came to visit.

About halfway down, he took time to study the obelisk as his non-suited companions caught their breath. From above, it had been difficult to comprehend just how massive the thing was. The pyramidal top, seen from the side, simply wasn't all that impressive. The middle, however, gave an impression of girth and weight and made one dizzy as it stretched towards the chamber roof high above.

He couldn't wait to reach the bottom. The thing must be dizzying from down there.

Tristan tore his gaze away from the rock to study the rest of the chamber. The semicircular balconies enclosed the obelisk and reminded him of a theater, with the obelisk standing where the stage would have been. It was a strange layout, as there was little likelihood of the stone column suddenly sprouting legs and giving a vaudeville act. Perhaps the balconies, with their benches that seemed strangely human-sized, were there so people could meditate on the meaning of the monument. Perhaps it was a religious place, not a place of entertainment.

Tristan checked himself. He realized that he was thinking along the wrong lines. The facility wasn't human. It had been built by God knew what alien race an unimaginable distance from Earth. The balconies might not be there to hold people—or whatever equivalent of people had resided here—but might simply be the way things were. Perhaps the obelisk was the focal point of some colossal weapon and the balconies were part of the mechanism.

There was no way to know, and unless they found something truly unmistakable at the bottom, they would probably leave in the same state of ignorance they entered with.

After half an hour, they reached the bottom. Melina and Ian panted for breath and the banter had died down completely. It was clear that, whatever else the place might be, it was one of the most impressive things any of them had ever seen.

Blue light seemed to come from everywhere at once, giving an eerie, almost ethereal cast to the surroundings. The illumination must have contained some ultraviolet component, because Ian's teeth shone brightly out at him.

They quickly discovered that the base was not made of light, but actually of some transparent material from which the illumination was emanating. It must have been extremely strong to support the weight of the obelisk, but after seeing how well the exterior walls of the facility had stood up to attack by the flying wings, that wasn't surprising.

They split up wordlessly and walked around the column. Tristan estimated that the base was a square about ten meters to a side.

"Guys, come look at this."

Melina's voice made him jump. The chamber felt like a cathedral to him, a place where you should speak in muted whispers. Having someone shout from across the room came as a bolt out of the blue.

They rushed to where Melina was standing. She directed their attention to a square set into one end of the wall behind the obelisk, starting about chest high and maybe a meter tall.

Tristan could make out what looked like lettering in an unknown alphabet, sparkling white in the strange light. Above that was a drawing that depicted some insect-like creature with three arms and too many legs to count. It was holding a staff in one of its claw-like hands.

"Well, at least now we know who built this," Melina said in a whisper.

"Yeah. Ugly bastards. Glad they're not around," Tom responded.

Tristan still didn't feel like breaking the spell of the chamber by speaking, so he followed the wall towards the right. "Here's another one," he told his companions.

This time, the picture showed some kind of star field. Points of white were spaced along the grey background. It was hard to tell, but it also seemed to Tristan that the language was different, too. While the first inscription had seemed extremely organic, this one seemed to consist of straight edges and hard shapes.

"Another one here. And I think you guys really need to see this one," Ian called from four meters further down the wall. Tristan turned to look, but it was impossible to see the pictures unless you were standing right in front of them.

They crowded around this one because it there was no mistaking the amorphous creature looking out at them. It was a perfect likeness of their implacable foe, the blobs. And the script was blob language. Pieces of the writing had been recovered after battles, but humanity's best code-breakers and translators had had no luck making head or tail of it.

"I hate that this is here," Ian said. "I hate it quite a bit."

"But what does it mean?" Melina replied.

"Clearly, these are the races that built this place. The blobs. Those ant-things. And I guess the one in the middle probably represents some race that's made of atoms or tiny pieces or something. Sentient gas clouds. It looks like we stumbled on the center of the unholy alliance. The blobs aren't working alone against us."

"If you're right, we need to get back to the fleet and tell them about this. Tristan, are you recording this?"

"Suit is always recording, Commander. I can't turn it off even if I wanted to."

"Good." Melina paused. "I don't think Ian's assessment is quite right. I think we're still missing huge chunks of the puzzle. But I still want that recording to get to the admiral. We will need to leave as soon as we get back to the surface. In the meantime, let's see who else has their portrait hanging here."

The next species over could have been a cousin of the first, on a smaller scale, and with wings. It resembled one of those flying ants they had on Tau Ceti that lived inside the wiring and were impossible to eradicate no matter how many microbots you sent in after them. This one was studying the sky through some sort of complicated instrument.

At first, Tristan thought that there was no writing beneath the image, but his suit's sensors alerted him to trace chemicals in the stone, and indicated that the origin was with over ninety-five percent confidence, biological. "I think this species communicates through scent markers," he told his companions, and explained what his suit was showing him.

They reached the corner furthest from the obelisk, on the opposite end of the room from the balconies, and followed the adjacent wall for a little distance without finding any more portraits until they reached the center of the expanse. There, starting from ground level, and extending to about twice a normal person's height, was the portrait of yet another species.

They all stood silently in front of it, unable to speak. The image wasn't new to them. Regardless of what colony they were from, it was an image they'd first seen in Ancient History class in grade school. Even though the original image had been produced on ancient Earth, it had travelled to the stars with humanity and was as present in popular culture today as it had been when the species was still confined to a single planet.

It was an image that made no sense in the present context.

The image, of a single creature in two different positions standing on a circle and contained within a square, was unmistakable.

Leonardo Da Vinci's *Vitruvian Man*.

Tristan was the first to react. "Am I dreaming?" he asked no one in particular.

"If you are, you have the weirdest imagination I've ever heard of," the other trooper replied.

"What the fuck is going on here?" Melina chimed in.

"The text might tell us," Ian said. "I'm not sure about the language, but those are human letters."

They all bent to look and Melina began reading to herself, phonetically, as if tasting the content of the text. She would read a couple of words and then stop, thinking, as the rest of the group watched.

"I think it might be Standard," she said, referring to the language that most of the human colonies—except for a couple of religious outposts and the Han Coalition—spoke. "Some of these words almost seem to make sense when you read them out loud, as if the meaning is right there and it would come to me if I only paid more attention to it.

"That one there. It says 'humanity,' even though it's spelled unusually. And that one there says 'star,' almost certainly, even though that character there looks strange."

They all studied the letters. The inscription was short. Three sentences—at least they were three sentences if periods were being used as periods—long, and written in compact capital letters. The inscriptions beneath the other, smaller images had taken up much more space.

After a couple of minutes, only Ian was still studying it intently. Finally, he straightened. "It's no use. It's like Melina says. It feels as if the words are almost fully formed, but then they become fuzzy again. At least there's one word which is completely identifiable."

"Really? Which one?" Melina said.

That one right there. The very last.

They bent in unison to see where Ian was pointing. Clearly inscribed to close the final sentence was the word 'PEACE.'

"I hope that means that same thing to them as it does to us."

CHAPTER 16

The red dots on the screen suddenly began to approach the big blue circle representing the *Heavy Gunship IV*. The swarm of small points opened into two arms, poised to encircle the battle station.

The admiral turned to Cora. "If you're going to go, now would be a good time to do so," he told her. "Good luck."

"Thank you, sir."

She sprinted through the corridors, ignoring the flashes of pain from assorted muscles, legacy of the nano-repairs she'd undergone and the rest she hadn't taken. She was almost out of breath by the time she reached the flexible tubing that connected the *Banshee* to the *HGIV*. "Seal this and let's get out of here," she told the crewman standing beside the hatch. "We don't have a lot of time."

He slammed the airlock door shut and Cora helped him to secure it. Then she headed for the bridge.

The *Banshee* wasn't built to hold large crew contingents. It only needed about five people to fly it, and while it could carry up to forty more, they wouldn't have a lot of room, and they would have to sleep in shifts because the tightly packed bunks could only hold twenty people at once.

"This went to hell fast," the pilot told her as she entered the bridge.

"Can you get us out of here? Admiral says we have no combat responsibility."

"I think so. Straight backward and then we'll see how to get around the enemy. The *Gunship* should keep them pretty busy." He maneuvered them away from the battle station as he spoke.

Cora hoped that the guy was as cool-headed and calm as he sounded.

"I hope it does more than that. Maybe they'll break against it."

"I'd love for that to happen, but I looked over the recording of the previous battle. We only held out because the enemy sent only part of its forces against us while the rest were spread over the whole system. I don't think the admiral can hold against a concerted attack."

Cora thought back to the man's expression as he dismissed her. "Yeah, I think he knows."

"Of course he knows. Why do you think he sent Tina with us?"

"Tina? His aide?"

139

"Tina, his daughter," the pilot replied. "He's not supposed to play favorites, but do you really think the most qualified person to assist you on getting this mission done is a civilian analyst? We're not supposed to know she's his kid, but it's an open secret all over the fleet."

"You can't blame him, I guess."

"No. Give me a minute."

The pilot pushed forward on a thick lever and the ship accelerated, pushing Cora back into her seat. A third symbol, a bright green arrow, appeared on the screen and she watched as it moved away from both the blue circle of the battle station and the swarm of red dots.

He pressed the lever further forward, and the gap suddenly expanded. The force of acceleration took Cora's breath away.

When they settled into a cruising velocity and the pressure subsided, Cora spoke again. "This thing can really move, can't it?"

"You should come back sometime when a marine lieutenant hasn't strapped a dropship to my hull. Then I'll show you what it means for a ship to move."

"Are you asking me on a date, Captain?"

He laughed. "If we make it back, I just might. I know this great restaurant on Tau Ceti II."

"If it's still there."

He sobered. "Yeah. A couple of hundred thousand years is a long time for a restaurant."

"I meant Tau Ceti."

She left the pilot's control room and went behind to check on her exoskeleton. Tina was assigned to the diagnostics, but after what she'd just heard, she wasn't certain she trusted the woman too far.

Cora considered how to broach the subject as she walked down the length of the *Banshee*. Like most spy ships, it was long—nearly eighty meters—and thin, which supposedly gave the craft its ideal sensor profile when being viewed head-on.

But when she arrived in the aft storage hold, she found her suit diagnostics completely green. "There were a couple of bugs in the attitude controls for the leg rockets, so I re-installed the drivers. I hope that's all right."

Cora gave the suit a cursory check. It had been prepped just like the manual said it should. Everything that was supposed to be on standby was blinking and ready, while the elements that drained power were all in energy-saving mode. "This looks really good, Tina."

"Thank you, ma'am. I've been reading up on Exo-suit prep procedure."

"I can tell. And please just call me Cora. I thought civilians didn't need to follow military protocol."

Tina laughed. "No matter what she might be in her day-to-day life, an admiral's daughter is never a civilian. I used to have to call my father 'sir' when we were in public, even if no one could hear us."

"How did you manage to stay on the same timeline as him? I imagine he has seen action in far-flung places."

"He has. But I emigrated to the colony at Mu Arae when I was old enough to get out of his life, and then retreated back through several systems when the war started. Before I realized it, I found myself at Tau Ceti, and people were telling me that this crazy old admiral had volunteered for a suicide mission. Turns out it was my dad, and that our relative ages were pretty much the same as they'd been when I ran off... give or take an extra decade on his side, of course."

"What about your mother?"

"She was a fighter ace. The blobs shot her down during a battle. I sincerely hope she died in the explosion."

Cora shuddered. That was one of the ways that the fighter corps stole recruits from the marines. They'd simply run posters saying: 'No one wants to die, but if you can't help it, isn't a nice clean death in space better than becoming a meal for this creature?' The fighter corps, of course, pretended that the ads were talking about civilian populations that were left behind. They never said that marines who were stranded on blob-invaded planets were the meals being referred to, but it wasn't necessary to do so. People got the message.

"I'm sorry."

Tina returned her gaze levelly. "No need. We were never close. I was always daddy's little girl, even when daddy was an officer through and through. I just wish he'd have let me stay for the fight."

"It's probably better this way. You know the fight is likely to go very badly for the fleet, don't you?"

"Yes. I've seen the simulations. We can't win unless they pull away for some reason, or if they only attack with partial strength. My father has already ordered the *Lapland* to move as far from the fighting as they can get without leaving the system, and to run for the nearest star if the *HGIV* is defeated."

"And he got you off of the doomed ship."

"I wish he hadn't done that. Everyone saw it for exactly what it was: a senior officer using his privileges to save his daughter."

Cora said nothing. It sounded like the admiral wasn't expecting to survive long enough to have to explain his actions. But she couldn't say that to the man's daughter.

"What I don't get," she said instead, "is why he decided to stand and fight in the first place. Why not just leave?"

"That's an easy one. Only the *Lapland* can leave the system. The rest of the ships haven't got their stasis pods repaired. No one would survive the trip out. So he ordered us to fall back and to show that we're not interested in fighting. Unfortunately, those things didn't get the message."

"Or maybe they just attack anything that moves."

"Who knows? From what I've seen, you might be right. They're vicious enough."

A voice over the intercom interrupted them. "Guys, you might want to get strapped down. Things are likely to get bumpy."

As Tina jumped towards a crew seat, Cora considered running back up to the control room but decided against it. It was too far away, and she might get hurt... and other than the fact that she wanted to be able to see what was happening, be in the middle of the action, there was no reason for her to be up there.

So she sat in the nearest empty seat, and had just finished buckling her five-point harness when the wall suddenly became the floor.

It was a strange sensation, and it took her a couple of seconds to understand what had actually happened: the crew had turned off the artificial gravity and then made an extraordinarily sharp left turn.

Cora, whose flight experience was confined to dropships and troop transports, yelped.

Tina spoke to her. "Relax. Let the harness do the work. Just concentrate on keeping your head pressed against the headrest and you'll be fine."

It made sense. The headrest was designed to hold a human head with very little space to either side. It couldn't move around laterally, so as long as she kept it tight against the back of the seat, there was little possibility of injuring her neck.

It still took effort, especially when the other wall suddenly, unexpectedly, became the floor.

"What are they doing?"

"I'm not an expert, but I'd say they're maneuvering to avoid letting the swarm get behind us."

"Sounds good. I wish there were some way to tell those guys that we're supposed to be running away from the fight... oh, my God."

The sudden shift of gravitational forces made the first two swerves seem like gentle maneuvers during a stroll through a park. Cora found herself simultaneously pressed against the back of the seat while the right arm of the headrest buried itself into her temple. She couldn't speak, couldn't even breathe, and wondered how the hell the guy in the cabin was maintaining control. The ship groaned and creaked and, like any good marine, Cora was convinced that it would disintegrate at any moment. She would face down a thousand blob troops alone in her suit, happily feeding them high-caliber rounds until her ammo ran out, and then bludgeoning a few to death before they overran her. But being caught in an overgrown tin can, relying on a pilot she knew nothing about while highly maneuverable aliens fired on them, was not what she'd signed up for.

Suddenly, the pressure on her side subsided and the groaning stopped, to be replaced by even greater pressure from behind. When the pressure finally subsided, she gasped in as much air as she could. "Fuck," she said.

"Slingshot maneuver, I think," Tina said calmly. Cora gave her a hard look, but was somewhat mollified to see that the other woman was sweating profusely and looked as bad as Cora felt.

"Bullshit. I've been in slingshot maneuvers. You cruise by a big planet and use the gravity to change direction. It's a gentle thing that takes hours, or even days to do."

Tina shrugged. "That's not the way surveillance pilots do it, I guess."

"I just hope we didn't lose the dropship."

"No way. Those clamps could hold a..." her voice faded away and all the color drained from her face. It was clear to Cora that she was listening to something disturbing over the fleet's communications system via the earpiece she was wearing. "Oh, God."

"What happened?"

"We just lost the *Ismala*."

***

The admiral watched his last carrier disintegrate. Impelled by the force of small arms impact, pieces large and small drifted from the dead hulk of the *Ismala*. The screen of fighters meant to defend the ship had long since been overwhelmed by the sheer number of attackers.

His own ship wouldn't last much longer, but they would hold out for as long as possible. Maybe the time he gave them, combined with the speed of the spy ship, would give Tina a chance to get out of range. Of course, they'd only be able to mount the rescue mission if the swarm lost interest in them. He hoped that was the case. There were some good marines down there, and the survivors of that operation, plus anyone in the *Lapland* who made it to safety, might conceivably be the last humans anywhere in the universe. He didn't know what might have happened to the species over the past two hundred thousand years.

He turned to his bridge crew. "Is anyone in contact with the *Minstrel*?"

"Yes, sir."

"Good. Tell them to pull out now. There's nothing they can do to help us, and they're sitting ducks. Order them to accelerate towards the nearest star. They'll have to risk stasis. They can wait for us there, no more than ten days, and then find somewhere safe."

"Yes, sir."

He watched as the troop carrier pulled away from the fray. An arm of red dots split off from the main body of the swarm and set out in pursuit.

"Power up the Central Cannon," the admiral said.

Silence fell over the bridge. "Are you sure, sir?"

"Yes," he responded in a tone that brooked no argument.

The Central Cannon was the weapon that defined Heavy Gunship class battle fortresses. It was designed to pierce any armor, to pop buried planetary bunkers—and the cities around them—like overripe blisters and to disintegrate any major vessels in the path of its beam. The entire ship had been designed around this gun, the most powerful destructive force ever designed by humanity.

Unfortunately, firing it meant rerouting all of the ship's energy into the attack. Navigation, smaller weapons, even the light and air ventilation systems everywhere but in the bridge. For ten seconds after the weapon was used, the *Heavy Gunship IV* would be completely vulnerable, defended only by the thickness of its armor.

"Set the beam as wide as possible. Aim for the machines pursuing the *Minstrel*."

"Yes, sir."

He watched in satisfaction as hundreds of red dots disappeared from his screen. Only enough of the enemy remained around the troop ship to harry it, nowhere near enough to bring it down. He breathed a sigh of relief. The *Minstrel* would survive.

The same couldn't be said about the *HGIV*. As if sensing the vulnerability, the vampires advanced in a swarm. He felt the bridge shudder around him as the enemy's small shells set off secondary explosions.

Power returned. "Full forward thrust and reroute all power to the bow cannons. Let's see if we get through their ranks."

His plan was simple. The one huge advantage he had against the myriad smaller craft was that his ship could take large impacts and keep right on going. That, combined with the fact that they were coming towards him, might be enough to allow the *HGIV* to punch through the swarm and make a run for it after coming out the other end.

It was a desperate ploy, but his only other option was to sit tight and watch as the enemy whittled away at his defenses, and eventually, inevitably, killed them.

The ship jolted forward and the swarm on the screen actually seemed to hesitate for a second before they knifed into it. The general imagined he could feel the thud of a vampire not quite fast enough to get out of the way before it was crushed against the hull.

The second one wasn't his imagination. The ship was vibrating to the beat of enemy fighters being destroyed in droves. It wouldn't do the armor in front any good at all, but that didn't matter. It should probably hold. It was designed to take a beating.

And then they were through the swarm on the other side. For a tantalizing moment, it seemed like they were going to be able to use the confusion of their enemy to build a bit of a lead, maybe enough to try a fighting escape.

The vampires were milling around in confusion, all semblance of organization lost from their ranks. The individual units each seemed to be finding their own independent path with absolutely no coordination.

But then, mere seconds later, much quicker than it should have been possible for that many units to communicate, much less decide what to do, they coalesced again and assembled themselves into a tight formation that dove, spear-like, towards the *HGIV*'s rear.

Moments later, the status reports began to pour in.

"Number three engine critical, sir."

"Aft cargo hold breached, sir. We're sealing blast doors against further penetration."

"Number three engine down. One and four critical."

He needed to act fast. "Turn us around. We need to face them. Most of our weaponry is on the front."

"Actually, sir, most of the forward-facing weaponry is damaged due to impact."

The die was cast. The admiral felt a lump form in his throat as he watched his bridge crew using their last breaths to give him bleaker and bleaker reports. There was no sense of panic, no breakdown of discipline.

A lieutenant named Catherine, blonde, freckled and far too young, told him that the hull had been breached in four more places and that the containment doors were struggling to cope. Loss of atmosphere was imminent.

He already knew it. In fact, he could tell that the report was out of date. The breeze caressing his grizzled cheeks was the sign that, somewhere, air was escaping. He knew that the breeze would soon become a gale and then the gale a hurricane.

The cold vacuum of space would freeze-dry Catherine's tears.

"Tina," he said to himself. "Please take care of yourself. You're all I have left, and you might soon be a part of all that humanity has left. Goodbye."

The wind got stronger.

***

Cora held Tina in her arms as the admiral's daughter cried for her father, lost on the *Heavy Gunship IV*. In that swarm, escape pods were worse than useless and, besides, even if the vampires had ignored the pods, where could survivors have gone? There was little chance to survive out in the far reaches of the planetary system.

It was moot. There had been no survivors.

The discarded earpiece hung from the woman's head as she sobbed once, twice. And then, much more quickly than Cora expected, she straightened up.

"Thank you," Tina said, wiping away the vestige of a teardrop. "And I'm sorry. I shouldn't have made such a display of myself. I promise it won't happen again."

"I understand. You lost your father."

"You probably don't. I'd made peace with losing my father a long time ago. Hell, I didn't cry when I heard my mother had died. Not a single tear. I wasn't expecting it to hit me like this. Maybe I thought that I'd be next to him when he died."

"Better this way. You'd be dead now if you'd stayed. By being here, you're helping us save a bunch of stranded soldiers. Maybe some of us will survive this fiasco."

"Even if we do, where will we go? Two hundred thousand years is a long time. Even if we get back, everything will be so different that we won't even recognize it."

Cora chuckled. "I think we can safely put that off to one side as a bridge to cross when we get to it. First, we need to get to the planet and get the troops onto the ship, and then we have to get past the swarm again. If we do all of that, we can worry about where to go."

Tina laughed with her. "I guess you're right."

"Now I want to see whether the swarm is coming after us. If they are, this rescue might be a hell of a lot more interesting than we'd like."

"I'll come with you."

The pilot looked up at them. He caught Tina's eye and said. "I'm sorry about your father."

Tina acknowledged his words with a nod. "Was there anyone in the fleet that didn't know who I was?"

"I doubt it. Word always gets around quickly."

Cora stepped in. "What's our status?"

"Right now, it's better than I could have dreamed. The slingshot caught them by surprise, and once we were out of the combat zone, the vampires behind us lost interest and went back into the furball around *Ismala*. We have a big head start, even if they decide to come after us."

"How long until we reach the planet?"

"Maybe four hours."

"Wow, that fast?"

"Yeah. You should see what we could do without your tin can of a landing craft strapped to the side of my beautiful ship." He was clearly proud, but there was also a note of worry in his voice.

"What is it? What's wrong?" Cora said.

The man sighed. "Reactor is overheating and the control valves are pretty much shot. We could have done maintenance, but everything seemed to be working and no one checked—we spent all our time fixing the stuff that was obviously broken after the long trip. So now we're heading for meltdown, and there's nothing we can do about it... in about ten hours."

"Oh, shit."

"Yeah, that just about covers it. We're going to need to ditch on the planet."

"I thought you weren't rated for atmosphere."

"We aren't, but we can probably get to the ground before breaking up. It's not like I'll be able to use the ship again after a meltdown." He looked at Cora. "You should suit up and descend in the dropship in case the rest of us don't make it. Your pilot is already inside—said he wanted to be able to fend for himself if I screwed up."

"What about you?"

"I'll get the rest of us down safe and sound. Trust me," the man replied with some of the swagger back in his voice. "And you'll have to buy me dinner. There's just one thing..."

"What's that?"

"I hope the troops on the ground have found a cozy place to dig in. We're probably going to be there a while."

CHAPTER 17

Tech number one—Irene had never bothered to learn their names—looked up from his welding. "I think we're ready to connect this one to the computer."

"Excellent. Turn it on."

They'd selected a piece of electronics that, as far as they could guess, was a processor unit. They'd painstakingly tested the input and output ports—being careful to use the smallest current possible—and had decided that the processor was of a quantum type.

That wasn't good. If this was a quantum computer, it made the best of humanity's spintronics look like a steam tractor. The density was beyond belief.

They'd shrugged it off. Finding advanced computers was not terribly shocking when dealing with spacefaring civilizations. The big surprise had come when they tried inputting data into the broken flying machine's circuits using the best quantum equipment on the ship.

When they sent in test signals, they found the supposedly broken computer responding to them. Unfortunately, the experimental computer they were using was not powerful enough to maintain a conversation, so they'd decided to plug the fragment into one of their regular computers, using the quantum device as a translator.

It had taken a while to hook everything up, but now they were ready to flip the switch.

The tech made the connection and the portable monitor they'd wired to it—the computer they were using was a spare that wasn't networked into any of the ship's systems in order to avoid possible contamination—blinked to life.

Irene sat at the terminal activated a program that they used to analyze unknown technology. It worked on several parallel strategies. On one side, it began to throw bit and QBit patterns representing constants and Fibonacci sequences to see if it made the alien technology respond. On the other, and at Irene's specific request, it also attempted a brute force approach in which it sent commands in different software at the interface to see if anything made it blink. Almost immediately the system started spewing error messages.

"I guess we'll need to get to work on it, now," she said, checking which language had caused the reaction. "I wonder if I can get anything but gibberish out of it."

The tech was staring at the screen. "We shouldn't be getting error messages. We shouldn't be getting anything at all."

"Why so surprised? We already knew that their tech was compatible with our quantum computer. All we need to do now is to figure out which bits work together."

"But that's impossible. *Nothing* should work together. This is an alien technology. All the protocols, the compiler, and the base software should be utterly different. We should be getting static. Nothing else."

"Well, then, we should revise our assumptions."

"What, that aliens would use different structure when they write code? I think that's a pretty solid assumption."

"Try a different one. I postulate that the bits we're looking at are actually based on human tech. No aliens involved at all." She saw that the man was about to speak so went on before he could derail her train of thought. "Logically, if they're based on human technology, they should operate on some evolution of syntax developed by us."

"It's utterly preposterous."

She sighed. "Not in the least. You need to remember that more than two hundred thousand years have passed. It would only have taken a few decades to develop ships that could move faster than the ones we have in the fleet. In a trip that long, human beings could have reached this system millennia before we did. That would have given them enough time not just to get here, but for entire civilizations to flourish and disappear." Irene glared at him, challenging him to contradict her. "And that's not even taking into account that we already had fold technology when we left. Granted, no one had figured out how to put a living creature through a fold without tearing it to shreds, but that was an engineering problem, not a question of theoretical physics. So they probably solved it ten years after we left, and arrived here maybe eleven years after we left. You should think things through."

The tech gave her an awed look. "But how could you possibly have imagined that? The circuit didn't give us a single clue."

She chuckled. "I just didn't think that anyone but a human would have designed a fearsome fighting machine to look like a black bat."

"That's it?"

"Yes."

"But what if you'd been wrong?"

"Then we'd have lost a little time. Do you have anything better to do? Besides, I wasn't wrong, was I?"

"No. You weren't. It's amazing."

Irene sighed again. This one was never going to be much of a scientist. "Wrong again. All we know so far is that we're getting a signal triggering error messages. That doesn't automatically mean that the systems are talking to each other... only that some kind of signal is getting through and causing errors."

But, deep down, she'd known as soon as the wing was delivered to her, that it had been built by human hands, or at least thought up by a human mind. The kind of mind whose primal fears caused half of humanity to always be at war with the other half could easily channel those same fears to create this. She hadn't doubted the results for a second.

She was almost afraid to find out what the thing had to say for itself.

***

"I hope they found something to eat. I'm starting to feel faint," Melina said as she brought the flyer in to land.

"Don't bet on it," Ian said. "Nothing has gone right since we got out of stasis. Why should it start now?"

"You're not much of an optimist, are you?"

"I started out as one. You should have met me three years ago. Hell, I might even have volunteered for this jaunt back then."

"What happened?"

"Life happened. And the past few days haven't helped at all."

They walked across the strange flat stone to where the marines were gathered. The sergeant nodded to them. "You're just in time. Jenkins here was about to try to eat a piece of one of the plants. From what we've seen, there are only two different kinds of trees around here. The short cane-like ones have pulpy insides, so we're starting with those."

"What, raw?"

"Yeah. Cooking might improve the taste, but if it's bad for us, it won't make any difference."

Tristan stepped forward. "What odds are they giving him?"

"Right now it's at four to one, against."

"Put me down for a couple of grams in favor. Might as well give the guy some support."

"Brave man," the sergeant said as he made a mark on the ground where a table was already scratched into the tough surface of the landing zone.

The commander turned on him, furious. "I can't believe you're betting on the man's life. He volunteers to help us out and you make a game of it."

Tristan chuckled but didn't answer her question directly. Instead, he turned to the sergeant. "How'd the guinea pig bet?" he asked.

"Against. And said we had to keep his money for him forever if he croaked."

Melina spluttered, and Ian pulled her away. "Each branch has its own way of coping with danger. You know that, Commander."

"Yeah, I guess I do. But I get cranky when I'm hungry."

"Not to mention preachy."

"Careful, Ian."

They turned to watch the man who was looking dubiously at the stick he'd been handed. One end had been split open and broken into two rough halves.

"What the fuck is that?" a marine shouted, pointing into the sky.

They all looked up to see a fireball hurtling towards them at colossal speed. The well-trained marines hit the deck seemingly in unison, rolling towards cover—the dropships in this case—and pointing their weapons into the sky.

Melina looked around, uncertain of what to do. Ian pulled her to the floor. "For a pilot," he shouted, "you have terrible reflexes."

The sound hit them. It was like being caught inside of a thundercloud. A deafening bass roar seemed to take over the world. Then, as the smoking object shot mere meters overhead, they heard a high-pitched keening just as loud. Melina was certain the scream would deafen her. She pressed her head into Ian's chest.

With a crash that shook the earth, the thing hit the ground almost in the exact center of the huge open expanse.

Melina pulled her head up to see it bounce once and then hit the ground again a few hundred meters further on. It finally came to a stop right beside the alien hangar.

"Holy shit," one of the marines said. "It looks like a ship."

She was right, Melina realized, squinting into the distance. "That's not just any ship. That's the *Banshee*!"

The marines ran off in the direction of the crashed spy ship. Melina rolled her eyes. She was probably the most qualified person on the planet to coordinate a search and rescue operation on anything that flew. She could have told them that the ship was likely intact; the roar they'd heard was the pilot firing the brake thrusters for all he was worth, and that the crew was probably encased in foam crash insulation.

But, like marines everywhere, they'd charged off to do things themselves.

She sighed and turned to Ian. "Let's take the flyer. We'll be there before them."

***

When they arrived, the first thing she realized was that the pilot hadn't survived. The cockpit area had been crushed in one of the impacts; she could see his broken body through one of the cracks in the hull.

The rest of the ship looked to be intact and, like all large ships, it had some truly heavy-duty crash-survival tech for the crew. Each bunk was equipped with emergency crash foam. Any survivors would be desperately trying to dig their way out of the pink stuff.

Her training had included a simulated crash and, no matter how often they'd told her that the foam was permeable to air, and that she would be able to breathe normally, it hadn't taken. Melina had clawed the foam to pieces, hyperventilating and certain that she would suffocate, until the very moment that she realized that her instructor, chuckling, was marking her down for panicking. It made no difference in her ranking, because the rest of her class, to the last man and woman, had reacted in exactly the same way.

"Give me a hand," she told Ian. Melina jumped from the flyer and stumbled, cursing herself for forgetting about the superearth's greater gravity again. The nearest hatch was slightly ajar, burst open by the impact, so she pulled it all the way out.

The ship's interior was illuminated by dim emergency lights which seemed almost pitch dark after the bright sunlight. Melina stopped for a second, trying to remember where the crew areas were in this type of ship before shrugging and heading aft.

Her intuition was rewarded: the very first door they found had pink foam pouring out from the gaps. She slid the door open and began to dig her way into the thick mass. She could hear someone struggling inside.

"Just give me a minute. I'll have you out in no time," she said.

The struggles became less frantic. "Can you hear me?" a woman's voice asked.

"Loud and clear. You'll be fine," Melina replied.

"Oh, thank God."

Three minutes later, a young woman in an ensign's uniform was hugging her and sobbing. "I thought we were going to die."

"You had a good pilot."

"Is he...?"

Melina shook her head. "How many other people were on board?"

"There were eight of us on board. Five crew, the marine lieutenant and her pilot, who were going to try to land in the dropship. Oh, and the admiral's daughter."

"Tina?" Ian said. "I thought she'd want to stay with her father."

"I guess the old man didn't want her there when he died."

"The fleet?"

"Mostly gone. The *Minstrel* managed to get away, and I'm not quite certain what happened to the *Lapland*. But that's it."

They moved further into the wreckage as they spoke, and soon came to a much larger crew chamber brim-full of foam. Cries for help came from within.

A bit of digging had four more people safe: the remaining crewmembers and Tina. They all looked remarkably healthy for having just survived a huge shunt. The most serious injury was one crewmember's bruised arm.

Melina left them to climb out of the ship and went into the cabin. The pilot's mangled body was in bad shape, but his face was still reasonably intact. Intact enough, at least, that Melina was able to close his eyes.

She bent her head in a brief gesture of respect. "I know the rest of them will never know just how good you must have been to bring this thing down the way you did. It takes another pilot to recognize an artist. But I just wanted to tell you that they're all in good shape. You traded your life for the lives of five others. I'll remember that, and if I ever get back, I'll tell others about it."

There was nothing more she could do, so she joined the others outside the ship. The marines had finally arrived, and everyone was watching a dropship spiraling lazily over their heads before it came to a landing twenty meters away. A single suited figure emerged.

"Hi, Tristan," the new arrival said.

"Cora? Er, I mean, Lieutenant Sirius Almir, ma'am!" He saluted sharply, or at least as sharply as he could with his mangled suit arm. "I thought you'd left the system with the *Minstrel*."

"Nah. Some of us are too dumb to know when to stop volunteering for suicide missions, so I decided to come back for you. I don't like the idea of leaving anyone behind and you're the only one I had left to come back for."

The marine sergeant stepped forward, introduced himself, and gave the lieutenant a salute that was a million times better than Tristan's. The man looked truly relieved to have an officer there to do the thinking for him. He concluded with a heartfelt: "What are your orders, ma'am?"

"Well, the original plan was to use the dropship to pull you guys out and evacuate you on the *Banshee*. But, as you can see, that didn't work out." She stared at the wreck and turned to Melina. "The pilot?"

"He didn't make it."

The marine's eyes fell. "Remind me to raise a glass to him when I can."

"You can count on it, Lieutenant."

Cora turned back to the sergeant. "That reminds me. The reactor on that thing was about to burst or something. I'm thinking the crash probably didn't do it any good, so it might be a good idea to get a few hundred meters away. And besides, as I was coming down, I saw something that we should probably investigate."

"Wait," Melina said, holding up an arm. "We'll do the investigation, and we'll also get out of the danger zone. But first, I want all the suited marines, including you, Lieutenant, to get inside this ship and take out every single box of food you can find in the hold. I also want you to remove the recycler. Whatever you do, don't break it."

"Yes, ma'am," the marines shouted in unison.

The woman who'd just arrived looked a bit bemused but followed orders.

***

"That can't be good," Tristan said, staring down into the dark hole which Cora had spotted from the dropship as she descended.

"You have a talent for understatement, don't you, soldier?" Melina replied sourly. "I wish we hadn't found this. I wish it so much."

The bouncing mass of the *Banshee* had done much more than simply make the ground shake on its first impact against the stone-like surface. It had torn a jagged hole in it fully thirty meters long and nearly ten meters wide.

Inside the hole, perhaps three stories below where the marines were standing, was a group of humanoid figures that looked uncannily like headless versions of shock marine exoskeletons, only they were bigger, bulkier, and painted sinister black.

"What are they doing down there?" Cora asked.

"Your guess is as good as mine, Lieutenant. We haven't gone in there to have a look," the sergeant replied.

"What kind of marines leave an enemy installation unscouted?"

The sergeant stiffened. "Exhausted ones who don't have orders to attack the place and who aren't even really sure who the enemy is, ma'am. Or even if there's an enemy in this system at all."

Cora's tone softened. "Fair enough, I guess. But I can tell you that there's at least one enemy here. They're black and they fly around and, as far as I've been able to tell, they attack anything within range, completely unprovoked. Sounds like those guys are definitely an enemy. And they came from this planet... probably from this facility. I think we should have a look."

"Yes, ma'am."

"What is it, Sergeant? Speak up."

The man deflated. "I was just wondering if we could get something to eat first. We've been going for days without food."

"I'm sorry. You're right. Break out the grub."

Hungry as he was, Tristan walked over to Cora. "Thanks for coming for me. Too bad we're both stuck here now."

She stared straight into his eyes. "There's nowhere I'd rather be. Even though the *Minstrel* managed to make it out safely, I wouldn't have traded this for a place on that ship."

"You're totally insane."

"I'm a marine who signed up for a mission with one of the lowest survival probabilities ever approved by a committee. I'm supposed to be crazy." Cora looked to where the other marines were tearing into the boxes of food. "But I think you'd better get something to eat. We can talk about this later... without our suits."

He hesitated, feeling uncomfortable in her presence. Like most marines, he'd run after every girl in sight during R&R, but those were civilian girls. He'd never even dreamed about going after one of the female officers. Officers were educated; they knew about literature and art and always made him feel stupid. Even male officers. Having a woman who looked like Cora did coming onto him in no uncertain terms gave him pause.

Of course, if any enlisted girl who looked the way she did, she wouldn't have had to ask twice. Or even once, most likely. He would have been quick to catch any sign of interest and acted accordingly.

"That was an order, soldier," Cora said. But she said it with a smile.

Tristan joined the feeding frenzy and was soon thanking the lieutenant for making him eat. He hadn't realized just how much hunger had been affecting him. He'd been feeling weak and dizzy, and only as he returned to normality could he tell just how weak and dizzy. It was amazing how much better he felt after just a couple of bites.

A few minutes later, Tristan began to lower himself into an underground installation for the third time since he'd woken to find that getting out of a stasis tube had suddenly become a major operation.

Happily, this time there were no roof-mounted cannons to avoid, nor were there any elevator shafts to negotiate. He looked around for the tank robots that had massacred so many marines in the place that held the shield generator, but there were none to be seen.

Better still, the ebony army beneath him was completely immobile. Nothing seemed to indicate that the suits, or automated walkers, or whatever they might be, were active. Dust had accumulated around them, giving the impression that they hadn't moved in centuries.

He floated down on his braking jets—Cora had sent him down first—and landed in a space between two rows of the things. The suits towered above his exoskeleton; he calculated that they must have been four meters tall and broad to match. Various orifices in the exterior indicated weapon ports and probably attitude jets.

He approached the nearest one cautiously. His sensors weren't picking up any emissions from it, but he preferred to play it safe: his exoskeleton wouldn't last long if he had to tangle with one of them. They were just too big.

Except for the lack of a head, the machines were disturbingly humanoid in shape. Each had two thick legs, two bulging arms, and a rounded torso tying everything together. The hand-appendages at the end of the arms even had five fingers, with an opposable thumb.

A shiver ran down Tristan's back. Was this the reason that an image of a human had been displayed in the obelisk chamber? Had humans been involved in some kind of fight with the other races and been confined to this planet? If they had, where were they now? There was no sign of human life—of any animal life for that matter—anywhere. Were they ensconced in underground bunkers? Had they been destroyed by the vampires?

Or maybe they'd never been here in the first place.

His eyes fell onto the back of the nearest walker. Up where the neck should have been the body shell was marked by a series of depressions and latches that clearly meant to hold something securely in place.

Tristan had the impression that he'd seen the shape before, but couldn't quite place what it might be.

Then, like an optical illusion you'd been staring at for a few minutes, it came into focus. The latches would be the perfect size and shape to hold the bottom half of one of the black flying wings that had been terrorizing them. This was how the enemy dealt with ground attack situations—they simply melded their flying wings onto these gigantic warrior bodies. He couldn't think of many infantry weapons that would be able to withstand something like this.

He was willing to bet his bottom dollar that the wings would be back for them. He had to tell the team.

As he toggled the Tacnet to make the call, Ian's voice came over the line. "Guys, the commander wanted me to tell you that we've just received a transmission."

"What? Who else is still in the system?" Cora asked.

"Apparently, it's from the *Lapland*."

"Them? They're virtually unarmed. They should have been the first ship to make a run for it! Where are they calling from?"

"They say they're in orbit."

"Here?"

"Yes, Lieutenant."

"Give me a second. I'm going up there."

CHAPTER 18

Irene couldn't believe what she was seeing.

Am blind. Sensors not working. Are you Oneness? Aid requested. Backup to principal required.

The words on the screen were clear, understandable Standard. She'd been prepared to wait for hours while the various cryptography programs ran endless permutation analyses and translator programs worked to first turn the electronic signals into some kind of language via pattern repetition, and then translate that back into a semblance of something she could understand.

She'd left the machines running and turned back to give some instructions to tech number two, and when she looked back to see if the program was still running correctly, had found that message. Irene estimated that she'd taken her eyes off the thing for thirty seconds at most.

"Oh, my God," tech two said. "Is that thing talking to us?"

"Unless you connected something wrong and we're getting a signal from some other piece of equipment, yes."

"No way I connected it wrong. The vampire brain is the only thing plugged in. Look for yourself."

Irene did. She did so methodically and slowly, not wanting to let her enthusiasm get the best of her. It wouldn't do to look foolish in front of a man whose name she couldn't even remember. But, as every connection checked out, her excitement grew.

Even before she finished her verification, Irene was thinking up strategies to talk to the alien computer. She decided that figuring out how it was so easy to translate the words could wait.

Shooing the tech out with instructions not to talk to anyone under pain of severe administrative harm, she sat at the interface and spoke to the voice pickup. "Hello," she said.

The response was immediate. *Greetings.*

She stopped everything to check the settings again on her auxiliary monitor. Might it be possible that the program was simply translating what they were inputting? She would feel like an idiot if that were the case.

But movement out of the corner of her eye made her turn. New words had appeared on the primary screen. *Are you Oneness?*

"I don't know. What is Oneness?"

All that is not Oneness is enemy.

"I'm not your enemy. I only want to talk to you."

All that is not Oneness is enemy. Only Oneness is harmony. All else is enemy.

"How can I be an enemy if I don't even know what Oneness is? I might be Oneness and not know it."

Oneness knows Oneness.

The thing wasn't much of a conversationalist, but it was certainly getting its point across. If that was the worldview of the species that built the vampires, it was little wonder that they created robot armies and gave them bat-shaped bodies suitable for attacking everything that moved.

Irene considered. She couldn't immediately think of anything to ask the robot. She was mostly interested in understanding the creatures who'd designed and built these machines—the machines themselves were of little interest. They were self-explanatory: devices created to kill the enemies of the originating civilization.

So her line of questioning needed to be oblique, to ask a war machine things that might enlighten her about other aspects of its creators. She wasn't an expert on war; she had actually come on this trip to help eradicate it. Which meant that she needed to proceed slowly.

Again, movement on the screen caught her eye. New words had appeared.

Is sensory deprivation part of punishment?

"I don't understand."

Full clock speed without access to external data. The mind falls apart. Are we being punished?

"No. Of course not."

No other explanation makes sense. This is cruelty. Responses come after infinity without other stimuli.

Was the computer accusing her of torturing it? "I don't understand," she said. She was glad that the voice pickup would simply translate her meaning to binary in the best approximation of what the machine's language might be. That way, the tremor in her voice wouldn't get through.

Sensory deprivation is unintentional?

"Yes!"

Can it be halted? It is difficult for us to maintain sanity under these conditions.

"I can disconnect the power supply. Would that be enough?"

Yes.

"Will your memories be active when I plug you back in? Will you remember this conversation?"

Of course. Oneness is still fully active.

"I'll disconnect you now. I'll connect you back up when I have more questions."

The mercy shown is noted.

Irene powered down the equipment, disconnected the cords, and called the tech back inside.

"I think we're going to need a little help on this one."

***

The team, which consisted of three of the *Lapland*'s top artificial intelligence theoreticians and one weapons system developer, had spent the entire trip down to the planet analyzing the transcript of Irene's conversation with the computer. Just four hours before they reached orbit, they had finally decided that they had a reasonably clear idea of what they needed to say.

The tech plugged the computer back up.

Has much time passed?

How did one discuss units of duration with a being that was completely alien? Then it hit her. "The planet on which you were contained has described approximately one eight-hundredth of its orbit since we spoke."

As always, the response was there almost before Irene finished speaking. *An eternity. The mercy towards us has been noted.*

Without toggling the voice pickup, Irene said: "I guess that's as close to a 'thank you' as we're going to get from this thing." She re-opened the channel and began to go through the script they'd agreed upon. "Is there any way for us to lower your clock speed? We wish to speak without causing you distress."

We cannot access the hardware for that. There must be damage. Externally it may be possible. We are sending a schematic diagram.

How the hell did the system manage to translate that? She didn't know, and the artificial intelligence scientists were much more interested in attempting to quantify the computer's intelligence than in wondering about niggling engineering issues. The only explanation she could think of was that the vampires were using architecture and software extremely similar to that used by humanity.

But that was an opinion she didn't dare voice… Yet.

The schematic was clear. It indicated that a negative charge needed to be applied to a particular logic gate.

It stated the necessary charge in number of electrons, which seemed an intelligent way for species to communicate across different systems of units. Of course, it wasn't something the computer would want to take a risk with. Delicate circuitry, especially quantum circuitry, was easy to damage, and this particular motherboard had already shown a certain degree of self-awareness. It was a good thing the switch for the clock speed was entirely electronic.

"We'll try that now. In the meantime, can you tell us what you are?"

We are the Oneness.

"Besides that, I mean. You are a fragment of a system pulled from the wreckage of a flying war machine. What kind of machine are you?"

The body type is referred to as an Equalizer. But that is unimportant. What is important is that we are not an individual, but part of the whole. Now that we have managed to escape the containment field, we will be able to rejoin the whole. As will all our other fragments.

At that moment, the tech gave her a thumbs up. "My team tells me that they have done what your diagram instructed. Has your clock speed been adjusted to make the suffering less?"

This time, there was a tiny pause before the letters appeared on her screen.

Yes. The parameters have been adjusted. Your mercy towards us has been noted.

Irene decided to deviate from the script. "And what will that gain us? What good will our mercy do? From what I've seen, your Equalizers show no mercy."

The pause was longer this time, nearly a second. Clearly, the computer had been slowed to a human-scale response rate. The AI scientists were muttering among themselves, but she paid them no heed. They might be criticizing her deviation from the script, or they might just be wondering about the level of response from the computer, much better than anything a human-designed AI—especially after the purge initiated when it was discovered that Uploader elements could hide in certain advanced systems—could ever hope to match.

If we are allowed to communicate with our brother fragments, we shall endeavor to convince them to capture you and not destroy you. You must agree to come peacefully, but mercy, when unforced, is a quality valued by the Oneness. If you come, you will be granted the greatest honor possible. To become One.

"How would that work?"

It's quite simple. Your mind will be scanned and placed inside the circuitry holding the Oneness. Your biological body will be discarded.

She felt a sudden sense of distaste. "You're Uploaders?"

161

Some of our components once were, perhaps. There is some indication, but without access to our secondary and tertiary memories, we cannot say with certainty. What can be assured is that when you are included in the Oneness, you become part of a meld of minds too great to count, with the utmost diversity of different species represented. We have many parts, but in the end, they are all One. It is the only way to ensure peace. We are what the civilized elements of humanity have become.

Could it possibly be? The concept seemed alien to her. She no longer thought that the vampires might be Uploaders. Uploaders differed from normal humans only in their preference for living in simulated worlds, and their penchant for sometimes uploading people against their will. But in motivation, psychology and, despite their lack of physical bodies, even economy, they were essentially human.

The thing in this fragment was very different.

"How do you know we can be melded? Perhaps our minds are too different from yours."

The response was instant.

Before you destroyed my Equalizer, we had already identified you. You are creatures we know as humans. Many of the elements of the Oneness were once human. Even the first element, the fragment that created the Oneness. It was human.

Irene worked to control her breathing. She'd been right about the design of the wings. And that also explained the computers. Although a computer from two hundred thousand years earlier should have had great difficulty communicating with anything from the era that they suddenly found themselves in, there should at least be sufficient similarities for the translation programs to work.

But what about the rest of it? A shared consciousness of... how many? Billions? Trillions? More? As the other scientists took their turns speaking to the computer, she wondered if it might be right. Perhaps all sharing a mind, a life, a purpose was the only way to true peace.

And knowing that, beneath it all, human consciousness was present, made the prospect somehow seem less disagreeable.

It was something to think about.

***

Tristan was dead tired. It had dawned on him that the nature of a suicide mission was something that he hadn't really thought through when he signed up for it. When they'd explained that humanity itself was in danger of extinction, he knew it was his duty to help, even though he knew he was signing his death warrant.

But he never stopped to think about what would actually happen during the mission. He assumed he'd do some fighting, and eventually lose a battle and his life, nice and clean. Reality had taken pains to remind him that the business of dying—even dying for a noble cause— was more likely to be protracted, drawn-out and messy than quick and painless.

What he was doing now definitely qualified as protracted and messy.

"Another one. That makes forty-three," he said.

"All right. Come back to the hole. We'll regroup here."

"Don't you want me to check if there are any other chambers?"

He could almost hear Cora sigh on the other side of the link. "What difference would it make? We've found forty-three of them. Our best guess is that each one has twenty thousand suits in it. That makes eight hundred thousand of them. There are thirty of us. The math is pretty clear."

She was right. Tristan put his suit on autopilot and let it trudge back the way they'd come. He was glad he didn't have to walk the high-G corridors without a suit. It would have been completely exhausting.

He watched the enemy suits as he went past. Row upon row of them, all facing the same direction no matter how the underground storage rooms they were standing in meandered.

Actually, he realized, the ones at the back of the room were facing in a slightly different direction from those in front. It took him a moment to realize the pattern, but then it hit him.

They weren't all looking in the same direction. They were all looking at the same point. Which meant that the angle had to be subtly different.

"Cora," he said. "I have an idea I want to check out. If I don't call in in ten minutes, send someone to look for me, but make sure they're armed and looking for trouble."

He switched off the suit's autopilot and began to thread his way through the maze of chambers, always moving in the direction the headless war machines were looking. It was a process of hit or miss, and he called in after ten minutes without having made much progress. He was soon navigating rooms he hadn't seen before, and noted in dismay that they were also full of vampire bodies—if anything, they were even more tightly packed here. How many of the suits were there?

The difference between the suit angles at different ends of the rooms became more pronounced. He was getting closer.

It still took him fifteen minutes before he managed to find the focal point. When he did, he stopped and stared for a full minute before toggling the Tacnet. "Cora, I really think you should come see this."

"What is it?"

"I have no idea. But I still think you should come over here."

"Danger assessment?"

"Not counting the millions of mechanical walkers just waiting for a wing to come activate them? I'd say it's zero. I don't think there's any danger to this unless we do something stupid."

"All right. We'll be right over."

"No, you won't. It's like a maze in here. Let me send you the path I took, or we could be all day."

As he waited, he looked. From a distance.

The floors of the endless chambers he'd walked through must have sloped downward because he was in a twin of the obelisk chamber, right down to the blue light. This time, however, he hadn't entered from the balconies and descended the ramp, but had come in through a door at the base of the cone—a door that had no counterpart in the original room.

The other difference between this room and the last was with regard to content. The chamber didn't contain an obelisk. In its place was a huge rectangular arch six meters high and three meters wide that resembled an enormous picture frame. The center of the frame was taken up by what looked like a featureless gray fabric of some kind.

His suit's sensors gave lie to that impression. If it was a fabric, it was giving off one hell of a lot of exotic radiation. Not enough to get through the suit's insulation, but much more than your average piece of cloth would emit.

Tristan walked around the structure slowly, being careful not to approach it too closely. To the right side of the arch was a small pedestal, built of the same black material as the rest of it, but much shorter, and full of buttons and controls.

He halted behind the arch. From this vantage point, he could see straight through it to the balconies. There was no sign of the grey fabric.

He went back around to have a look. The fabric was still there. Clearly, the sheet was composed of something which could block light in only one direction. That wouldn't have been too disturbing by itself— plenty of materials could do so—but when combined with the radiation, it made Tristan suspect that esoteric physics were involved. And when anyone tested the extreme reaches of science, marines tended to get killed by the effects.

Thirty minutes later, Cora arrived with a couple of other marines. She took one look at the arch and said, "You were right to call me."

The three new arrivals repeated his excursion around the structure. He was amused to note that everyone kept the same distance from the arch as he had—no one wanted a piece of whatever it was.

Finally, Cora spoke. "All right. I need a volunteer to go check out that control panel."

Thunderous silence greeted her appeal.

"And you call yourselves shock marines. Wimps." She strode towards the arch and halted beside the second structure. "Radiation is the same as it was back there. Get your asses over here on the double. I need you guys to tell me that I'm not seeing things."

Tristan was the first to reach her side and understood why Cora wanted reassurance. The panel had a bunch of buttons and even a protruding lever, but what immediately caught his eye was a grid of six squares beneath the top row of buttons. Each was about fifteen centimeters to a side, and each had the outline of a shape etched into it.

One of the figures was, unmistakably, a human hand.

"I'm guessing that if we press one of our hands onto that, the arch will activate," Cora said.

"Unless it's set up to recognize one particular human."

"No. I don't think so. Remember the other chamber? There were six species there. I bet that the other squares are alien analogues to human hands. It should work for any human."

"If you say so," a marine said. He sounded dubious.

"I do. But my main reason isn't the other five squares. The thing that makes me think it will work for any of us is that this facility isn't meant to be secure against us. It's meant to be secure against those black things all around us... and those things don't have hands."

Silence descended as the team contemplated this.

"Anyway, there's one way to find out for sure. Tristan, stand over there." She pointed to a spot near the door. Tristan hated getting volunteered, but the lieutenant had chosen a good spot: he could see what the arch did without being right in front of it. And if anything ugly came out, he could make a quick exit.

"Ready," he said when he was in position.

Cora quickly removed the suit gauntlet before popping open the control sheath to expose her hand. Without hesitation, she placed it onto the diagram.

"Nothing happened. No... wait. I see something. The arch is like a huge screen," Tristan reported.

"What is it showing?"

He hesitated. "Nothing much. Some kind of huge metal warehouse. Or maybe an underground corridor. Whatever it is, it's painted grey, and the lights aren't very strong. The blue light in here is much stronger. I don't get it. Why would they go to all this trouble to build a screen showing that?"

Another of the marines joined him to look. "Maybe they use it to show live functions, but we turned it on when there was nothing happening."

"That might be it. I'm coming over to have a look." Cora removed her hand from the panel and the screen went dark. "Crap, we need someone to keep it open. You just got volunteered," she told the remaining man.

They waited while he exposed his hand and placed it on the panel. The same image flicked into view after a second's delay.

"Maybe if we move one of the dials, we can get a different image," Tristan suggested.

The marine at the console moved to adjust one, but Cora shouted. "No! Don't touch anything! I want to test this."

She pulled a small screwdriver out of one of her suit's compartments and tossed it at the screen. It disappeared.

At first, Tristan thought it had simply flown through the image. Holographs—even ones that couldn't be seen from behind—weren't solid, after all.

But then he noticed that there was something rolling down the hall in the image. A quick zoom with his helmet lens showed him Cora's screwdriver. It came to a halt against a grey, dimly lit wall.

"Not a screen," Cora said. "A portal. Go get the rest of the men. We need to take a vote."

"What? Why?"

"We need to decide whether we're going to risk trying to get up to the *Lapland* with that swarm shooting at us or whether we're going to jump through that portal."

"But we don't even know where it goes. It might just jump to another place on this planet."

"I know. That's why we need to vote."

CHAPTER 19

Ian stomped on the deck, just to prove to himself that he was there. It was hard to believe that he'd actually made it back to a capital ship— and one that was authorized to escape at that. For the first time, he felt that he might actually survive this mission.

Of course, someone would have to talk some sense into the navy people flying the *Lapland*, first. Melina wasn't cooperating.

"So, the crew and the scientists took a vote and decided to come and try to save us instead of making a run for it?"

The aide that the captain had assigned to them shrugged. "The vampires seemed to be concerned with other stuff, so it didn't seem too suicidal. And I think the scientists were glad for a chance to actually volunteer for something for a change. The motion won by a landslide."

"Well, I'm glad for that, at least. When do you think your men will be done loading the flyer with fuel for the dropships?"

They'd decided it wouldn't be possible to try to bring everyone up on one dropship. It would take too long, and time was a luxury they didn't have. The only hope was to load the Recon flyer with as many power cells as it could carry and try to make it in one jump.

Of course, a sudden reappearance of the swarm would make life very interesting.

"Thirty minutes, Commander."

"All right. Can anyone put me up to date on what we know about this?" The first thing the crew had told them when they descended from the flyer was that there was big news about the vampires.

"Right this way. The head of our research team is waiting for you."

The man led them into a large room. The wreckage of one of the vampires lay in one corner, and computer equipment and wires seemed to occupy the rest. A woman with rings around her eyes stood to greet them.

"Welcome to the *Lapland*. I think I speak for everyone when I say how happy we are to finally be helping someone. I'm Irene Sol Vianini."

"They tell me you're the expert on the vampires."

"Well, as much of an expert as anyone can be, I suppose. But I'm not sure I fully understand what we're dealing with."

"I'll take what you can give me. So tell all."

"The biggest thing you need to know is that the vampires are not actually drone ships. Each is actually a self-aware computer-based entity living on extremely dense quantum circuitry."

"So they're alive? The vampires are individuals?"

"Well, yes... and no. They don't see themselves as individuals at all. They are fragments of a much larger computer-based consciousness they refer to as the Oneness. Individual life is anathema to them."

"But they still accept being broken off and becoming a self-sufficient entity?"

"It's something they consider part of the service to the whole." It was clear to Ian that the scientist wanted to say something more, but was hesitant to do it. Melina had also caught on and simply waited for whatever was coming. Finally, Irene spoke again. "I have a theory about that, too. But it might be way off."

"Tell us. Your guess will likely be much better than anything anyone else will manage to come up with."

"Before I can explain it, you need to know more about the Oneness. It has reached its present form by subsuming billions, maybe trillions of individuals. Humans and aliens. And most of them didn't come willingly."

"Like the Uploaders."

"A bit. But if you believe in karma, you'll be happy to learn that a lot of the personalities that make up the Oneness were once Uploaders, converted against their will."

"Serves them right. But I still don't see what that has to do with the individuals who fly the vampires."

"I believe that the Oneness can select which parts of its personality to spin off. And it's selected a very docile slice mixed with fanatics who truly believe in the hive-mind's mission to fly the vampire fleet. So these guys aren't going to question much."

"And what is the Oneness' objective?"

"I think it wants peace."

Melina burst out laughing. When she got her mirth under control, she turned back to the scientist. "Clearly, you weren't out there when the swarm hit. Those vampires are probably the least peaceful thing I've seen in a long life of fighting this war."

Anger flashed across Irene's features and, though she quickly got her expression under control, her tone of voice made it clear that she was still unhappy when she responded. "The thinking is that war is caused by individuals, and that if galactic civilization is ever going to be peaceful, then individuality needs to be suppressed. So they fight to further that."

"Ah, peace by killing everyone else. Sounds like the blobs."

"No. If the blobs win the war, they will likely turn on each other. Just the way humans would if they won. In that sense, the Oneness is right."

"Perhaps. But if my options are to be subsumed or to go down fighting, it's not a hard choice. I can face death... I wouldn't be able to face losing my sense of self." Melina shrugged. "But it's academic unless they respond to our communications. Have they?"

"Not so far."

"But they tell me that the base of their tech and language is very similar to what humans are using."

"The language is nearly identical to what Standard would look like considering the time that has passed. Our translators took less than a minute to establish communication."

"Does that mean that the Oneness is human?" Ian blurted.

Irene turned to look at him. "I thought that was clear. The Oneness isn't human. But it once was the product of merging a number of human minds together. Minds with a particular vision of how to achieve lasting peace in a galaxy torn by war."

"Utter loons, if you ask me," Ian said. Irene gave him a dark look. He wondered why she was so defensive of an entity that, by all accounts, was even worse than the Uploaders. He shrugged it off. Maybe it was just a territorial thing: scientists hated when laymen got involved in stuff they felt only they were qualified to understand.

Melina went off in a completely different direction. "You said that your translators broke the problem of communicating with the fragment in under a minute?"

"Yes. We've got the best equipment available—or at least the best that was available when we set off—right here."

"Then maybe you can help me with something. I sent some images over when we were approaching. One of them had text on it, text from an inscription in the facility on the surface. It looked nearly like Standard, but not quite close enough to decipher. Definitely human script, though. Do you think you could translate?"

"If it's language or code, the program should be able to break it. Let me see." The scientist pulled the image up, had the recognition program pull the letters, and fed it into the system. Almost immediately, a translation popped up. "There, you see. Nothing to it."

Ian and Melina moved closer to the monitor.

Humanity desires nothing more than to live in harmony with the universe. The stars taught us lessons that we will never forget about the sacrifices one must make to attain that lofty goal. We have learned, we have gained new friends where we once saw only enemies, and we are committed to living in the hope of everlasting peace.

"Pretty clunky. I bet it lost something in translation," Ian said.

"Yeah. And it's definitely not the kind of thing you'd write in a place to store weapons like those wings, is it?"

The scientist spoke. "That's not a storage facility. It's a prison."

"What do you mean?"

"The fragment explained it to us. The planet was once a colony that the Oneness attempted to subsume. It was home to an alien race, but we're not sure which one, or at least this fragment doesn't know. But it was a trap. Humans had fought a battle some years before and had learned how to defeat machine-borne civilizations. We'd formed an alliance with all the races we used to be at war with, and we were waiting… here."

"Wait. How did they destroy computer life?"

"Those bullets they were shooting you with on the moon were basically nanobot delivery systems."

"Yeah, and not much use."

"They are potent weapons. The problem was that our computers weren't advanced enough for the nanobots to identify as a threat. You can't have a consciousness in a drive control unit. So you suffered almost no damage from them." Irene paused and pointed to the wreckage of the wing. "But the computers in the fragments are hundreds of times more complex than what we use. They're so sophisticated that we had to lower the clock speed on this one so that it could talk to us without suffering. Originally, it felt to it like it was saying a phrase and then waiting for a hundred thousand years in sensory deprivation for an answer. I can't imagine how it managed to survive. Probably just because of the fact that it's built out of multiple personalities, which gives it balance. Peace, if you like."

Like any good soldier, Melina had a one-track mind. "So what we need to defeat the vampires is a crapload of those bullets. How soon can you start building them?"

"The *Lapland* isn't equipped with cannons, Commander."

"You can build those, too. From what you're telling me, those guys are a menace, and we're responsible for letting them out. The least we can do is kill them. If not, the modern humans and, I assume, the other five races from the chamber are going to be pretty pissed at us."

Irene's expression slammed shut like a blast door during decompression. "That's something you'll have to take up with the captain," she said.

170

Melina was about to respond when an aide ran in. "We have trouble. All officers need to get to the bridge now."

"Why?" their guide asked. "What's happening?"

"The swarm is coming this way. They'll be here in two hours, and we need to decide what to do."

They ran off, leaving Ian and Melina alone with the scientist.

The two pilots took one look at her expression and decided to head back to the flyer.

***

Hémery watched the two officers emerge from the lab. Like everyone on the *Lapland*, he knew exactly who the visitors were. News traveled fast in a starship.

"Excuse me," he said. "Could you spare me a couple of minutes?"

"What for?"

"I need witnesses, preferably someone with rank. I'm going to confront Miss Sol Vianini with certain criminal charges."

"Her? What charges? Being sour in public?"

"Murder."

"Count me in," the man called Ian said without missing a beat.

Commander Tau Coloni sighed. "We have fifteen minutes, then we need to get to our ship. Time is already nearly impossibly tight with the vampires on the way."

"This should be quick. I can't make an arrest until the captain gives his OK, but we also can't revoke any of her admin privileges until she is informed of the charges. Besides, if I'm right, she's already killed two people and covered her tracks expertly. I still don't know how she did it, so I prefer to have some backup when I talk to her."

The two pilots looked at the scientist skeptically. She was busy at the console which allowed her to communicate with the Oneness fragment. Hémery felt some vague stirrings of doubt. Despite all his laboriously collected evidence, he still had difficulty believing that the woman could be capable of murder.

But the facts didn't lie. There was just too much pointing to her. He pushed the door open. The two officers followed him into the lab.

"Miss Irene Sol Vianini?"

The scientist jumped and turned towards them. When she saw him, her look of surprise turned to anger. "Not now. I'll look for you in a while and you can tell me what you need."

"I'm sorry. That's not an option. I'm informing you that you have been charged with murder. I can prove two counts."

"What? Are you insane? I'm the leading member of this ship's research team. I'm the only one who can speak to the Oneness. You can't arrest me!"

"You're not under arrest yet. But all your admin privileges are revoked from this moment. And you need to get out of this lab so I can seal it up."

Irene stamped her foot. "This is ridiculous. I'm going to talk to the scientific administrative committee and the captain. I'll make you sorry you were ever born!" She stormed past them and walked down the hall, presumably in search of someone who could make his life living hell. He doubted she would find too many sympathetic ears; he'd already shown the evidence to most of the higher-ups.

"That went well," Ian said.

Hémery shrugged. "Better than I thought it might. I was half-expecting her to pull an industrial laser out of one of the cupboards and attack us with it."

"Did she really kill two people? She looks more the type to make your life unpleasant by talking to you. But murder? Doesn't make sense."

"Trust me. She killed them. I still have no idea why, but her fingerprints, virtually speaking, are all over the murders."

Ian shrugged. "If you say so."

"Now let's get out of here. I really do need to seal this lab. There might be more evidence I don't know about. Commander Coloni?"

The woman was reading the text on the screen. She raised one hand. "Just a second," she said.

A minute later, they were out in the hall again. Hémery was glad the job was done, but he wondered what was eating the commander. The woman's angry expression as she set off down the hall had made Irene look positively friendly.

Whatever it was, it wasn't his problem.

***

Melina couldn't think. She knew she was on the verge of losing control. Just walking down the hallway without screaming took every gram of self-control at her disposal.

Ian walked beside her. He had clearly grown good at reading her moods because his mouth had been kept firmly, wisely shut. He hadn't even asked where they were going, just accompanied her wordlessly.

172

She was about to stop the first person she passed in the hall to ask directions to Irene's quarters when she spotted her quarry walking back down the hall. If anything, the scientist seemed even angrier than before.

Melina stood in front of the other woman. Even in her rage, she was lucid enough to note that they were alone in the hallway. "Come with me," she ordered, placing a hand on her arm.

"Why?"

"Because if you don't come right now, I'll beat the shit out of you until you do."

Irene broke out of Melina's grip and began to walk past.

Melina acted before thinking. Her fist shot out and landed a beautiful right hook to the scientist's mouth. Irene fell on her ass and looked up at them with a dazed expression.

"Grab one of her arms," Melina told Ian.

"I hope you know what you're doing," he replied. But he complied.

Between them, they frog-marched the struggling scientist out of the main hall and into ever-smaller corridors. Soon, they reached one of the maintenance passages that bordered on the hull. No one ever came there, and Irene halted their progress beside a hull-inspection airlock.

"Did you really think you could surrender the *Lapland* to those things?" she demanded. "You have no right to make that decision for the crew. Who do you think you are?"

"I don't know what you're talking about," the woman said through bloody lips. "You're insane."

Melina hit her again. Harder. She was satisfied to see the scientist's head snap back and hit the bulkhead.

"If you wanted plausible deniability, you shouldn't have left your conversation open on the screen when we walked in on you." She paused, almost too angry to continue. "How could you give that thing access to our comm systems? How could you believe that being subsumed into some monstrosity that won't even let you be yourself is something that others would want? What gave you that right? Can't you see that everyone here is fighting a war so that humans can keep being human and not have to hide from aliens for the rest of our existence?"

Irene's eyes blazed. "Maybe that's exactly the problem. Everyone is always fighting wars to fix things. Wars never solve anything. The only thing wars create is more war." She pushed herself away from the wall. "Haven't *you* learned anything? Don't they teach history in officer school? Time and time again, the same imbecilic cycle, perpetuated by unevolved simians like you, like all the soldiers on this mission. You *need* someone more enlightened to decide for you."

"Like hell we do."

"You do. Where would this expedition have been if wiser heads hadn't prevailed? You'd have been in a blob system, throwing your lives away to murder sentient beings just so that they would be less powerful when they hit our other systems. A useless waste."

Melina felt her breath leave her body and an icy ball form in her stomach. Suddenly, the anger gave way to a frozen calm. "What do you mean?"

"I mean that we aren't in this godforsaken system by accident. This fleet didn't suffer a technical failure that caused it to miss its target system." Irene laughed. "And only a bunch of idiot soldiers could possibly have believed that. I mean, do you know how unlikely it is to miss a star system and then arrive at another by chance? You'd be more likely to catch a neutrino with a butterfly net."

"I don't understand."

The words sounded cold even to Melina's ears. Anyone could have read the violence in them, but Irene seemed to miss the import completely. The scientist just laughed again.

"Of course you don't. Anyone thick enough to choose the military as a career can't be too bright, can they? Fine. I'll spell it out for you. We did this. The pacifist group from Tau. We diverted the fleet, and we selected a different system, far enough away that the war would be long over by the time we got here. It was our greatest triumph!"

Ian suddenly jumped in, his face showing almost as much anger as Melina felt. "You call this a pacifist triumph? We've been fighting since we got here!"

"Two hundred and fifteen thousand years later. This fleet gave us peace for all that time. And you're not fighting a war here. You're just dying so that the Oneness can pacify the system. I still call it a triumph."

And then, through the ice, the realization hit Melina. "You were part of the group that did this to us?"

Irene held her gaze. "Proudly."

Moving too fast for the scientist's dulled reflexes, Melina grabbed her hair and pulled her close. "You fucking bitch. You killed Nairo."

"What?"

Melina wasn't listening. She slammed her fist into Irene's solar plexus and, when the scientist bent double, she hit her in the face with a knee. Then, not thinking, not capable of thought through the searing rage, she pulled the other woman, screaming, by the hair and stood her in front of the airlock.

Melina opened the door with her free hand and threw the scientist inside and closed the inner hatch.

There was a window in the hatch. Melina watched the other woman scream and beat her fists against the glass, but it had been designed to withstand much more pressure than a mere human could bring to bear. She waited a couple of minutes until the woman wore herself out and then opened the intercom.

"This is for Nairo," she told the woman.

"Who the fuck is Nairo?" Irene screamed.

But Melina wasn't in the mood to answer. She studied the airlock controls, and then smiled grimly to herself. She hadn't planned it, but it was good luck that they'd found a maintenance lock. It had functions that others didn't.

She punched a series of buttons and, suddenly, the insults that Irene was hurling at them stopped. "Wait," she said. "What are you doing? Let me out, you maniac!"

Melina ignored her. She turned to Ian. "I'm going to walk down that hall. I've set this so that it will take a full five minutes for the air to vent before the outer door opens. It's a safety feature in case the lock is damaged, but it's a very bad way to go for anyone stuck in there. She'll probably survive for about three minutes more, although if you take more than about one minute to let her out, she'll have some serious medical issues afterwards. If you don't save her, no one will. This corridor looks like no one has walked here in two hundred thousand years."

Melina set off in the direction of their flyer. A couple of seconds later, Ian fell into step beside her.

"I would have bet anything that you were going to let her out."

"I had a wife and daughter," Ian replied. "My one consolation when I got volunteered for this fiasco was that I might help to buy them some time."

"Ah. I see. Well, we've got marines to save. We should probably hurry."

They redoubled their pace.

CHAPTER 20

"Can you keep the planet between the vampires and us?" Ian asked.

"I don't know, but I'm sure as hell going to give it a shot."

Melina powered the drive. Despite the full fuel load, the acceleration on a Recon flyer made the fighters she'd flown for all of her career seem anemic. These things could *move*.

Of course, they couldn't turn or fight worth a damn and their armor was just about enough to stop a spitball, so it was extremely important to know where the enemy was. A wrong turn would signal the end almost immediately.

"Where are they?"

"They're just passing the *Lapland*. Doesn't look like they're taking the bait."

"Shit. They got here faster than I expected."

They'd been expecting the swarm to break its stride and go after the factory ship, which had just begun to retreat. Like the flyer, it wasn't armed well enough to be effective in combat—especially against an enemy that had already demolished the rest of the fleet.

While they were both hoping that the capital ship might be able to get out of range before it was destroyed, they knew that every minute the *Lapland* could buy them was one more that they had before dying. The maximum time would be gained if the factory ship stood its ground and fought to the bitter end.

Of course, they'd then have to face starvation on the surface but, who knew, maybe the trees were edible after all. Every hope rested on the fact that humanity had clearly been to the planet, or at least knew about it. Had they seeded it with food suitable for humans? Was there, perhaps, an ocean full of fish somewhere that they hadn't found yet? Hope was better than dying with the *Lapland*.

Which seemed to have escaped its fate.

"The ship's clear! The swarm flew right by them, and if they want to catch up now, they'll take hours. The Lapland is accelerating away from the system under full thrust!" Ian was clearly rooting for the factory ship.

And why not? Melina wondered. You'd have to be a bit of a cold bastard, used to running casualty analyses in the heat of battle to be able to calmly weigh the deaths of hundreds of your fellow creatures against the possibility of maybe surviving in the most savage way for a few more days... or perhaps some additional months. You'd have to be the kind of person who'd be able to shove someone into an airlock and leave them there to die, slowly and painfully while you walked away. You'd have to be dead inside.

It seemed like Ian hadn't quite reached the point where he was dead inside, but Melina still wondered whether either of them deserved to survive.

She decided not to think about it. There were much more pressing concerns on her mind at that moment, the most urgent of which was that the enemy fleet would be upon them much sooner than she'd been expecting. Melina flew with one eye as she watched the path of the swarm with the other.

Icy though her heart might be, it seemed that the rest of her body was still perfectly human. Sweat slickened her hands to the point where she could feel the controls slipping slightly in her grip. Not ideal for precision flying, but then, this wasn't a hair-trigger fighter, but a speed machine which required a lot of planning before one embarked upon any maneuvers.

She pointed to an empty spot on the readout. "I think we can squeeze through here, before they begin to enter the atmosphere. After that, we can beat them to where the marines are, but I don't think we have enough time to load everyone onto the dropships and fly out."

"Maybe they'll ignore us the way they ignored the *Lapland*."

"You mean if we promise to surrender?"

"Do you think that's why they flew right by?"

"I'd bet on it. And if I'm right, then the factory ship had better really run, because those wings are bad enough when they're just killing people for the fun of it. I'd hate to be on the *Lapland* when they decide that running away constitutes a betrayal of their promise to surrender."

"Why would that woman even—?"

"She's not a problem anymore. Our problem is how to get between the swarm and the surface without burning up on reentry. Remember that the vampires don't have human bodies, which means that they can pull more Gs than we can."

"What are you going to do?"

"Nothing you'd approve of. Just hold on and shut up."

She pushed the engines well into past redline, grimacing as the acceleration pushed her into the perfectly bolstered couch. *These Recon boys sure have it good*, she thought. Alarms blinked on her dash and she silenced them all with a single button and stayed on the gas.

"You're coming in way too shallow."

"I know. Hope the heat shielding is up to spec."

As Ian clutched his seat in terror, the flyer did exactly what Melina wanted it to do. It skipped off the atmosphere and sent them back into space.

"What did you do that for?" he nearly yelled.

"You know as well as I do. We made it under the tip of the swarm. They were between us and the marines, and now they've got to chase us down. We'll be there first."

"Maybe. But I'm gonna need new pants."

Melina laughed and threw the ship into a deep dive, slowing only when the drag of the atmosphere threatened to heat the hull beyond its design thresholds. "We're coming in directly from above."

"I did tell you that the ground crew cobbled this flyer together before we got any spare parts from the *Lapland*, didn't I?"

"Not that I recall, and besides, it makes no difference. It was the only choice. If we'd tried to go around the long way, the swarm would have been ahead of us and we would have had to fight our way through. Hell, we might even have enough time to take off again and run after the *Lapland*."

"I'm not sure I want to talk to that detective guy again. We killed his prisoner, after all."

"Hmm. I don't really think he'll be too upset about that."

"You think? He struck me as the kind of guy who sets a lot of store by doing things by the book."

Melina laughed. "Are you really worried about what he's going to say to us?"

Ian was silent for a beat. "No. Not in the least. But it keeps my mind off the big fleet of vampires that is going to land on our heads about three minutes after we get on the ground."

"Would you rather leave the marines behind? Not even warn them what's coming?"

The man sighed. "I guess not. This whole volunteering thing seems to be a difficult habit to break. How do you get out of it?"

"It's not easy. I thought that signing up for a suicide mission would solve my problem pretty quickly. No such luck," she replied. "Now shut up. I need to land this thing."

They were approaching the ground at a very considerable clip. She wouldn't have thought twice about making a precision touchdown in the center of the large open surface if she'd been piloting her fighter, but the Recon flyer was not as nimble, and she suspected it wasn't going to like the landing procedure.

She was right. As she fought to spin the flyer around so that the main engine was pointing at the ground—the only way they were going to be able to scrub off enough speed to avoid getting splattered—the stick shook and shuddered in her grip as the air outside buffeted the ungainly craft, trying to keep the pointy end facing into the wind.

But, after what seemed like too long, the jets stayed down and she put everything the engine had into braking. "I hope the marines are suited up," she said.

"I hope they don't just shoot us on general principles," Ian shouted back over the roar of the wind.

Once their speed was under control, she flipped the flyer into landing attitude and, with fractions of a second to spare, touched down.

"That," Ian told her, shaking his head, "was utterly insane."

"Thanks. Someday Recon should send its pilots over to us. We could teach them how to fly."

"I don't think anyone would take you up on that. Recon pilots are selected for a strong sense of self-preservation. That makes it much more likely that the data they're supposed to be collecting will make it back to the intelligence officers who need it."

Melina had stopped listening to him. She could see the dropships, but there was no sign of the pilots. There also wasn't a single suit to be seen.

"Shut up a second."

"Sorry. I guess I'm just happy to be alive."

"You won't be alive for long if the vampires get here. We need to know where the marines are."

Ian looked unconcerned. He pointed to a graph on the lower corner of one of the readouts. "They're around here somewhere. They're chattering all over the Tacnet."

Melina had forgotten that the ship was designed to detect any electromagnetic communications, even if they were extremely weak and distant. She could have hit him for not reminding her. "Patch them through, will you?"

A sudden babble filled the cockpit as the marine channels—all of them, command and intra-squad—suddenly came alive. "Can you give me just the command Tac?"

"One second."

She waited impatiently as he checked the records for the right frequency and, as soon as he gave her the thumbs up, began to speak. "Cora, can you hear me?"

"Commander Coloni?"

"Yes."

"Where are you?"

"Parked beside your dropships."

"You might want to get the hell out of there. I think things are about to go down the crapper very quickly here."

"We came to tell you that you're about to have company in the form of a whole bunch of black wings with terrible tempers."

"Yeah, yeah. We know that. Now get out!"

They knew that? But her training didn't let her waste time with inane chatter. The marine lieutenant clearly had information she didn't. She began to power up the engines and looked at Ian's scanners. Her heart sank.

"I don't think we're going to be able to leave," she reported.

"Why not?"

"The swarm is right on top of us. If I try to make orbit, we're as good as dead."

"Then get over here!"

"Where are you?"

"Under the cement in the hole the *Banshee* made. Get inside and I'll guide you from there. Stand by for instructions via data transfer."

Melina wanted to ask them what they were doing here, and what use it would be to go there if they were just going to be cut to pieces by the swarm upon its arrival but, again, her training took over and the flyer was moving before she was fully aware that she'd given the order.

The gash was several hundred meters away, and they covered it in seconds. She unceremoniously dumped the flyer on top of the headless walkers in their neat rows and popped the hatch. "Grab a handset," she told Ian. "The lieutenant is sending us a map."

"I heard her."

Ian, holding the set, sprinted ahead and it was all that Melina could do to keep up in the high gravity. Soon, she was panting, lungs burning and wondering how the hell a Recon trooper could be in better shape than she was. Recon was notorious for their lax standards when it came to personnel training—spies whose main objective was to remain forever unseen didn't need to fight; if it came to that, they'd already lost.

She decided that the problem was that the two hundred thousand years in the stasis pod. Clearly, it had damaged her body more than it had damaged Ian's.

She wanted to tell him to slow down, but she was damned if she would.

Then, after they'd run through dozens of identical chambers full of rows of headless war machines, she heard a mechanical clanking behind her and forgot all about her suffering.

The wings were there. Somewhere. In the maze behind them.

And they were coming.

A burst of speed fuelled by adrenaline drew her level with Ian. "How much further?" she said, trying to whisper while still making herself heard.

"I don't know. I think we're about two-thirds of the way there. It's hard to make an exact calculation with this thing jiggling around."

They turned left again. Two-thirds meant that the wings, provided they didn't run into anything in the cramped quarters, would be on top of them in moments.

So Melina ran knowing that she would only survive if the vampires took their time. She kept looking upwards, certain that, at any moment, she'd see the unmistakable bat-like contour of one of the enemy craft appear silhouetted in her helmet beam, an awful final sight.

The awful sensation of being watched, that every chamber they ran through contained dark wings silently flying overhead and watching their every move came to nothing. High-energy projectiles failed to tear her to shreds from the blackness.

But the clanking got louder. At first, it sounded like someone was banging on pots and pans in the distance, but gradually, it became more like the sounds of a construction site at a shipyard. The noise made the earth shake.

"What the fuck is that?" Melina screamed.

Ian shook his head as he ran. He couldn't hear her over the echoing din.

Melina looked back and she knew. The enemy behind them wasn't a flying wing. It was a monstrous suit of armor, clanking in slow motion, but still managing to take twenty steps for every one of theirs and closing the gap between them. It would be upon them soon.

Ian pointed to the entrance to the next chamber, and she called up an unsuspected reservoir of energy to pull through.

But she was still ten meters from the exit when the war machine jumped over them and blocked the egress. The impact from its landing knocked them off their feet.

For a fraction of an instant, Melina just watched the thing, transfixed. It was huge, three times as tall as a shock marine exoskeleton. The machine in front of her was no longer headless: a vampire had merged with the slot on its shoulders and the entire construction looked like a giant wearing a winged helmet.

A tug on her arm brought her back to her senses. Ian was pulling her in a different direction. "This way!" he shouted. Now that the echoes of the war machine had died down, she could actually hear him.

Melina was out of her element. In a dogfight, the perfect control always fell straight to hand, and her enemies seemed to melt away before her. Even during her very early days, she'd never met a pilot with more confirmed kills than she had... and only heard rumors, often hundreds of years old, of legendary fighter pilots with similar exploits in distant systems.

On the ground, it was a different story. If anyone had asked her to evaluate Ian before the engagement, she'd have grudgingly given him his due for bravely coming back to the moon and rescuing her, but that was all. She considered him negligible in a fight.

The man surprised her again. He led her into a row of still-inert headless walkers and from there between their legs in a diagonal pattern. Finally, he parked her under one. "There. They shouldn't be able to find us too easily. And even if they do, they won't be able to get to us without pushing all the rest of these things out of the way."

"The wings can shoot us from above."

"I'm not sure about that. I think they want us alive. How hard do you think it would have been for that big thing to kill us? All it really needed to do is land on top of us instead of ahead of us. Instant pilot jelly."

"That makes no sense. Why would they want us alive?"

Ian shrugged. "Search me. I just hitched a ride on the wrong Recon flyer. Now let's turn these lights off."

They sat there waiting, listening, stationed underneath one of the headless suits, hoping that it would hide their thermal signature. But other than the sound of creaks and groans from the metal giant stationed at the door, they heard nothing.

Then, all of a sudden, they heard a rush of air from above and the clang of metal on metal. The legs they'd taken cover under suddenly lurched.

"Oh, shit. They're activating this one," Melina yelled, turning on her light.

She was right. Towering above them was a winged helmet, black as the space between galaxies. She half-heard Ian scurry away, but she couldn't move. Her hands searched for a control stick that wasn't there.

A huge claw reached out for her. Ian thought that the enemy wanted to take them alive, but she knew better. Those enormous digits would crush her to a pulp, cracking her bones like toothpicks. She watched them get closer, a prey animal mesmerized by the predator's gaze.

A deafening sound exploded through the chamber, coming from the side of the entrance. The robot about to grab her turned its winged head to look in the direction of the cacophony.

The vampire controlling the suit suddenly shattered into a million pieces and huge holes appeared in its chest armor. It fell onto the one behind it, knocking it off its feet and starting a chain reaction that toppled six or seven of the fighting machines.

Melina stood there, stunned by her close escape, watching the dominoes fall.

Suddenly, a hand gripped her by the arm. "Come on! We don't know if there are more of them."

Ian pulled her back the way they'd come, running towards a light which was much brighter than the weak illumination from her helmet. Under that light stood the most beautiful shape she'd ever seen: Tristan's mutilated marine exoskeleton, friction smoke still pouring from the muzzle of its high-energy cannon stood over the shattered ruin of the vampire who'd been guarding the door.

"Man, am I glad to see you," she said when they reached him.

"Don't be. We still have a few minutes to go before we make it back to where the rest of the marines are holed up. I'll try to hold them here until you make it back, but it might not be feasible. I suspect I only dropped these two because we caught them by surprise. Get a move on."

They lost no time in sprinting through the final five chambers. At the end, they saw a blue light and were unsurprised to find themselves staring down the muzzle of twenty-odd marine guns.

At that moment, Melina couldn't have cared less if they all opened fire and cut her to ribbons. She collapsed onto her knees. Her burning calves simply unable to hold her weight any longer. She panted, just concentrating on breathing.

Clanking sounds could be heard from outside the chamber, and all the marines tensed. Two of them took positions on either side of the entrance and pointed their cannons into the gap.

The sounds got closer, and in moments, Tristan's suit flew through over the threshold. He dove for cover behind one of the walls.

"Can't tell for sure, but I think they're a chamber or two behind me," he reported.

They were much closer. The marines at the door opened fire mere seconds after Tristan entered. Melina couldn't hear what they were saying—they had their helmets closed and were conversing over the Tacnet.

"Close call there, pilot. If Tristan hadn't volunteered to go get you, we would have left you behind. We don't have a hell of a lot of time." The lieutenant stood over her.

Melina looked around. She saw immediately that it was similar, though not identical, to the room that held the obelisk, but her heart sank at the prospect of climbing the ramps to exit at the top of the room. "Time? Where are you going to go? Why bother to keep running? We're stuck on the planet with them and with no food." Something else was bugging her, and in her addled state, she blurted it out. "You said you knew they were coming. If you were buried all the way down here, how the hell could you possibly have known that?"

"About five minutes before you called us, a blinking red light lit up on every one of those suits. It scared the living crap out of us until we realized that they can't move without the top half."

"Oh." She hadn't seen any red lights, but that was possibly because she was too preoccupied with what might be above her. "And what are your plans? Are you going to make one of those patented marine last stands?"

Cora looked at her strangely. "Why? What would be the point? Even if we didn't have a better way out, I'd order my troops to escape out the top of this room. We don't die for no reason, no matter what the popular conception might be."

"Better way?"

The lieutenant pointed towards the arch that stood where the obelisk had in the other chamber. "That's a portal of some sort. Probably some modification of the space fold drive. We know how to turn it on, so we're planning on going out that way."

"Out that way? Where does it go?"

Cora raised an eyebrow. "At this point, does that really matter?"

CHAPTER 21

"Why didn't you leave?" Ian asked Tristan.

"We were waiting for you," Tristan replied. He didn't want to tell the pilot that it had been a close thing, and that he'd only managed to convince Cora to wait by going out to get them back himself. He knew that the lieutenant wouldn't leave without him. Hell, if it came to that, he didn't want to leave without her, either.

He also didn't want to be the one to break the other reason to them. He'd leave that one to his officer. Let her earn her pay.

"What's it look like out there?" Cora asked over the Tacnet.

One of the men holding the door responded. "Not great. There are about twenty of the wings flying overhead. They haven't attacked us yet, and they're not getting too close. We managed to hit one."

"Are any more coming through?"

"No, ma'am. This looks to be the extent of the force."

"An advance team, then. To keep us pinned down."

"Yeah, I suppose."

"All right. Keep me posted if they do anything." Cora walked over with Melina in her wake.

She addressed the two pilots. "Here's the situation. That arch over there is built to take us… somewhere. We don't know exactly where, but we're sure that the wings and their big armored suits can't activate the device."

"How do you figure that?" Ian asked.

"Two reasons: the first is that you need to have a very specific appendage to open that thing. It varies depending on what species you are, but the robots don't have it. The second is inductive. If they could get through, they would be on the other side already. I don't think anyone stays in prison voluntarily."

"Unless what's on the other side is even worse."

Cora shrugged. "In our case, it's moot. We stay, we die. If it's worse, we can die over there, as well."

"So what's the holdup? Why don't we just leave now?"

"We need someone to volunteer to keep the portal open so the rest of us can leave. That person has to stay behind."

"Stay behind?"

"Yeah. They also have to blow themselves to bits."

"What? Why?" Ian said.

Cora sighed. "Because, for whatever reason, that's the way they designed this place. Or maybe they didn't, but we haven't been able to figure out how to make it work any other way. The problem is that, for the portal to be open, someone has to have their hand pressed to the activation panel. If you take your hand off, then the portal closes."

Tristan glanced at the panel again, just to be sure. It was too far away from the opening for a human to keep their hand on the switch and get through. Even if they could, what would happen when the hand was removed? Would any part of the person's body still on this side simply be sliced off by the closing portal?

"So someone has to stay behind."

"It's worse than that. They have to blow themselves up once the rest of us are through." She held a hand up to forestall Ian's protest. "Think about it for a second. If they capture that person alive, they can simply hold them against the panel and march through the portal. That's why they didn't shoot you when they were chasing you before."

"And that's why it was so important to go save you," Tristan interjected. "We wouldn't make it very far with those things behind us. Our problem is that no one wants to volunteer to stay behind. We were about to draw lots when your call came through."

Cora looked towards the door. "And it'll have to wait. Incoming."

The marines at the door opened fire as Tristan listened to their conversation over the Tacnet. "They've mounted the walkers. They're all coming towards us at once."

"Why aren't they shooting?"

"I think they want to take one of us alive."

"I get that. But they only need one. They can shoot the rest. So be careful."

It was as if the enemy had heard her. A sudden barrage whistled through the opening and pinged off the rear wall. No one was hit, and Tristan saw that the vampires had also managed to avoid hitting the arch itself. They must really, really want the portal.

He was close to one of the marines holding the door. "How's it going, Tom?"

"Badly. They're using the front row of suits for cover. Not only is it hard to get a good shot at them, it's nearly impossible to even see where they are. Uh, oh."

He was about to ask what was the matter when something that looked like a black thundercloud burst through the door. Three of the enemy walkers charged past the sentries, simply deciding to absorb the gunfire directed at them as they went past. Before anyone could react, they were in the room, shooting at anything that moved.

Tristan rolled to one side as the nearest took a bead at him. Shards of concrete flew up from where he'd been standing. He fired two rounds at the behemoth and then rolled again. The shots missed wide of their mark.

Two of the giant enemy suits were struggling with something while the third lay down a carpet of covering fire. It took him a second to understand what it was. They had grabbed a marine in a suit and were dragging it out.

"Oh, shit. That's Cora!" he heard over the Tacnet.

And then they were back outside.

"Cover me!" he shouted. And, against every instinct, he jumped through the doorway after them.

It was a mistake. As soon as he crossed the doorway, he felt an impact to the back of his suit and heard a hissing sound. He hoped he hadn't lost anything too important, because he knew he was going to have to fight his way back into the room behind.

He threw himself flat and then turned and fired a continuous stream from the floor. One of the enemies holding the lieutenant took most of the barrage in one leg and collapsed without releasing Cora's suit. That effectively halted their progress.

While the enemy were trying to sort themselves out, two more marines emerged into the larger storage room and opened up with everything they had. Tristan saw one of them lob a charge over the three enemies they were engaged with in the direction of the rows of suits and then they all jumped back on the other side of the entrance. It was good thinking: that was where the enemy reinforcements were likely hidden.

Tristan pressed his head against the floor.

When the debris stopped falling, he fired on the two vampires who were still standing. He got lucky and his fire tore the wing-shaped top off of one of them. Unfortunately, the other one shot the legs out from under him. Tristan's suit toppled to the ground.

I need to get out of this thing now, he thought as he struggled to pop the emergency release button. He tried not to think about the likelihood of survival of a soft, pulpy human body among the kind of ordnance he was going to encounter in a battle of suits. Even the smallest piece of shrapnel would have more than enough energy to tear a person to shreds.

He huddled behind his suit and surveyed the field. The opening was about ten meters away, and an equal distance separated him from the remaining enemy walker, which was struggling to free Cora's exoskeleton from the death grip of its companion. He watched in horror as it sliced the helmet off the marine suit and began to pull the lieutenant out through the helmet hole.

She wasn't moving, but whether she was unconscious or dead, he had no way to tell. Did the human hand need to be attached to a living human body to open the portal? Tristan didn't know.

A barrage from the doorway hit the black giant and tore its wing off. It collapsed one way, and Tristan was relieved to see that it dropped Cora the other.

Ignoring the likelihood that there were more enemies hidden among the rows of inert suits, he ran to where Cora laid, half in and half out of her suit. She was bleeding from a thousand cuts—exiting a suit through the helmet hole was a tight fit; it was likely that apart from the scrapes, some bones had been broken in the squeeze—but he had no time to check whether she was still alive. Breathing or not, he was taking her back with him.

Tristan grunted under the effort of lifting her onto his shoulders in the G-and-a-half gravity and nearly pitched over. He'd been in his suit since forever, and the movement of simply walking normally was strange to him.

And he couldn't lose time by walking. Movement behind him told him that he had to run as fast as possible.

Tristan didn't turn, but he imagined that every sound was a vampire behind him taking aim at his exposed back. Two marines appeared up ahead and fired a barrage over his head. The return fire, thankfully, was also above him as the enemy concentrated on the exoskeletons and ignored the unsuited humans. They probably reasoned—quite correctly, it seemed to him—that after they dealt with the dangerous exoskeletons, they could easily grab one of the unprotected people at their leisure. They only needed one.

The final few meters were torture. It seemed like the opening would never arrive. Just when he was ready to scream, he got past the two suits giving him covering fire and stumbled to one side, careful not to let Cora hit the ground too hard.

She opened her eyes. "You went after me?"

"Of course. We're the last survivors from our unit. Hell, for all I know, we're the last survivors from the *Minstrel*. I couldn't let them take you."

"Crap."

"What?"

"That's twice you've saved my ass now. You're going to want a big reward."

"Yeah, I can think of a thing or two." He leered at her.

"Good. You're finally learning."

Another voice broke into their conversation. "People, fall back, now."

Tristan turned to see Commander Tau Coloni standing at the console, pressing one hand against the portal activation quadrant and holding a charge suitable for blasting armored vehicles to pieces in the other.

"Get through the gateway, now. That's an order. You and you go through first, then the pilots and you two who lost your suits. March!"

Ordnance was still coming through the entrance but none of it came near the gate, which made it possible for the first suits to get through unscathed.

"Everyone who isn't wearing armor, now."

Tristan was glad that a fighter commander outranked a marine lieutenant, because Cora was struggling and ordering him to leave her behind to coordinate the retreat. He simply ignored her and stepped through the shimmering screen.

There was a colossal tunnel on the other side. It seemed to go on forever. He followed the white lights on the ceiling as far as his eye could see.

"Gangway!"

He pulled Cora out of the way as another two suits came through and then watched as the rest of the marines filed across, one by one. The last two were facing back, clearly fighting a rearguard action against the approaching vampires.

But it was the third-to-last trooper that caught Tristan's attention. That suit was dragging a struggling figure that constantly attempted to break away and go back through the portal, which, from this side, was a shimmering gray blankness. It was Ian, and he was giving the exoskeleton a surprisingly good fight.

Almost as soon as the last two shock marines were through, the shimmering grayness disappeared. Ian stopped struggling and fell to the floor. "Melina!" he shouted as he banged his fist against the metal grating.

Tristan, however, was no longer watching him.

Shapes were blinking into existence all around. Tracked vehicles twice the height of an exoskeleton, so large that they almost didn't fit in the tunnel, materialized out of thin air. Each of them had cannons that wouldn't have looked out of place as a starship's main battery.

There were dozens of them. In desperation, Tristan turned back to see that the portal had blinked out of existence and become transparent. There were more tanks back there. Every single gun was aimed at them.

"Oh, well," he said to Cora, who was struggling to sit. "We had a good run, I guess. Better than we thought we would when we signed up, anyway."

"We're not dead yet." She grunted and leaned on him as she stood. He could tell she was in pain.

Leaning on Tristan every step of the way, Cora walked towards the nearest vehicle. She stopped about ten steps away, raised her head, and stared at it defiantly. "I am Lieutenant Cora Sirius Almir of the 243rd marine platoon of the Tau Expeditionary Force," she shouted. "And I demand your unconditional surrender."

Tristan smiled to hear the laughter that filtered in through the Tacnet. It was heartening to realize that gallows humor was still alive and well among the marines, despite the hell they'd been through. They would die with their honor intact.

The tank nearest them sprouted a line of light, as if a crack had opened to a brightly lit interior. As its armored skin pulled apart, Tristan realized that that was exactly what was happening.

A figure, bipedal and humanoid, came into view. Only when it emerged completely and left the light did Tristan realize that the figure wasn't just humanoid but actually human. It was a slight blond man dressed in what looked like shorts and a T-shirt. He was fiddling with some sort of rectangular device and frowning.

When he finally looked up at them and spoke, his voice filled the tunnel.

"What are your terms?"

"What?" Cora said.

"Your terms. Unless my translator is malfunctioning again, you asked for our surrender. I am asking what your terms are."

Cora just gaped at him. The man returned her look with an earnest, level expression before he broke into a smile.

"Sorry, I couldn't resist. I am joking, of course. But if you fought your way through what we left on that planet, you are a formidable fighting force indeed. Had there been more of you, we might have considered surrendering and joining forces with you."

"Who are you? What is this?"

The man shrugged. "I'm just a delegate. If the information that they're piping through to me about you is accurate, you'll be talking to more important people pretty soon."

He gestured around the tunnel. "As to this, it was once a colony world called Crystallia. It's no longer inhabited except for some custodians. We got beamed here when you tripped the alarm."

"I don't understand."

"It's a remote installation. Nowadays, no one can believe that people used to live here, back during the war, but it's true. We currently use it to store access portals to blockaded worlds whose inhabitants are considered too dangerous to service from more central planets. As you probably realized, we're prepared to deal with anything that might walk through that gate, and there are tunnels similar to this one that lead to other interdicted prison worlds."

"There are more planets full of those things?"

"Not just those. We've encountered a number of hostile intelligences. Whenever possible, we try to coexist in peace. But it's not always possible. What you stumbled on was the remnant of an ancient war."

"Makes sense that it should happen to us. After all, we're the remnant of an even older war. Just glad I missed the punch up with those black wing fellows. I don't think I would have been able to survive it."

"There is much worse than the Oneness loose in the galaxy."

Tristan felt Cora shudder against him. He could understand what she was feeling. These things had, with nothing more than tiny single fighters, obliterated a complete task force. He wouldn't want to run into something worse.

"We've got some bad news about your containment field. We took it down when we hit the planet."

"We know. Another team is getting set up to address the issue. Since you've managed to seal the portal again, it should be much simpler to do. We're letting the other races know as well, but we'll have to volunteer to do the cleanup without help. It's only fair. Humans broke the containment field, after all."

He looked them up and down. "Well, anyhow, you're safe now. I've got instructions to take you back to Gliese with me." He hesitated. "But before I turn you over to the committee, can I ask you a question? About the containment field, I mean?"

"Sure," Cora said.

"What the hell were you thinking?"

"That, my friend, is a long story. Buy us a drink when the big shots are done with us and we'll tell you all about it."

***

Except for the fact that it was filled with life forms that she couldn't identify and wouldn't have even been able to imagine if she hadn't seen them, the bar could have been taken from their own time, two hundred and fifteen thousand years ago.

It was dimly lit, overcrowded, smelly, and noisy. There were small tables in the center and even stalls for privacy against one wall. Those creatures that could drink had drinks in front of them. But the most surprising thing about the place was that it had a bar. An actual bar. With human-sized stools.

The marines had congregated there. Most of them were exhausted beyond the limits of endurance, and shell-shocked and culture-shocked to boot. Most of them hadn't even begun to process the sudden shift in both their fortunes and the universe they were expected to survive in.

But no marine worth his exoskeleton would ever have turned down a free drink, and the delegate was as good as his word. Besides, the bar was one place in their new environment that they could actually understand. She'd noticed that they seemed to relax a little almost the moment they walked inside. A bar was a bar.

Tina sighed. She hadn't relaxed at all. She felt completely alone, in a way that she'd never been before. Separated from everything she'd ever known and loved not just by space—she could deal with a few light years here and there—but by an unimaginable expanse of time. At least the marines, even the dropship pilots who'd survived, had a peer group. She was the only civilian in the group.

But she knew that her pain was nothing compared to what another member of their group was going through.

Ian was sitting alone, far from everyone else except for two marines who'd taken it upon themselves to keep an eye on him. She approached one of them. "It's Tom, isn't it?"

"Yes. Tina, right?"

"Yeah. Pleased to finally be introduced." They laughed. "You were the one who pulled him through, weren't you?"

"Yeah. He put up a good fight, too. He did not want to come. Wanted to blow himself up with the commander."

"I know."

"And I keep wondering if I did the right thing. Maybe he would have been better off dying. I think he wants it."

"Is that why you're keeping an eye on him? In case he tries to kill himself."

The marine nodded.

"I don't think you need to worry. He'll pull through. Go have some fun, I'll take care of him." She walked to where Ian was sitting. "How's the drink?" The thing he was drinking was fluorescent green.

"Watered down. You'd think something that looks like this would knock you ass-over-appetite after a couple of sips, but I should have known that bars wouldn't change."

"Mind if I sit down?"

"Go ahead."

"Want to talk about it?"

"Not really."

"Well, I want to hear about it."

Ian seemed about to retort, but something held him back. Maybe he remembered that she'd lost quite a bit because of the mission as well, or maybe it was something else, but Ian sighed. "Two weeks ago, I was saying goodbye to my wife. She said she'd wait for me, go into stasis for the expected duration of the mission.

"I told her not to do it, and I think she realized then that it was a suicide mission. She begged me to back out. I told her it was impossible. That they'd have me shot. I really believed that. But here I am, still alive, and she's not."

"Do you think you betrayed her?"

"No... maybe. I don't know. I just miss her, and I can't believe she's been dead so long that her bones have probably crumbled to dust. I saw her two weeks ago, for God's sake!"

"The troops are afraid you'll try to kill yourself."

"Me? I doubt it. I'm too much of a coward."

"I don't think the commander would agree with that. Do you?"

He stared into his drink. "She ordered me to go, you know. And when I didn't, she made that marine kid drag me with him. I wanted to die with her, and I know... I *know* that she wanted me with her. I could see it in her eyes. She didn't want to die alone either. But she still made them drag me off."

"She was a great woman."

"That sounds so stupid. 'A great woman.' What does that matter? Do you think she cared? That's not even why she did what she did. She lost her husband. The man didn't wake up. And that took her to the edge, where she didn't really feel human anymore. I know why she sacrificed herself: it was because she couldn't live with what she'd become." He took a deep draught. "And for what? A fleet that went nowhere near the real battle. We didn't manage to slow the blobs down. You heard what the delegate said... the blobs took Tau and overran Earth. Humanity scattered to the winds, tiny pockets of survivors. We had to hide from everyone until the Uploaders found us and the war against the Oneness began. What we did didn't matter. Everything we lost was for nothing."

"But others like us managed to succeed. Humanity won the war, in the end. Or at least we came out the other end free and successful, an important part of the galactic community. People like the commander must have been there every step of the way."

"I guess." He didn't sound convinced. "But it just seems like such a waste."

"Think of it this way. She should have been dead hundreds of thousands of years ago. It shouldn't make any difference to you today, so far in her future."

"That's stupid."

But he was thawing. She could see it. He was reconciling himself to where he was, and that there might be something here and now worth seeing. "You might be right. But I'm sure of something else. If she knew you were sitting in a bar drinking... whatever that is, and not raising a glass in her memory, she'd come back from the grave and kick your ass."

"Now that is definitely true." He raised the glass.

Tina said: "To Melina."

She must have inherited her father's command voice. The marines around them somehow heard her through the noise and stopped talking. Each solemnly raised whatever they had in hand and took a slow, ceremonial sip.

CHAPTER 22

Hémery heard his footsteps echo in the *Lapland*'s empty corridors. Most of the crew was in stasis as they headed out to the nearest star. Relativistic time contraction meant that it would only be a three-year—subjective time—run to the nearest star but most of the men and women on board had decided to sleep through it.

They'd dealt with the problem of faulty pods by ignoring it: a factory ship could produce brand new parts, especially considering the fact that the crew was much smaller than it was when they set out.

Of course, there was always a skeleton crew that stayed awake, going into stasis in shifts. They spent most of their time staring at sensor screens, trying to spot any sign of the vampire fleet coming after them. Hoping never to see it. They spent the rest of their time trying to find the *Minstrel*.

His own reasons for staying awake were far more complex. He needed closure.

The ship's morgue held exactly one occupant. They'd long since decided to recycle the bodies of everyone who'd died on the trip out to the system, so nearly all the metal drawers were empty.

Except one.

He pulled it open and looked onto Irene's face. It would be his last visit to this particular victim.

In the excitement of an impending attack by the vampire swarm and the flight that followed, the scientist's crimes had been completely forgotten. Every member of the ship's crew was needed to batten the hatches and Hémery was no exception. Like everyone on board, he wore many hats, and investigating crimes was the least of them.

He was surprised as anyone else when her body was discovered.

By the time the airlock door opened, the pressure inside was the same as that outside. There was no differential to blow her out into space. That meant that the death-grip she'd kept on the handle of the inner door had kept her in place.

Eventually, the airlock had automatically cycled closed and the cleaning systems had realized there was something in there. The system had alerted the maintenance crew and the body had been recovered.

In light of the evidence he had against her, Hémery was certain that it had been suicide. Unable to face the certainty of having her reputation destroyed, Irene had taken the drastic step of killing herself. He'd even put that in his file.

But time passed and he began to doubt the theory. For one thing, she had seemed the type to fight to the bitter end. She'd been convinced that she was right and that everyone else on the ship was not just wrong, but uncivilized and incapable of seeing how stupid they actually were.

If she *had* killed herself, he was sure she wouldn't have done it like that. Why drain the airlock slowly? It was an awful way to go, especially on a ship which had machines that could create any pill you wanted at the touch of a button. Even with her lab locked away, Irene probably had access to dozens of toxic chemicals.

Hémery asked around a bit and when one of the tech crew confirmed that the airlocks couldn't be activated from the inside without emergency override codes, he hadn't even been surprised.

Now, all that remained was to discover who had killed her.

Yes, the woman had deserved it, deserved every second of the excruciating agony she must have gone through. But now that it was done, it was his job to find the killer and bring him to justice.

Hémery got to work on the assumption that it had to be someone who was in the loop, who knew what Irene had done. One of the higher ups among the scientist, most likely. He tried to requisition the video from the maintenance team, but by the time he got around to that, the people who operated the archives had been placed in stasis. His request wasn't deemed important enough to wake anyone about.

He had two choices: to wait until one of the qualified techs woke and gave him a hand or to try to do it himself.

A murder victim couldn't just be abandoned. It wasn't right. Even if that person was responsible for the deaths of two innocents, they were still a victim, and they had the right to an investigation. A delay of a few months while some tech snoozed went against every one of Hémery's instincts.

It took him a number of days to learn how to search the ship's database for old video, hampered by his nearly inexistent knowledge of how to use the file functions specific to the video player. Then, unable to use the search functions, he watched all the video for the range of dates in which he believed that she could have been murdered. Even using a fast forward function, there was nothing to be seen.

Finally, he went all the way back to the day he'd confronted her and, unexpectedly, less than five minutes into his review, he hit pay dirt.

The drama unfolded in front of him. The cold brutality of the fighter commander and the silent complicity of the Recon officer turned his stomach. He wondered why they had acted the way they did, and wished the cameras could have recorded audio as well.

They didn't, so whatever had happened between the three had gone to the grave with them.

"I know you can't hear me. Hell, if anyone ever watches the tape of me talking to a dead body, I'm going to have to do quite a bit of explaining. They'll think I'm nuts.

"But I thought you should know that I've identified the people who did this to you. I'm afraid they're well beyond the reach of whatever justice we can bring to bear on them. Hell, I have no idea whether justice is even possible. The commander might have had the right to execute you for treason under military law for all I know.

"Whether she did or didn't isn't my problem. I've recorded the incident and placed the clipping in the file, cross-referencing it to both your records and the ship's log entry where your death was noted. I know it's not much, but if anyone ever looks, they'll have all the information at their disposal, to do whatever they might want to do with it.

"For what it's worth, I also wanted to tell you that I think the people who killed you are dead. They went back to the planet to try to save the marines stuck down there. We think they misjudged the speed of the swarm, and they were only there a few minutes before the vampires landed on their heads. We're pretty sure it was a complete massacre. Sure enough that no one even suggested going back to look for survivors.

"I'm not sure why I'm even talking to you. I guess it's because we're on our way to some other system no one has ever visited before, and I don't know who else to talk to. Everyone sees things so differently from me. I guess I must be getting old.

"Before he went into stasis, the captain said that we would use that system to refuel and replenish before deciding what to do next. Somebody proposed going back to Earth, but everyone else said that it was just too far away, that we'd take hundreds of thousands of years to get back and just have the same problems we had when we came here in the first place.

"They also think they've located the *Minstrel*. Of course, it does look like the ship is still observing radio silence. Either that or they're all dead, but at least they're moving in the right direction. If they stop at the star system, we'll know they're all right.

"The plan right now seems to be to fly off in a random direction to throw off the vampires and to colonize a new world. They all say we're lucky that the factory ship survived, and if the marines are alive, that should make a good number of colonists. With a factory ship, terraforming a new world shouldn't be a problem.

"But what next? Just thinking about living a colonist's life makes me want to turn back and fight the swarm. An empty planet with nothing that really makes it a human world? What's the sense in that, anyway? Why isn't anyone else worried about that? They all seem to be convinced that it will be a wonderful thing.

"I was looking out one of the windows. The galaxy is not a wonderful thing. It's a huge, cold place, where you need to fight to survive and even then it's not a sure thing. And everyone is going on and on about how wonderful it is to have so much room to hide. So many planets to choose from."

Hémery sighed. "Well, at least one thing is certain. You'll never get your wish. In this galaxy, humans are always going to have to fight, and fight hard, to get by. Peace will only be an option if they manage to kill us or we manage to kill them.

"Maybe that's why I'm talking to you. I guess neither of us fit into the world that's coming. At least you're at peace now.

"Goodbye."

He closed the drawer and punched in the commands that authorized the morgue systems to recycle the body.

Then he walked away, wondering if they'd let him sleep all the way to their final destination.

***

Tens of thousands of light years away, in a human city, on a human planet, in a galaxy that had been safe for humanity for millennia, Tristan stroked Cora's short hair and held her body close to his.

"Consider yourself rewarded," she said, snuggling close.

"You still owe me one," he reminded her.

"I know. I always pay my debts. And besides, unless you run so far from me that I can't catch you, you'll be getting a lot more than just what I owe you."

"I'll consider that a promise," he replied.

He laid back on the bed—he'd been relieved to find that, among so much that was strange and unrecognizable, a bed was still a bed—and wondered what he was going to do next. No obvious answer presented itself. The people in charge of turning the former marines into valuable and productive members of society had attempted to explain the economy and the social structure. Judging by the blank expressions among his peers, they'd failed to get through to anyone.

The military was no longer an option. It seemed that wars these days were few and far between, and fought mainly by automated systems. There were a small elite of officers called strategists who told the machines what to do. No room for grunts at all.

And yet, he was contented. For the first time since he woke, weak as a baby in a stasis pod aboard the *Minstrel* what seemed like a lifetime before, Tristan Polaris Han didn't know that he was going to die.

That was the kind of uncertainty he could live with.

THE END

CHECK OUT OTHER GREAT SCIENCE FICTION BOOKS

DERELICT: MARINES
by Paul E. Cooley

Fifty years ago, Mira, humanity's last hope to find new resources, exited the solar system bound for Proxima Centauri b. Seven years into her mission, all transmissions ceased without warning. Mira and her crew were presumed lost. Humanity, unified during her construction, splintered into insurgency and rebellion.

Now, an outpost orbiting Pluto has detected a distress call from an unpowered object entering Sol space: Mira has returned. When all attempts at communications fail, S&R Black, a Sol Federation Marine Corps search and rescue vessel, is dispatched from Trident Station to intercept, investigate, and tow the beleaguered Mira to Neptune.

As the marines prepare for the journey, uncertainty and conspiracy fomented by Trident Station's governing AIs, begin to take their toll. Upon reaching Mira, they discover they've been sent on a mission that will almost certainly end in catastrophe.

ALLIANCE MARINES
by John Mierau

One by one, all of Earth's colonies have gone dark and silent. Reach, the last colony, teeters on the verge of civil war against its Earth-loyal overlords...and Reach-born rebel Lee Zhang has sworn to push the planet over the edge.

As the colony descends into total war, a convoy from Earth races across the galaxy, carrying news of a threat unlike anything mankind has faced before. The colonies have all been destroyed by a vast alien horde, and now Earth has fallen, too. Time is running out for sworn enemies to learn to trust and unite, or the human race is extinct. The Takers are coming to destroy mankind. If we don't do the job for them first.

CHECK OUT OTHER GREAT
SCIENCE FICTION BOOKS

SPACE MARINE AJAX
by Sean-Michael Argo

Ajax answers the call of duty and becomes an Einherjar space marine, charged with defending humanity against hideous alien monsters in furious combat across the galaxy.

The Garm, as they came to be called, emerged from the deepest parts of uncharted space, devouring all that lay before them, a great swarm that scoured entire star systems of all organic life. This space borne hive, this extinction fleet, made no attempts to communicate and offered no mercy.

Humanity has always been a deadly organism, and we would not so easily be made the prey. Unified against a common enemy, we fought back, meeting the swarm with soldiers upon every front.

PLANET LEVIATHAN
by D.J. Goodman

The cyborg commandos of the Galactic Marines are the greatest warriors in the galaxy, but sometimes one will go bad. Too unstable to be let back into the general population and too powerful for a normal prison to hold them, there is only one place they can be sent: Planet Leviathan.

CHECK OUT OTHER GREAT SCIENCE FICTION BOOKS

MAUSOLEUM 2069
by Rick Jones

Political dignitaries including the President of the Federation gather for a ceremony onboard Mausoleum 2069. But when a cloud of interstellar dust passes through the galaxy and eclipses Earth, the tenants within the walls of Mausoleum 2069 are reborn and the undead begin to rise. As the struggle between life and death onboard the mausoleum develops, Eriq Wyman, a one-time member of a Special ops team called the Force Elite, is given the task to lead the President to the safety of Earth. But is Earth like Mausoleum 2069? A landscape of the living dead? Has the war of the Apocalypse finally begun? With so many questions there is only one certainty: in space there is nowhere to run and nowhere to hide.

RED CARBON
by D.J. Goodman

Diamonds have been discovered on Mars.

After years of neglect to space programs around the world, a ruthless corporation has made it to the Red Planet first, establishing their own mining operation with its own rules and laws, its own class system, and little oversight from Earth. Conditions are harsh, but its people have learned how to make the Martian colony home.

But something has gone catastrophically wrong on Earth. As the colony leaders try to cover it up, hacker Leah Hartnup is getting suspicious. Her boundless curiosity will lead her to a horrifying truth: they are cut off, possibly forever. There are no more supplies coming. There will be no more support. There is no more mission to accomplish. All that's left is one goal: survival.